My Broken Compass

Printed in the United States of America

ISBN: 9798986035208

Library of Congress Registration Number

TXu 2-301-480

First Edition: October 2022

Compass Heart Press LLC

Sacramento, CA 95833

To My Mama Jene

Every journey I have started in my life has been possible because of the love and guidance you gave me. You gave me the confidence to make huge moves in my life, both physically and mentally. The words on the following pages are an example of a huge move I was strong enough to make because you made me brave. You taught me to love with my whole heart, even if those around me did not understand. To leap, even if I wasn't sure how strong the ground was beneath me. To see things in the world that others were blind to. To have the strength to move across the county alone. The humility to turn around and drive home when I realized it was a mistake. Above all else, you taught me what family meant. You made the world a better place, and you continue to impact the world, even after you have gone. You are iconic, you are a legend. I will spend my entire life trying to be even half as inspirational as you were. Thank you for everything.

ONE

Samuel **sat outside** under the night's green sky. He did most nights now. With every broken breath, his lungs filled with the sweet, aromatic flavor of freshly damp foliage. Exhausted emerald eyes stared into the distance, searching for answers. His overworked mind was lost in the gradual motion of the rise and fall of his shoulders with each breath. As always, he was engulfed in the moment. He let his mind drift like a buoy at sea. The surrounding stars danced a secret little dance, capturing his attention. Emerging patterns formed and shifted, making it impossible for Samuel to think about anything else, holding him trapped inside himself.

These days, Samuel always felt misplaced. Near-perfect nights like these were the most difficult to stay focused. This night's breath had a tangible chill, colder than usual for this time of year. This corn-filled town had long been a distant memory for him, but the feeling remained familiar, as if he had run through these fields just yesterday as a carefree child. Samuel fought against the glacial chill for as long as possible, his breath escaping his cracked lips and vanishing into the night. His desire to stay and watch the stars dance their promenade was trumped by the need to seek refuge from the bitter, unyielding elements. Finally, giving up his already-lost battle with Mother Nature, he headed home.

"It's getting late anyways," he reconciled.

There was still so much left to do before resting tonight: meals to be prepped for the kids' lunches tomorrow, clothes to be washed and the house to be cleaned. Samuel rose on unstable feet and lost his balance slightly as he pushed forward and off the awkward stump where he had been resting. He staggered for a few steps and plunged his hand into a dark bush armed to attack. He had anticipated that it would serve him as a crutch, but he was disappointed. Pain pricks from briars flooded his senses immediately. He recoiled his hand too quickly, and the sudden thrust sent him stumbling backward. A new patch of shrubs had appeared behind him suddenly, tangling his shoes and pushing him to fall even harder. Samuel landed on his butt with a ferocious thud.

"Do I give up?" Samuel whimpered slightly and lowered his head in defeat. "Or do I muster on?"

"Of course, you can't just win," Samuel mumbled, defeated. "You have to crush me." His dark opponent showed no reaction to his words, so Samuel, too impatient to wait for a response, got up and started his shameful saunter home.

Several field lengths separated him from shelter. Samuel stepped forward with a purposeful pace, hoping to generate more body heat against the growing cold. The wind was not going to allow him any remaining dignity; it grew stronger and colder as he walked straight into its trap. The sharp edges of his silent enemy stabbed with precision at his eyes, nose, and cheeks. Samuel lowered his head, burying his neck into his shoulders for what little protection they could muster against his attacker.

Home was close now, less than a mile. Most nights, the distance was never a thought, but this night was different. On this night, the dancing stars made his distant memories seem somehow closer, beckoning to be relished longer.

He resolved to watch the stars as he journeyed home. Through the chaos, one star claimed his attention. At first, it seemed dim, but when he looked away, the star seemed more pronounced in his peripheral vision. Its wattage vibrated up and down, making this star of the stars dance, out of the steady rhythm of its brethren. Samuel wanted to understand the cadence of its dance, but each time he turned to look at the entertainer directly, the relentless enemy forced him to keep moving.

Time to wave the white flag, Samuel thought to himself just as the tough wind finally paused.

It did not slow down or decrease; it was like God reached down and pressed the pause button, stopping it dead in its tracks. The little star's dance changed from a whimsical, uncharted pattern and appeared to edge forward in a singular, focused path seemingly directed towards Samuel's home. He became concerned when he noticed its brightness swell.

Samuel stopped and looked at the star directly. It seemed as if the star noticed his attention and stopped mid-ballet. The twinkle seemed to mute when Samuel's gaze caught it, as if it were a child playing possum who had been caught after bedtime.

"This isn't possible," Samuel muttered to himself. "I know I'm not seeing a star move towards me. Stars don't move like that."

Shaking any thought of a phenomenal star from his head, Samuel continued his march home.

Imagined scars from his frosty opponent warmed and replaced by a memory of dancing flames waiting right inside. Samuel started a fire barely an hour earlier, to keep the family warm before slipping away into the night for a few moments of privacy to reflect on the day. The house was so close that he could imagine the sounds of the faint crackling of the fire, filling the air. Already, he was imagining the million little embers joining forces against the wooden dam that was built to keep them at bay. He had almost forgotten about the trailing star - the fiery nova - that passed over in a great bright beam, recapturing its spotlight. It flew straight into the distance towards his home, disappearing into the verdant sky above Fort Anderson.

At that moment, childhood sentiment took over, and Samuel dropped to the ground on both knees. He clasped his hands, closed his eyes, and made a secret wish, all sprung forth from ancient instinct. The wish was locked away per tradition, for no one to know but him. No audible hint released from his shivering lips. It was a contract between the mighty Star God and a peon. As the moment passed, it felt silly giving into such a childish impulse, as these days Murphy's Law was everywhere. Then again, any plea for change was worth a try. Samuel got back onto his wavering feet and started to mosey slowly across the wet field toward his tiny haven.

The house wasn't much to look at. A white, three-bedroom ranch home set back in the tree line, with weather-stained shutters not hanging quite flush with their windows. The outside could use a coat of paint or three—the elements had won their battle on the little home's epidermis, with unmatching shades of snow, ivory, and smoke peppering the house, the lightest ivory on the most exposed sides.

Over the years, minimal upkeep was done, but nothing for aesthetic purposes. The shingles on the roof were mismatched, doing their job well but not looking pretty. There were only a few minutes of hot water at a time, and the only heat provided was from a "smurf-sized" wooden stove in the joint living room/home office. The house needed lots of repairs, but for now, it was held together with love, duct tape, and hope.

The walls barely contained the huge personalities of the four children that shared it with Samuel. The girls shared the north-facing room, and the twin boys shared the southern one. Moving here was an adjustment for them all; the country living, the small quarters. But it was all they had since... Well, since Matthew's extended absence.

"Why Matthew, why did you have to..." Samuel muttered, then stopped himself.

He never let himself dwell on the past; in any case, it wouldn't help him or his family. Matthew loved him and their family, but he said he had to leave and couldn't be in touch. He had no idea when, or if, they would be reunited. Samuel knew he had to trust his partner's choices, even though he didn't understand them. He knew Matthew and trusted him to do right.

It was time to end me-time and restart we-time. Samuel took a quick, steadying breath, centering his balance between his undependable feet as he reached out for the rust-covered doorknob. His eyelids fluttered away the creeping tears as the door opened. Stepping over that broken threshold, it was time to be Daddy again. Samuel loved his family more than anything, but he was not a natural at this. Matthew was the born Papa; he had patience for days and could see around corners.

Samuel had always been a great sidekick, supporting Matthew from the passenger seat while thoroughly enjoying their adventures. Now, without Matthew, Samuel was lost. There was no time to be sad. His family needed a rock to lean on. The kids would be up soon.

The doorknob, piercing cold to the touch, initially resisted being turned. With a little more effort and a subtle grunt, the knob gave way and the door opened with a loud creak. Samuel held his breath, hoping that the noise was not enough to wake the twins. A few seconds passed, and the peace remained. The coast was clear to continue with nightly routines. As the door closed, Samuel could smell a mixture of burnt embers, brick dust, and the sweet scent of freshly baked cake in the air. It had been a long day, and he had rewarded the family with a well-deserved home-baked dessert earlier. The succulent perfume still hovered.

TWO

Something on the wall the living room demanded Samuel's attention. The judgmental mirror on the wall cast the truth back at him; he had not been taking diligent care of himself. His normally short, black hair was overgrown and starting to curl up at the ends, peppered with gray hairs beginning to make their debut among the frizz. His beautiful, green eyes were buried behind dark bags - fighting bruises that no one gave him.

No steak would fix this, he thought.

His typically clean, crisp-shaven face was starting to gain grassy scruff. Never had he cared so little about his appearance. Matthew would never have allowed this.

"Stop right there," Samuel whispered to himself. His voice was raspier than usual. "It's time for chores." Tomorrow he would have to groom the man in the mirror, if only for his family. Hopefully, they didn't notice how badly he'd let himself go before he remedied the situation.

Samuel quietly pulled the twins' clothes from a homemade wooden drawer in the hallway, to ready them for school in the morning. The smell of cedar paused him for a moment as he thought back to his childhood, how he had pulled his own clothes out of a similar drawer.

This isn't what the circle of life is supposed to feel like, Samuel thought. He stopped himself from drifting further down memory lane and urged himself to get back to the task at hand. His instinctual urge to match the twins' outfits was impossible to resist tonight. He loved it when the boys harmonized. Matthew had always been very much against it. Even at the tender age of four, Matthew and Samuel could both see that the two boys' personalities were far too varied to expect them to wear the same clothes. Five now, he reminded himself. He made a mental note to put together a hasty party after the move was complete.

Matswell, a half attempt at combining their names, was quiet. He was reserved, a thinker, a planner. You would think he was a perfectly quiet boy until his plan was fully formulated. Then the wheels went into motion. Whether sneaking a cookie to bed or invading Fort Knox, Matswell had a plan for every potential obstacle. He could plan how to triumph before ever taking the first step toward victory. As many times as Matswell had bested him, Samuel knew that his son would either grow up to be an evil mastermind holding the earth hostage or the CIA's greatest asset. Either way, Samuel figured it was best to always stay on his good side. There was no denying that he was Matthew's little mini-me.

Nickelias, or Lias for short, was the other twin. He was the overconfident, outgoing, look-over-here type. Always holding the room's attention, Lias was all impulse, with no time to plan. If it weren't for his mastermind brother, there was no doubt he would have been in so much trouble, even at his young age. Matswell was always intervening at the right moment on his brother's behalf. There was no denying that Lias was Samuel's son through and through. Just like their fathers, the two boys complemented each other well. With the two of them together, everyone in their path knew they should watch out.

With the kids' school starting tomorrow, Samuel was afraid for his boys. He knew Lias would be fine on his own, but he would never agree to leave his brother. Even back home, Lias would never agree to do anything that Matswell couldn't do. It didn't even matter if Matswell didn't want to do it. Honestly, it was Matswell that Samuel was more worried about. But he was also fully aware that the boys' fates were tied; when one struggled, they both would.

Matswell was a very routine creature, and he struggled the most with changes to his surroundings.

Samuel speculated that this was because Matswell did not like obstacles that he could not predict or overcome. A new school, new kids, new teachers; Samuel knew it would all be a lot for Matswell to take in.

Lias would be the one to find trouble, and he would bring Matswell along for the ride. Samuel was afraid because the local kids had all been raised around each other's families for generations. This was something he knew all too well. His boys would be the outsiders, targets for ridicule. The thought of their taunting knocked the breath out of Samuel every time. He didn't want his boys to go through what he had gone through here.

Even with their older sisters just across the schoolyard, the boys would be in for it for sure. At least until the girls caught wind of it. At sixteen, Eternity would tear the school to pieces over her brothers. Octavia—Tavia to her family—was two years younger, but Samuel knew she would burn the bricks to ashes and stamp them out with her bare feet.

Matthew and Samuel had always instilled in their children the importance of family unity; you survive as a family, or you crumble as a family. Both girls remembered the struggles it took for the boys to come into existence: the many close calls of losing the twins week after week, the 8 long months until they were born, then the neonatal unit in Memphis Hospital.

The whole family was shaken. If not for the scare with the boys, Matthew would have pushed for a dozen more kids. Both dads agreed that they would not push their luck any further, and instead, adore the family they did have.

The children did not know that Matthew had to leave. They were used to him being away for weeks at a time for work. For now, Samuel was content to let them believe that. After all, he didn't know much more anyway. He put a spin on the move, telling them that it was necessary for Papa's work. It made the kids sad, but Papa was out trying to save the world—or at least, the people in it. They embraced their lot to the best of their ability. All four kids were exceptionally well-adjusted and brilliant, thanks to Matthew. All four had a strong aptitude for abstract and creative thinking, thanks to Samuel.

The bureau creaked shut as Samuel selected the perfect outfits for the boys' first day of school. This time of evening when his hands were busy, but his mind was free, allowed Samuel a chance to guess what Matthew had been up to. Whatever his reasons for not being around, Samuel knew it must have been necessary for him to leave when he did.

Samuel never knew another soul more loving than Tater. Tater was the pet name he had for Matthew, a relic of their youth together. Samuel knew little of Matthew's work at NASA. The only insight he ever got from Tater was in blips during his sleep. During their final days together, Matthew would often mumble in his slumber. Soon, the mumbles would be followed by screams of fear. Matthew's hands would form a protective shield across his face.

Helpless against his husband's struggles, Samuel did the only thing he could do—the only thing he always did. He got close to Matthew's ear and whispered into it the stories of their youth and their love. This always eased Matthew's dreams back to what Samuel imagined was a happy place, and a lone tear escaped down Samuel's cheek before he composed himself again.

"That will be quite enough of that for today," Samuel choked out, wiping away the evidence of his body's betrayal.

Time was often a blur for Samuel lately. The ticking clock hanging on the wall tried to remind him that he had only been home for a few minutes. It hadn't taken long to gaze in the mirror and remove already-folded clothes from a drawer for the boys. Even though inside of him years had passed, his body had only experienced a few minutes since he'd walked in through the front door.

With the boys' clothes laid out, it was time to move onto the small kitchen quarters to tidy up before breakfast. Generally, Samuel had a schedule of meals planned and prepped out for the week, not because he was naturally organized, but because without such a schedule, he would easily forget some of the necessities, and the kids would end up eating random junk. Without Matthew, most meals were planned mere hours, if not moments, ahead of time. Sometimes the junk food won.

Most meals consisted of different variations of rice, beans, and minimal meats. Samuel often served them with homemade rolls or biscuits. Today it would be biscuits and gravy for breakfast. Samuel sorted out the necessary supplies in his mind. This was a favorite breakfast of his growing up; it always gave him a euphoric feeling. Even now it brought delight to his heart.

He quietly pulled the flour from the cupboard, then the measuring cups. As he reached for the oil, something glinted in his peripheral view. A bright glow from outside the kitchen window. It was the star from earlier. "What are you doing, following me home?" Samuel said, not giving a thought to whether anyone might hear him. "Are you here to hand-deliver my wish?" He turned towards the window to give the star his full attention as the roar of a distant freight train disrupted the quiet household.

"*Shit!*" he screamed. How had he missed the signs? The last few moments were a blur as he sprang into action. The extreme weather, the sudden drop in wind, the eerie silence before the storm, the green tint to the sky - he hadn't been exposed to this kind of weather in years, yet his instincts should have been more alert.

A hue of white dust filled the kitchen and spilled onto all corners of the dark home as the flour hit the floor. Samuel rushed to the twins' room, calling out for Tavia and Eternity. "Girls! Get to the nursery, now!"

Matswell and Lias were up crying from the night's screech. The girls were in the hall in seconds, quickly catching up to what was going on. Each girl grabbed one of the brothers. "Get into the tub," Samuel ushered them into the bathroom. Even with the girls cradling each of them, the noise was terrifying. Having never lived there, the boys were disoriented and confused. They had no idea what was happening or why the house was shaking.

The boys continued to scream as the noises from outside pierced their ears. Samuel quickly folded over towels and instructed the girls to press them against the twins' ears. He knew that if there was something crashing toward the house, the cast-iron tub would be the best defense against the blow. Samuel slammed the rickety bathroom door shut to dampen the noise, but the house continued to shake. Samuel crawled into the tub and curled himself over the kids with the blanket. "It's okay, it's okay," Samuel said, trying to reassure himself as well as the children. He caressed the twins' heads through their sisters' embrace and prayed that he was right.

The boys' heads were buried in the girls' laps. The girls pressed against their Daddy's chest with fear, trying to keep their obvious tears from showing. Samuel looked directly at them and simpered a fake reassurance the way only a father can. He tried to show them that it was okay, that they need not worry. There was no way of knowing what they were up against but seeing the family bond together in crisis was the most beautiful thing the father could hope to see in his children.

Whatever they were about to face, they would face it together. They would care for each other through it all. Through the chaos, Samuel's heart and mind were at peace. The girls could feel his mixed emotions and acknowledged it with frightened half-smirks. They subtly tilted their heads down and leaned into Samuel's protective embrace. The house continued to tremble and roar as the wind turned into a high-pitched whistle. It sounded like something was headed straight to the tub they were sheltering in.

* * *

From his office, Matthew stared at his screen, hands grasped into tight fists against the cold countertop. There was nothing to do now but trust Samuel to keep everyone he loved alive. Matthew had done all he could from the confines of his self-entrapment to warn Samuel that danger was coming. His eyes were glued to the screen as he replayed the last hour in his head, making sure he had done all he could to warn his family.

Matthew had monitored the incoming pressure changes on the doppler and had hijacked multiple secret NASA orbiting star satellite stations hovering over what would appear to be Samuel's head. He had used his pull to dim and increase the stations' exterior reflective lights by maneuvering the alignment of the solar panels and releasing stored energy bursts till he had Samuel's attention. He played with the stored energy bursts on every station aligned above Samuel's position, making them each dim out as the next one in line brightened, giving Samuel the illusion that a star was moving. Samuel would feel the draw to follow this "shooting star" back home where the kids were alone and unprepared.

It was working. Samuel was following the station's bright bursts, just as Matthew hoped. Then, out of nowhere, he saw that Samuel had stopped and dropped to his knees. Matthew knew exactly what Samuel was doing. "Not now! This is not the time for sentiments, Samuel! Get up and get to our kids NOW!!" Matthew yelled at his massive screens in anger. He shut the station bursts down till Samuel stopped being silly and looked back at the sky. With the last burst of energy left in its power, Matthew forced the remaining light in the station to spark bright and darted the station forward in a blazing trail until it had nothing left and died. Matthew would have to answer for his hijacking tomorrow, but right now it was the additional protection he could give to his world. It was the only thing he could do to protect their lives.

* * *

Watching the screens, Matthew knew Samuel had made the right move. Getting everyone into the sturdy tub was the smartest thing to do. It was the same thing Matthew would have done, although to be fair, he would have noticed the impending danger much earlier and moved the family outside of range, avoiding the fear Samuel had wrought upon them.

Matthew magnified the scene inside his former home, peeking through another satellite station into the east-facing bathroom window. They had known how frequent tornadoes were in the area when they built the house, which is why Matthew had chosen the cast iron tub and why its clawed feet reached ten feet underground, attached to a two-ton slab of concrete, to give them the best possible protection from tornadoes such as this. His heart ached as he saw his boys in terror. All he could do now was wait and hope for a miracle.

Matthew watched as their love-nest shook and rattled but held its own against the storm. He had never imagined having to come back here with the kids for more than a short vacation, so he had never upgraded the place's security as he had to their Atlanta home. Samuel had made the right choice in moving them back here. Matthew remembered forcing Samuel to promise that if things ever got bad for them, he would return here, to their first home. That promise was now decades past, but Samuel's loyalty was faultless.

Matthew could see the winds shifting on his screen; the storm was breaking up. His fists began to relax as he took deep, ragged breaths to steady his heart rate. He leaned back in his chair and stared around the room for a moment. The solid white columns held strong to the faux-glass walls that surrounded his workspace. Matthew had worked, dreamed, and cried in this room, having to watch his family grow without him. He sucked in a final ragged breath before exhaustion overtook him and spoke softly, "You will cure this. You will be with them again."

THREE

As the first light of dawn burned Samuel's neck through the stained window in the bathroom, he woke up from his exhausted slumber. He instinctively sleep-swatted away the rude distraction without success. The minute current began to intensify until it could no longer be ignored. Samuel's eyelids fluttered quickly around the room for his ducklings. All were quickly accounted for. The four were fast asleep, embracing one another in the cast-iron trench they had found refuge in.

"Thank you, Matthew," Samuel whispered. Matthew had planned for such a moment decades ago. The appreciation was swiftly replaced with remorse and heavy-heartedness. Samuel remembered his impatience and irritation with Matthew being so picky about designing this very tub to withstand such a beating. His face winced, remembering he had only cared about the temporary inconvenience of the bathtub being unavailable. How much he had resented Matthew dragging it out seemingly on purpose.

Matthew always thought of everything. He could look at an empty room and see every potential hazard, even ones that wouldn't come to pass till the end of a chain of seemingly unrelated events. Years before Samuel would realize a problem was coming, Matthew had already identified, isolated, and solved it. That was their dynamic.

Leaning the girls against one another, Samuel attempted to gracefully slide out of the tub and head back to the kitchen. Of course, that was too much to ask. He bumped his knee and elbow on the edges of the mighty tub and lost his balance trying to quickly swing his body over the side of the tub, causing him to stumble backward into the hallway. Samuel's head whiplashed against the hardwood, and he whimpered in defeat. Surprisingly, the commotion was not enough to draw attention from any of the children as they rested peacefully together. He staggered to his uncooperative feet and shuffled off to the kitchen.

The trail of heavy white power was scattered along the floor from the bathroom all the way into the kitchen. There was not a single inch of the kitchen that was not covered, ceiling to floor, in flour. Samuel knew it would take hours to clean up. Perhaps it was his sleepy imagination, but it appeared as if flour still lingered in the air like a thick fog, difficult to see through.

Samuel decided that it was going to be an oatmeal kind of day instead. He stared blankly at the mess in front of him, closed his eyes, and took in a long, heavy breath of the grained, gluten-filled air. He squared his shoulders back as he released the flour-filled air from his lungs.

It was time to get the day started. Samuel brushed off the teakettle and filled it with tap water. As soon as the burner was lit, crackles and pops sounded from the tiny gas flames sizzling off water droplets and flour that lingered on the outside of the whistling pot. It was early still, but Eternity would be up soon. She had taken to an early schedule years ago when Matthew thought her old enough to understand how important his work was. Matthew had sat her down and told her he needed her to keep an eye on his world at home while he fixed everyone else's out there. He informed her that he would have to be gone for long stints of time for work and that he needed her to be a rock for the family. That is exactly what Eternity became. She was young in years but old in age, just like her Papa. As the oldest of Matthew's kids, she had maturity and insights decades beyond her time on this earth. Matthew had a way with all the kids. He could have asked her to be a tree and she would have buried her little feet in the ground and stood there till Papa told her what he needed next.

You could not help but fall in love with any plan that escaped his lips. His words were dazzling, and his passion was transparent. He promised her a few more years in the director's chair then he would be home with them 24/7. Eternity devoted herself fully to the cause, just like her Papa asked her. As if Samuel's thoughts were a bell to awaken her, Eternity entered the kitchen rubbing her eyes, stepping softly against the creaky, dust-covered floor. Awake and alert instantly as always, she could see the heavy steam threatening to escape the kettle.

She took hasty steps to grab it before it had a chance to wake everyone. Without a word, she took the kettle from the stove and quietly filled a cup, as she reached for a cocoa pack. Like every other morning, Samuel stood in quiet observation, watching Eternity be so "on" all the time. He always found it amazing. He knew she did not get that from him. Samuel had watched Matthew's similar state of total awareness of everything around them for decades.

As Eternity helped clear a clean space for the family to eat together, she shared her thoughts with Samuel quietly. "I was scared last night. The storm, crazy lightning, the shaking house, it was all too foreign to me. We never experienced that type of weather back home." She lowered her head as if in defeat as she admitted her fear out loud. Samuel's index finger caught her chin and forced it back up until their eyes met.

"Honey, you were amazing," he affirmed. "No one can know everything ahead of time. You helped me get everyone to safety quickly and kept us all calm. Your Papa and I are both so proud of you."

"I hope that will be the last we see of these storms while we're here," Eternity proclaimed. She smiled softly and embraced her Daddy. As she pulled away, he brushed back her long, coffee-colored hair.

"It could be," he admitted. "Or there could be ten more. It's never consistent season to season." Eternity collected placemats from the cupboard, clearly unimpressed by his answers.

Placing a bowl at Lias' chair, she asked, "Do you think the boys will fit in well at the school here?"

She placed Matswell's bowl on the table before Samuel could collect his thoughts. He cleared his throat in an attempt to respond. "You are all going to be great. Each one of you is so smart and so special. How could anyone not want to be friends with all of you?"

Eternity rolled her eyes and turned away from Samuel to continue her trip around the table. As mature as she was, she was also a teenager, and it was made apparent that she had no time for such a supportive comment this morning.

Samuel wasn't clearing or preparing anything. He watched Eternity lovingly place the family's bowls around the table. She kept her head tilted down, her long hair parted in the middle, curtaining down both sides of her face like a chocolate waterfall. Samuel again found himself wondering what Matthew would do if he were here. His mind drifted to Matthew and how long it had been since he felt—

Samuel's dream was interrupted by Matthew's brilliant voice in his head: "Listen to our daughter, she needs her Daddy right now."

Samuel followed Tater's order and tried to listen. He tried to decode and figure out what Eternity needed. She was visibly slouching, her energy vulnerable and dim. *This isn't like her at all*, Samuel thought. He was mortified to have not noticed it before. Eternity was always the strong one, the big sister.

Samuel wanted to pep her up, to counter her sadness. "And the award for 'Big Sister of the Year' goes to... Eternity Anderson!" He declared in a playfully theatrical voice. "And the crowd goes wild!" Eternity smiled at him and rolled her eyes. Like any father, he wanted his baby to feel confident, secure, and valued.

She got to Tavia's spot, laid another bowl down, and said, "Tavia was talking in her sleep last night, before the storm. I can tell she really misses her friends back home."

Samuel took his seat at the table and countered, "We all do, baby. It's normal to miss people and to feel worried in a new place. It'll all work out, you'll see. Today's gonna be a momentous day."

Eternity quietly moved around the rest of the table. She set the last bowls in front of her and Samuel. Samuel sat in silence while she began to wipe another space clean at the table. With her head cocked downward, she pressed the rag firmly against the wood and scrubbed a sixth designated area with the heart and conviction of a Daddy's little girl.

Samuel extended his arms and walked towards her. She allowed his embrace for a moment before looking up with her large, hazel, sparkling eyes and said, "Papa's spot is clean just in case he makes it home today."

Samuel held her tight against his chest and confirmed, "Yes, baby, that spot will always be kept clean and ready for when Papa returns." Tears fell from their eyes, streaming down their faces, landing straight on Papa's spot.

Eternity admitted, "Last night was crazy. There is so much I don't like about Nebraska. Now there are crazy storms with winds trying their best to kill us. I'm not liking this place at all."

Samuel spoke softly and calmly. "I know the move was rough on you, baby. It's been rough on us all." Samuel relaxed his hold on her and turned away slightly.

Realizing that her dad was on the verge of becoming really upset, she shifted the conversation. "I just miss the old house, it was home, and this isn't... yet." She paused. "But I understand."

Samuel hated lying to everyone, but he knew it was necessary. He told the kids that they moved for his work, which was partially true. To friends and neighbors close enough to notice Matthew's extended absences, Samuel said that he wanted to move closer to his family for support. Nothing could be farther from the truth. They would be physically close to his family, but Samuel had no intention of interacting with them.

For now, he couldn't draw attention to the change. He had a role to play, honoring Matthew's wishes. Even if he didn't understand yet why, he trusted Matthew with all their lives. Samuel refocused his thoughts and spoke to his daughter. "Go wake your sister, please."

* * *

Samuel waved goodbye to the kids as the bus drove off, then exhaled deeply. Even though Samuel or even Eternity could have driven them to school, Matthew always insisted on the kids riding the bus. He always spoke so highly of the thousands of life lessons that one could learn on a school bus that had changed his life. No one, not Samuel nor the kids, ever attempted to fight Matthew on this.

They were far from school. The house was the bus's first stop in the morning and its last stop in the evenings. This allowed Samuel about 10 hours to tidy up, put in a day's work, and prepare for the kids to return home.

As he swept the last of the flour in the kitchen, Samuel noticed a powdery glare on the living room wall. He dusted up and down the wooden panels. While he wiped the wall hangings, he read them for the thousandth time.

Matthew Anderson, Masters of Biogenetic Engineering from Harvard hung on the left. His *Masters in Robotics Science from MIT* hung on the right. Between the two, but slightly lower, Matthew hung his *MSc in Space Systems Engineering*. Matthew was always so humble about his accomplishments.

In fact, it was always Samuel who dug them out and re-hung them on the walls. Matthew just needed the educational credentials for his end goals. He never bragged that every college he applied to offered him a full ride. Learning and solving problems came naturally to Matthew. Samuel remembered Matthew double-majoring at Harvard and MIT concurrently with ease, while he struggled to stay afloat with his law degree from Andover. Andover was not Samuel's first choice. It was not even on his list, if he was being honest. When Matthew made up his mind about Harvard, Samuel found an accommodating school so he could be with his young love.

Back then, the idea of being far apart was too hard for Samuel to imagine. Matthew's scholarships and awards allowed them to afford a charming studio apartment in Woburn and pay for Samuel's tuition. Samuel had refused, of course, but Matthew did not exactly ask. He never really asked when it came to finances; he just did.

Thinking back on the Woburn years, Samuel couldn't help but smile. He remembered their 3 AM cram sessions there. The apartment always smelled like coffee and pizza. Their backs touching, eating cold Chinese food out of a box sitting on the floor. Then there was the year they spent living in a tent while building their starter home in Nebraska. Oh, how they hated that house! Matthew was set to start at Georgia Tech barely 6 months after it was done. That was when they moved into their "real" home.

Samuel spent his time in court cases fighting all over Georgia for LGBT rights. Matthew took a dual role, reporting to the CDC and NASA simultaneously. The changing world around them necessitated a bridge between the two agencies. Matthew was the one to build it. Samuel didn't get to know much about Matthew's work. He didn't need to. It did not matter to Samuel what Matthew did for a living.

Samuel loved his time on the bar, but there was not a second thought in his mind when they decided to start a family that he would be the one at home with the kids. After all, Matthew had done, it was the least he could do in return. Matthew's work affected so many more people. It was a fair trade-off. Consulting from home still allowed Samuel to make a difference in the world while being present for his family.

His computer chirped, interrupting his daydreaming. An email had come through. His heart hoped it would be Matthew, but his brain knew that it was work. Matthew never emailed him in all of their time together. He didn't trust emails. Samuel did not understand Matthew's reservations, but it was never a battle worth having. Matthew did not email outside of work, and he never texted. The email turned out to be from a small law firm in Ohio that Samuel had been consulting for. "I guess it's time to work," Samuel muttered.

* * *

Matthew stared into the mass of computer screens on his desk. Watching five screens at once could easily be overwhelming, but by now it was second nature to him. He had been doing it for almost fifteen years. He had to do little more than observe the screens' progress and dictate any necessary changes for the field engineers to execute. His attention drifted off the screen as he thought of his family. Matthew was shocked out of his daze by an incoming video call. It was his assistant, Julia. Julia was so sweet; no matter what Matthew asked of her, she went above and beyond.

Everyone who knew Matthew Anderson knew not to cross Julia. They had been together since the beginning of Matthew's career. Matthew did not like having an assistant and rarely used her for typical assistant stuff. Julia was charming and ambitious. She was never his walking, talking datebook. Matthew often used her skills in negotiation follow-ups. Her responsibilities were unheard of for an assistant.

Julia's pleasant face filled Matthew in on recent assignments. "Please follow up with Big Tech," Matthew instructed her. "I need better quality data coming from Rover dash cams. Their satellites need to be adjusted; I can't see everything I need to see. Also, please secure 25 more automated bobcats and 5 more planters en route and spread out to the 5 test planets by month's end." Julia leaned her head and smiled slyly at him in assent. "Also, I really hate to ask..."

Julia stopped him immediately. She had been his friend long enough to know just what he was going to ask. "I know the family's in Nebraska, and they miss you terribly. With your permission, I'd like to work remotely for the next week and see them on your behalf."

Matthew smiled a tired smile. "Thank you," he said. There was nothing Julia wouldn't do for Matthew; she thought of his family as her own. She had been in the room with Matthew and Samuel when each of the kids was born.

Julia always volunteered to be the family cinematographer for every major event. Since her kids were long grown and her grandkids were so far away, she found Matthew just when she needed another family to be part of. As Julia's face winked out of existence, Matthew glanced back across his screens.

He was thankful for her unbreakable loyalty, as it gave him the necessary strength to focus on his work, despite everything else that was going on in his life.

FOUR

Samuel quickly lost focus at his makeshift desk in the living room of his small Nebraska home reading a lengthy email. His mind drifted to the twins on the bus, on their first day of school. He allowed his mind to wander back to his first day in Verdigre. His heart began to quicken. He had been newly adopted by his family and had to move clear across the state to start over here. His adoptive parents hadn't taken much care to ensure he was prepared for the long bus ride.

He was not much older than the twins were now. As the new kid on the bus, it was only a few moments before he became the target of the others' tomfoolery. The older kids asked if he wanted to see a magic trick. They did not wait for him to answer before removing his shoes. When they finally returned them, the laces had been tied together.

He had not yet learned how to tie his shoelaces properly, let alone how to tackle such a jumbled knot. Thankfully, the shoes were hand-me-downs, too big for his feet. He was able to slip back in them with ease.

He was the last one off the bus once it arrived at school. He tried to scoot along without lifting his feet off the ground. Samuel recalled the way he tumbled down the bus steps, scraping both his knees and palms. The other kids laughed at his peril before any adult bothered to intervene. The unison of laughter from everyone on the bus made it clear that it was acceptable by all the kids to treat the outsider so cruelly.

Even as he eventually made friends at the school, Samuel remembered how he always felt like an object of ridicule. Now his babies are on their way to the same school with the likely descendants of those very same children.

* * *

Tears ran down Samuel's cheeks. Before he knew it, he scooped up his keys and rushed out the door. The bus had half an hour's head start, but Samuel knew he wouldn't have any trouble catching up. He pulled up to the schoolyard and looked around. Not much had changed since his time there. Samuel quickly found a parking space and made his way to the bus loading zone. He found himself jogging there for no reason. The lot was empty; the school bus hadn't made it there yet. Still, he felt like he had to be there.

He had to wait for his boys with open arms, ready to support them when they needed him the most.

Looking at his watch, he realized he still had a few minutes before the kids arrived. He had rushed out of the house without a thought to his appearance. The last thing his family needed was faculty and students seeing him out of sorts. Small towns talk; he didn't want that.

Samuel rushed himself to the all-too-familiar restrooms outside the cafeteria to make himself a little more presentable. The kindergarten mirror did not offer much help. He had just finished toweling off water from his face when voices began to fill the hallways. He closed the bathroom door behind him. The windows that stretched the length of the hallway showed kids jumping down from yellow school buses. Samuel paused awkwardly in the hall. There were no other adults—let alone parents—in the vicinity. Woe weighed on his heart as the first of his tribe exited the bus. It was Eternity of course: strong, composed, and confident as always. She was holding hands with Matswell and followed by Lias. She was looking out for them, of course. His boys were not alone on the bus as he had been that day as a child.

He'd worried for nothing. But, he was already there, so worry or not, he was going to say good luck to his boys one last time before leaving. Eternity had barely stepped off the bus when she spotted him from across the parking lot. She must have quickly gathered why he was there. She took one knee and pointed him out to the boys, who took off running across the small parking lot. She waved to her dad as she rose back to her feet and turned in the opposite direction with her sister.

Samuel had already walked them back and forth to their classroom a few times the week before, so after a long hug, the boys were ready to walk the now familiar path to their class alone. Lias grabbed his brother's hand and led the way forward, unaware of what he was dragging his brother into.

Despite their youth, both boys were tough as nails. Lias had more confidence than most adults ever gained in a lifetime. He was grinning excitedly from ear to ear, ready to be rid of his adult interference already.

Matswell tried to keep up with his brother's optimistic stride, but there was just too much data for him to take in at once. He stumbled a bit as his feet struggled to keep up with his brain. The schoolhouse back home was brightly lit, clean, and full of kids. Here, the hallway looked like it had been pulled straight out of a scary movie. The dim lights barely hung on to their fixtures. The walls and crevices were coated with a layer of dust, making it clear that there was not enough cleaning staff in the building. The absence of students filling the halls even this early alerted Matswell to danger.

The boys made it to their classroom and walked inside, no longer holding hands. They remembered well the face of their teacher, Mrs. Hogeland. She was slightly shorter than most adults, making her instantly more relatable to the children. She had short hair that framed her small face. Her hair was shaven skin short on the sides of her face. It made the boys look at her as "tough." She had big framed purple glasses with a stitch sticker on the side that made her seem like a big kid to them. But her most remarkable feature was her huge warm smile, so large that her cheeks seemed to struggle to keep it below her topaz eyes. From her unique appearance, it was obvious she was new here. No generations of her family had walked these halls before her. She was a transplant, an outsider as well. This gave Samuel the smallest bit of relief.

The classroom was quite different from what the boys were used to. Back home, the classrooms were very tidy and stocked with computers, projectors, and dry-erase boards. This new classroom had no computers or projectors. The aged look of the classroom was out of place to the boys. The unfamiliar smell of chalk was very unsettling to them, especially to Matswell. Their desks were small and separated from each other in rows and columns. All chairs and tables faced toward Mrs. Hogeland's large cedar desk. This was nothing like the group-learning environment they had experienced in Atlanta.

Meanwhile, Samuel sneaked towards the boys' classroom surreptitiously. It had hurt him a little to learn that the boys were so independent. They did not need or want him to accompany them to class. He was not surprised, though. After all, they were Matthew's sons. He recalled the boys' first day of preschool when they had only needed each other. As long as they were together, the boys didn't mind being left alone, even if it was for hours on end. On that first day of preschool, neither boy shed a tear.

Samuel was hurt by their feat, but Matthew was proud of them. Samuel was not ready to have independent kids. He had spent the last sixteen years finding comfort in being needed. But even his youngest needed him less by the day.

It was eerie to walk these halls again after all these years. He knew this building all too well. Samuel remembered walking into this very room himself as a boy, not much older than the twins. Samuel still knew where every door would lead, and which teacher was likely behind each.

He sat with his back against the wall, just out of view. He didn't want to break the boys' rule of not coming in with them. He needed to be near them now. Samuel did not know why. It wasn't ever like this with the girls. Or even when the twins were back home. Here it felt like he needed to be around, to linger a bit longer.

Slouching down the wall, he remembered what a rough time he had had at the school in his youth. Even though everyone eventually treated him well, for the most part, he never felt like he fit in. He never truly belonged there. The feeling continued throughout all twelve years of school. Samuel struggled to breathe as he imagined the boys feeling the same way. He was panting, so lost in himself that he did not hear the approaching footsteps. A woman snuck up and placed her hand on his shoulder. He jumped in surprise.

It was Mrs. Hogeland. "Your boys are inside, safe, without incident," she whispered, putting her finger to her lips. "I will take good care of them, don't you worry." Mrs. Hogeland backed into the classroom again, closing the door behind her.

Samuel was a little embarrassed to be caught but was thankful she hadn't made a bigger deal out of it. Though he had been cast away, he found he couldn't move quite yet. He allowed himself to linger a bit longer. He could feel the cold vanilla-painted bricks against the back of his neck. It reminded him of when he was five years old. He had waited for his parents to come and walk him to class like the other parents did. They never showed up. He was tossed on the bus alone and expected to figure it all out. Only he wasn't strong enough for the journey. He yearned for support back then, but the support never came.

Samuel realized that he was projecting his past trauma and insecurities on the children. That was the true answer to the question of "Why am I here?" The boys were fine. He stole one last glance inside to remind himself that he was overreacting. Then, it was time for him to go home.

* * *

Tavia looked slowly around from the back of the room. She was not a particularly attentive student, so she was glad that Mrs. Grear had placed her in the back of the room. She thought to herself how different this school was compared to the one she was used to. Apparently, very few kids here had phones - or at least, were brave enough to have them out on display.

She looked at her wrist to see the awkward callbox watch she wore. It was a small, rudimentary version of a smartwatch Matthew had designed just for his family. Tavia had always hated wearing the watch. *Why couldn't Papa let them have phones like all the other kids did?* she thought. But Papa was peculiar with things like that. He did not like anyone besides him and Daddy to be able to track their location. Papa called cell phones a distraction from intelligence.

Leave it to my Papa to invent a watch with GPS reporting only to the parents' watch, and only allowing them to communicate with preprogrammed numbers from the parent's unit, Tavia imagined. Thankfully, no one here seemed to know what the unique watch was. No one would know that her dad had invented it. She tapped the tiny screen and looked at her call/message options. Dad's box, 911, Matswell, Lias, Eternity.

She always found it funny that Papa had invented this device but couldn't even wear it himself because of his work. As she fiddled with the watch, a group message came across; it was a heart emoji from Dad. Mrs. Grear must have noticed that Tavia had been ignoring the algebra lesson, so she called her to the board to write the slope-intercept form of an equation. Tavia was a little dramatic, pretending to have to think hard before writing y=mx+b. She knew math like the back of her hand—no way was she going to let anyone here learn that secret. Mrs. Grear gave her a few coordinates and different y-intercepts to test her knowledge before thanking Tavia and ushering her back to her seat.

Before sitting back down, Tavia noticed her reflection in the mirror. Her short, cropped russet hair had almost overgrown all the red highlights. She would have to fix that soon, but which of the children of the corn could she trust with her hair? Her face looked paler than usual... he had spent too much time indoors lately. She needed to get out more in the sun. She missed zipping around outside on her roller skates. Her ink-like eyes looked even more piercing than usual because of the purple bags under them. She was not sleeping well lately. She would have to plead her case again to Samuel for colored contacts. She never won, of course; she didn't actually need contacts, but she would have to try. She could slightly make out the tan line from her choker that this school forbade her from wearing. *What a stupid dress code*, she thought.

She shook her head, sitting down. Looking around the room, all the kids were cookie-cutter versions of one another. There was no variation in skin color. Everyone dressed the same. There was very little variety in hair color. Apparently, this school did not encourage any form of individuality. Hopefully, they would go back home soon and exit this cult.

FIVE

Samuel spent the day aimlessly wandering around Verdigre and reminiscing about his childhood here. He would drive the twins home from school today. "Just this once," he justified to himself. His extra worry about the boys settling into a new school was too much to bear. They were so young. Besides, he knew how much distaste this community had for anyone different; anyone who wasn't from around here.

The decision to drive them today was not just for the boys' sake. Rather, it was for Matthew's, too. Samuel didn't want to add any extra stress to Matthew. He had no idea what Matthew was involved in, but he did know that this piece of their life could be controlled. At this moment, Samuel would do his part to relieve Matthew's nerves.

"That was a good reason, right?" he asked himself, seconds before the twins hopped into the Jeep.

Samuel wasn't used to the bumpy ride that the old Jeep provided, nor were the boys. The green paint had faded from years of being tucked into the barn. The rocky Nebraska roads were too rough, and he didn't want to subject Gabriel to their dangers.

Gabriel was Samuel's pride and joy; a slick, black BMW he bought for himself last year, after closing out a case he consulted on for over a year. Matthew thought it was too flashy, but Samuel had always wanted a BMW, so he treated himself. Samuel had always been thrilled to be a dad but did not enjoy the expected transportation that came along with that territory. The day he traded in his old SUV for Gabriel, he felt free.

They all jostled around like bobblehead dolls as Samuel made their way down the dirt-covered road. Matthew had maintained the Jeep minimally through the years, working on it whenever he brought the family for an annual camping getaway. Matthew chose to come back here yearly to help them stay humble. He wanted the family to remember where they came from. He was afraid the kids would grow up without the basic life skills that could only be learned in the country. The weekend trip often turned into a four-day adventure of uninterrupted family time.

When the kids were younger, entertainment was as easy as handing them a card game, building forts, or having campfire cookouts behind the house.

The backyard was open land, connected to the acres of wheat and corn that stretched to the horizon. With the family never spending extended time there, there wasn't any point in adding too much to the yard. It lay empty except for a hammock and a tire swing.

The front yard faced a small forest grove that ran to the highway. The only indication that a home sat behind the trees was a broken mailbox post. A driver had run off the road and destroyed it, but no one was ever charged. The family did not need the landmark. They opted for a post-office box instead. Each of them could tell the location of their house by the subtle slope of the hill they drove over, just before they arrived at their discreet driveway.

Samuel made a game out of the bumps with the boys. "The tires must be shaped like octagons, what do you think, boys?"

"I think they're triangles, Dad!" Matswell said with a smile.

"They could be squares," Lias added.

"Do you guys remember what an octagon is?" Samuel questioned.

"Yes, Dad," they said in unison.

Matswell added, "It's a shape with eight sides, like a stop sign."

Samuel smiled with pride. He secretly wondered if the boys were going to be challenged enough in Verdigre. He could still vividly recall his struggle when he left here for the "real world." The education system here had not set him up for success; Matthew had to coach him for years to come.

Though the ride was bumpy, Samuel drove much faster than necessary. It was "boys' time." The girls insisted on riding the bus. No need to be the nerds seen with Dad on Day 1 of a new school. Compared to the smooth streets of Atlanta, driving in the bouncy Jeep was just like monster truck riding.

The trail smoothed as the Jeep breached the forest and climbed onto the highway. "We made it boys!" Samuel exclaimed.

He passed the time by talking to the boys about the fun memories they had from back home. He reminded them of the summer evenings they spent together when the cool evening air of June cleared the sky and revealed an entire galaxy of stars above them. Matthew taught them all about constellations. He always had a captivating way of talking and would often pique the kids' curiosity about the different possibilities hidden within the stars. He was grooming them to become free thinkers, that much was certain.

When they pulled up to the driveway, Samuel saw that an unfamiliar car was already there. Samuel's heart skipped a beat. He instinctively reached over to lock the Jeep's doors, his fight-or-flight mode kicking in. He slowed the car and started scanning the perimeter for intruders.

It was Matswell who first noticed the visitor. "Uliea!" he beamed and pointed. Samuel noticed Julia standing in the yard, looking out into the fields.

Samuel stopped the car just in time for the twins to leap from their seats and lunge toward Julia. She smiled a grandmotherly smile as the boys plowed into her. She instinctively lowered to the ground and reached out both arms into an awaiting embrace.

"Easy!" shouted Samuel as both boys hit her at once.

She held them and kissed them both until Samuel ordered them inside. Julia got back to her feet and stepped forward to embrace Samuel. As soon as they touched, Julia could feel him collapse into the hug. She knew that collapse. She knew the weight on his shoulders. Julia knew everything. Samuel did not realize how much he had built up inside till there was a chance to let it all go.

She held Samuel as he sobbed in her arms. Samuel tried muttering a few incoherent words between sobs.

She didn't need to hear the words to know what he was asking. "He loves you. He misses you, but he still isn't able to return."

Samuel cried even more. It was as if a dam had burst open. Julia leaned in close and whispered into Samuel's ear, "He's been watching you. He's definitely watching you now. It's tearing him up not to be here for you. Seeing you like this isn't good for him."

Lost and confused, Samuel whipped in a quick breath and held it for as long as he could. He wiped at his eyes and put on a fake smile for Matthew; though, the smile was not completely fake.

"It's so good to see you, Julia," he said.

Samuel loved Julia. He always felt much calmer around her. "Let me show you inside. Things are in a bit of disarray after last night's fiasco. I hope you're staying for a bit."

"A few days maybe," Julia replied. "You know I can't leave him alone for long." Samuel nodded. They both stepped inside.

* * *

A few hours later, Julia was stirring the tea bag in her cup and staring intently at Samuel. The kids all said their hellos and chatted with Julia before they were sent outside for training. Matthew had required each of the kids to learn karate, so Tavia was leading the lessons for now since there were no teachers around the area.

"Samuel, I know this has to be tearing you apart. You know he loves you and the kids with all his heart. And you know his clearance makes it impossible for him to share anything about what's going on.

Matthew is doing what he must. At least this way he's able to see you and the kids daily."

Samuel already knew that, of course. He knew the man he loved. He knew safety would be the only reason Matthew would stay away. "I know," Samuel agreed. "But that doesn't make it hurt any less, Julia. He isn't here."

Julia's understanding smile and eyes were always Zen to Samuel. But this time her presence, here in Verdigre, warned him that Matthew was in worse shape than he had thought.

If the only contact Matthew could muster now was Julia, then... Samuel banished the thought quickly before Julia could read it on his face.

"Shall we sit by the fire with our tea?" he asked. Samuel knew that the living room was the only room in the house with no windows; no windows meant no onlookers to disturb their privacy.

If he was going to get anything from Julia, he had to subtly suggest that direction to her.

"How was your trip?" Samuel asked in a soft tone.

"At my age, traveling always wears me out," Julia countered.

"Did you have to travel far?" Samuel probed.

"It felt like forever, but sometimes a trip to the corner store can feel like forever," Julia chuckled.

"The weather has been crazy around here lately. How has it been for you?" Samuel questioned with a caring smile.

"I haven't had much chance to notice, honestly. Sunup to sundown inside most days. It could be beautiful outside, or a hurricane, and I wouldn't notice." Julia sidestepped in that slippery way Samuel recognized all too well from his partner.

The chat continued in this way by the fire. Samuel looked for any opening to ask questions she could answer without realizing she was giving anything away. He was a distinguished member of the bar, so he was used to reading people. She evaded questions about work, how long her drive was, and whether the airport experience had been nice to her. Matthew had trained her well—too well in fact, for what Samuel needed right now. Julia's high clearance meant she had to be able to keep information in. After tea, Julia excused herself and headed to town to find herself a room for the night.

Samuel didn't even try to get her to stay; he knew she needed privacy to work. "I'll see you all tomorrow," Julia pledged as she rolled up the car window and drove off.

She was barely out of Samuel's earshot when her phone rang. She heard Matthew's soft voice on the other side. "Stop the car at the end of the driveway," he instructed. Julia followed his instructions without question. "Eternity's hidden her call box under the license plate, no doubt to act as a tracker to me. I didn't realize she knew something was wrong," he said. He couldn't be surprised she was brilliant—she had her Papa's genes, and he would have done the same.

Julia beamed with pride at Eternity's innovation. "I'll call you back," she said to Matthew. Eternity was truly her father's daughter. Julia turned the car around and drove back to the house. She knew she had to return the call box to its owner. Matthew would need it back on Eternity if he were to sleep tonight. These days, even that modicum of sleep was in peril, and therefore all the more precious. Julia smirked to herself with a grandmother's pride as she knocked on the door.

Samuel opened the door with a puzzled look. He saw Julia grinning and holding Eternity's callbox in the palm of her hand. She extended the device out to Samuel. "I'm sure Matthew would want Eternity to have this back," she said. "Besides, it will be more useful on her wrist than under my license plate." She chuckled as she said the words aloud.

Samuel looked down and tried to hide his expression. "Kids do the darndest things, don't they?" he lied to her. He faked surprise at her actions. Of course, she was just as worried as he was. He wore his best fake smile and shrugged it off. He thanked Julia for returning the call box and gave her another hug for the road.

Closing the door, he leaned against the wall and allowed himself a moment to be truthful with himself. Eternity had realized that something was going on and was worried enough to feel like she needed to track down her Papa.

"Why didn't I put that together myself?" Samuel muttered to himself under his breath. He had known that something was off with Matthew, but he hadn't imagined a situation where Matthew might need rescuing. Matthew was the strongest person he knew. Things were bad enough that Matthew was actively watching the family. His scrutiny was close enough that he wouldn't be found. The implications of this thought were scary.

Matthew had always watched over them. That was normal. But he had never watched them as closely before. This was profoundly serious. *It's time to do something*, Samuel thought. He knew he would have to be extremely cautious. Matthew was a planner; he would be looking for anything out of the ordinary to alert him to trouble. If Samuel was to succeed, he couldn't deviate from his normal routine. If he did anything spontaneous, he would be caught in an instant.

Samuel could see Julia's blinker through the kitchen window. She indicated left but turned right.

Samuel took it as another sign that something was not right. Dust swirled in the air. He watched until she drove beyond the coverage of the trees.

Meanwhile, Matthew's weak, hoarse voice continued to broadcast through Julia's car speakers. "How are they? Please give me all the details. I want to know what they are thinking about, how they feel, what they smell like, everything!" This was typical of Matthew. It was like his brain was going down a list of items. He needed all the details to know how to react. His voice cracked, "I really miss them."

Julia sighed to herself and took a deep breath as she prepared to answer him. "They all look healthy and happy enough. They miss you terribly but seem optimistic that you are returning soon. I just spent a little time with each of them. I fear your absence will affect the twins the most. They made it a point to mention that their birthday wasn't the same without you this year..."

"I'll be missing that for many more years, I fear," Mathew interjected in a disappointed tone. "I've never been away for this long. I don't know how to be an absentee dad."

Julia stopped him before he could drown in self-pity. "Don't be so certain of your future. The twins did say they wished for you as their birthday gift. They also mentioned they'd like to move back home. They're not fans of the new school. Matswell said the teachers are boring and Lias is confused by how the other kids act toward them. I'm not sure what's going on yet, but they haven't settled into things well."

"You're right," Matthew answered.

He was not used to feeling powerless when it came to his family. Now he had no choice but to watch from a distance the struggles his family faced without being able to step in and save the day. The Papa bear instinct was high, but his energy level was low—too low.

SIX

After karate, it was Tavia's turn to hang out with the boys. Her job for today was to bathe the boys and get them ready for bed. Eternity sat somberly at the table with her Daddy as the twins passed out hugs. Samuel waited until the younger kids were out of sight before quietly pulling his call box from his pocket. He extended out his arm and cradled the large watch in his palm. He tried to inject a light-hearted tone into his words.

"You'd have to get up pretty early in the morning to pull one over on your father, baby," he tried his best to chuckle, hoping she'd buy it. But Eternity saw right through him. Samuel knew he wasn't a good liar. Furthermore, his daughter was incredibly observant.

Her response baffled and confused Samuel. "I never intended to fool him, just to observe him. There were only two scenarios to play out. 1. Papa does what he always does—tracks the call box periodically to protect us and notices it is out of place eventually—or

2. He is watching closely to maintain secrecy and notices right away. The latter tells me something is wrong." Samuel lowered his eyes to the ground. Of course, she had a plan. Now he had to lie to protect her—to protect them all.

When he raised his eyes back up to meet hers, he had a more convincing laugh on his face. "Occam's Razor, my sweet daughter," Samuel challenged. "You are forgetting the most obvious solution of them all. Julia is great at her job, and you are not a spy. She noticed the watchband dangling out from behind her plate as she approached the car and brought it back in."

Eternity's soft peach complexion darkened with embarrassment as she realized how silly and amateur her actions were. Samuel helped her transition quickly, "No more Mission: Impossible movies for you, young lady." They both laughed the awkwardness away.

The room went silent as Eternity shifted gears. She tucked a few stray hairs behind her ear and reached for her backpack. She pulled out a permission slip for blood-type labs in biology and passed it over to her dad.

Samuel looked at it, took a deep breath, and checked the box that said, "I do not permit my child to take part." Eternity was not surprised when she reviewed the form. She had already known this would be his decision, as it always was when it came to anything medical in nature.

Eternity noticed that Samuel and Matthew were more private than most with medical history, but she never had a reason to be pushy about it over the years. After her defeat with Julia, though, Eternity wanted a win. She looked at her father defiantly and began to form a question. Samuel stopped her right away, lifting his left index finger to his lips. The truth was that he had no answer for her. He had no idea what he could say. Looking at Eternity's wide eyes and flushed cheeks, Samuel could tell that she was conflicted. He had seen that look in court thousands of times before.

His gesture was shorthand he had used with the kids over the years when he was caught off-guard. It was a stalling tactic, designed to give him another moment to gather his thoughts before responding. There was no reason to suspect that Eternity was onto him, so he dragged the moment out, pretending to listen for tiny little ears on the other side of the wall.

Samuel knew his daughter. He knew she wouldn't settle for anything less than a plausible explanation. The problem was, there was no such reason he could offer her. Instead, there was only the truth.

Samuel's time was up. The harsh huff of Eternity's exhaling and the genie-like way she folded her arms told him she was ready to plead her case.

Samuel had always dreaded this day. Eternity was going to hear the truth, and Samuel was going to have to be the one to give it to her. He regretted the fact that Matthew was not there to help him deliver the news.

"Get your coat, baby," he whispered.

Eternity was surprised. She had often tried to mentally square off with her dad, but his courtroom wit usually bested her. She had not expected this victory. She took note of Samuel's fidgeting and the way he shifted his weight from one foot to the other. It was clear that he was uncomfortable. *What could he have to tell me that would make him this uncomfortable?* she thought. *This had better not be an expanded sex talk...*

Eternity resolved to strike while the iron was hot. She was already mentally preparing the battalion of questions she would fire at her dad as soon as they were alone. She yelled out to Tavia that she was going out for a walk with their father. Tavia was mature enough to look after her brothers, so Samuel wasn't afraid to leave them alone for a short time. The twins could be a handful, but if anyone could hold her own against them, it was Tavia.

The early-night breeze nipped at their backs as soon as the antiquated door closed behind them. Samuel took in a breath and began talking.

"Sweetheart, you are growing up so fast. Faster than I'm ready for, to be honest. There are some truths in our world that you need to know. It was always our plan to tell you when the time was right. We've always tentatively scheduled this talk for after you turn 17. We'd hoped that you'd have some time to spend at home before we let you out into the world on your own with this knowledge."

Samuel allowed a moment to try to shake the cold off. Eternity studied him intently without interrupting his monologue.

"Given that life is hitting us all so fast, I don't see a point in waiting a few months longer. You are ready to know the truth of your world," Samuel admitted.

Eternity was staring ahead and watching her steps closely. She zoned in on Samuel's choice of words. She noted that he had said, "the truths of *your* world," not "the truths of *the* world." Before that, he had said, "the truths of *our* world." Whatever he was about to share with her did not apply to everyone.

Though she was bursting with questions, Eternity held her silence. It looked like Daddy was on the cusp of sharing something big with her. She knew that if she interrupted him, he was more likely to change course. She racked her mind, calculating the different possibilities until Samuel laced his hand in hers and brought her focus back to the present.

"You may not know this, but this house was the first home your father and I built after college," Samuel opened.

"I didn't realize that," Eternity interjected. "I guess I just assumed that you came straight to Atlanta after you finished school. Why would you come here?"

"I grew up here," Samuel answered. "Your father moved here from Idaho during his sophomore year. We took a liking to each other immediately. Papa had lived in many big cities before moving here. He knew more about the world than I did when we met, more than I could imagine. I was still coming to terms with my sexuality at the time. Back then, homosexuality was taboo here. I imagine it still is."

Samuel slowed his pace and held some branches out of his daughter's way. Once she had passed, he continued.

"But your father was brave. He could see a future where the world would see couples as couples, no matter what. He foresaw the legalization of gay marriage decades before it came about. Me, I never bought into it. Growing up here, I couldn't see any future that didn't revolve around hating anyone different than the rest. I really liked your father, and we spent all of sophomore year inseparable from each other. But I thought there was no loving future in the cards for us. No happily ever after. No family. No acceptance from God."

It hurt Eternity to hear her Daddy speak like that about his doubts. She swallowed down the lump in her throat and hoped that Samuel couldn't see the tears welling up in the corners of her eyes.

Samuel led them into a small clearing in the woods along the edge of a country road. They were out of sight of the house. The wind pushed past them, overwhelming them with the smell of iron and rust. They could feel the dirt in the air. Samuel wiped his eyes with one hand and pointed ahead of him with the other.

"There used to be a small house here, smaller than ours. It was where your father lived when they moved here. This is where I came to visit. Sometimes I'd drive by just to see him thinking in his hammock outside. I had such a tight curfew, so I rarely had any time to stop. All I could do was imagine the conversations we'd have if I could stop. Back then, I didn't think anyone would notice me driving by. I was sure I was incognito. Looking back now and knowing what I know about your Papa, there was no way he missed it. He just never called me out on it."

Eternity considered the information and agreed; that did seem like her Papa. But despite her best attempts to stay patient, she couldn't imagine what any of this would have to do with her blood-type assignment. Still, she would hold her questions till Samuel was done. She did not want to derail him.

Samuel paused for a moment, looking at his daughter before moving on with his story. He lowered his eyes to the ground, already feeling shame for what he was about to share. A deep breath brought his shoulders up to his chin.

The tale started very meekly, and Eternity had to strain to hear. "I worked a closing shift at Bubba's Burger Place, which has long been torn down, a few nights a week. It was a Wednesday night. There was a large religious party for the last hour after services were let out. As I served them and bussed trash, I overheard them talking about the day's sermon. The preacher warned them of the dangers of homosexuality and how God turns his back on 'those people.' Seeing the struggle his daughter had hearing him, Samuel tried to speak louder: "It was tormenting to hear. I tried my best to block it all out. After work, I walked to my car. It was late, and as usual, I was the last to leave. I was parked alone in a far corner of the parking lot. As the lonely breeze pushed against me a shiver went down my spine. I imagined the moving air to be the exhale of Satan himself. I felt naked, scared, afraid, and lonely. Being raised so religiously, God was with me no matter what. But this night he was not there to deflect the wicked wind. I felt forsaken, and it scared me disturbingly."

Eternity wanted to interject, to understand how any of this had anything to do with her blood typing assignment, but she allowed her father to continue, "I made it to the car, then I drove right here. Your father was alarmed when I pulled up so late. He rushed to the car and got in the passenger side. He asked me what was wrong. I told him that what was happening between us was not right. Being with him was not the plan God had for me. I shared that more than anything in the world I wanted a future. A partner society could accept. That my family could accept. I wanted to share a home with someone. More than anything I wanted a family that was all connected. I wanted kids that were half mine and half my partner's. With him, I could never have that connection. So, I thanked him for all his kindness toward me for the last year then asked him to leave me alone." Regret began to flow down Samuel's cheeks. He pawed at it, but the river continued.

Samuel wiped at his nose and eyes searching for the strength to trudge on. "Papa was so strong even back then. He let me speak without interruption. He did not argue or beg me to stay. When I finished speaking, he nodded his head as if he were tipping a hat. Then he got out of my car and went inside without turning around to see me leave." Eternity was wiping away a tear from her own eyes. By now she had forgotten what lead them to this story. She was caught up in the moment her father was now reliving transparently. Samuel paused, softly pinched the side of her cheek, and lifted her chin slightly to meet his stare. It hurt him to see through his daughter's eyes the pain that must have been cast on Matthew that night. No one besides Matthew knew this story. This was the first time Samuel was seeing how an outsider reacted to his actions. His rib cage tightened around his heart as the realization of that sunk in. He took in a few quick, sharp breaths of the humid dirty night before continuing with his recollection before he lost his will to continue. "

I drove home that night more alone than I felt before I got there. I guessed that God did not notice yet I severed that connection. That he was now welcome back into my heart fully. After all, God had used those patrons to deliver his message. I was going down the wrong path in my life. I had no choice but to act on God's wishes."

As Samuel admitted the last few sentences, his voice slowed, and his words slurred. Falls of tears leapt down his face. Eternity moved next to her father and offered one arm awkwardly around him.

"When I got home that night, I wiped tears from my eyes before anyone saw me. No one knew we were dating. No one would or could understand that we had broken up. I summoned the courage to walk past my foster parents. They were always waiting to catch me coming in even a minute late."

Samuel paused. Sharing all this for the first time drudged up his long-buried pain. He was on the verge of reneging on his commitment when he looked into his daughter's eyes. This was her moment, not his. He was there for her. He would go on.

"My foster parents asked me where I was. I explained that I had stopped on the way home to see Mathew. Right when I mentioned his name, they called him the devil and blamed him for my negligence. I explained to them that I told Mathew I couldn't spend time around him anymore. They were pleased about that and postponed my punishment for missing curfew. I noticed them smiling at each other in approval as I limped down the hall, crushed." Eternity scoffed under her breath. Her anger was written plainly on her face. But Samuel was not done sharing. "For the rest of junior year and through the summer Matthew never crossed my path. It was like he knew my every step and intentionally made sure not to be anywhere around me. I longed to see him, of course, but feared the pain I'd feel if I did. God never came back to me after that night. No matter how much I prayed for him, I never felt that connection return."

Samuel paused and took a stretched steady breath in and out. Eternity sat speechless at the mounds of information she had just received. Samuel could not meet her eyes as he continued.

"At the end of the summer before senior year was to start, I was walking down the street a few blocks from my house and my heart stopped. In my driveway, I spotted Papa's old car. I lost my calm in the moment before remembering that my family was all gone. The thought of seeing him after all this time was scary enough without having to explain his presence here. I hurried up to the truck and started to speak to him when he held up a mountainous palm and stopped me demanding that I take a ride with him. I was shocked. It was a commanding and scary presence at that moment. I felt like I owed this to him, so I did as he demanded. Partly for him, but if I'm being honest, I mostly did it to get him out of my driveway before anyone noticed."

Eternity looked shocked to hear her Papa be so stern, so angry. Samuel could guess from the puzzled look on her face.

"Papa was a teenager too honey. We all have moments where we act out of character. Those are the moments we learn the most from in life." Samuel offered.

Samuel looked down at Eternity before continuing. She was captivated. Samuel and Matthew never shared their story with the kids. It was a part of their history that Samuel didn't like to remember, and Matthew figured there wasn't any benefit in them knowing until they were older. Samuel continued.

"I waited as we drove off for him to speak. We rode in silence for some time, I assume he was gathering his thoughts. He told me that he knew I was lying that night. My heart panicked as I did not want to be confronted about any of this. I just wanted to forget this all happened and go back to my boring life. I was unprepared to defend my words. I could not even remember at that moment what my words were."

Samuel wiped at the edges of his eyes with his shirt sleeve as he recalled, "I was trying my best to remember my words that night. I all but blocked out the specifics from that dreadful day the best I knew how. Matthew told me that five countries had already accepted gay people getting married. He told me we could move to one of them if I was too impatient to wait for the United States to catch up. He shared that he refused to argue God with me. He told me that if I needed family support, I could have his. His parents already thought of me as part of their family. Unlike me, Papa's family knew he was gay and were supportive of that."

The wind was picking up. Samuel scrunched into himself. He tried to smile through the dark at his daughter as he shared more.

"Next, Matthew shared that over the time we were apart, he spent all of his time researching and learning everything possible about genetics and biology. He changed his course load to science and biology courses. Matthew promised that if I would accept his word for it, he would figure out a way to create a family from both of our genes."

As he looked at Eternity, Samuel could see that her eyes were overrun with tears. This was a lot for her to hear. It was a lot for him to share; but if he lost his momentum now, he would never get it all out. She did not speak or interrupt him in any way. Samuel continued his reminiscence.

"Now I was shocked with all this," Samuel admitted, "and all I could muster up to say was that it looked like he had a solution for everything. Your Papa told me that we would always be equal in all senses. He pulled my hand to his and placed a small gold band in it. He asked me to trust him to give me everything I asked for. He asked me to marry him when it became legal in the USA. He told me that even though I broke up with him almost a year ago, that he never broke up with me."

Eternity's eyes widened in the dark as she imagined the moment unfolding in her father's memory. She never knew when her parents got engaged.

As she dreamed it Samuel kept sharing. "I was confused and lost but, at that moment, the only thing I could think of was why the ring was so tiny. It would never fit on my finger. Papa told me that if my answer was yes that the ring was to go on my toe. A hidden symbol that the world need not see until I was ready for the matching companion ring to go on my finger."

At this point, Samuel sat down on an old stump and was pulling off his shoe to show his daughter a small toe ring on his left foot that she never noticed before.

The moonlight did not make it easy for her to see, but Samuel finished his story. "I didn't know anything that night except that I missed your father so much. Taking in all that he had done the last year for me in silence it only made sense to accept his proposal."

Eternity interjected finally, "If it had been a year since you two were together last and you knew nothing that went on in that year really how could you know at that moment that it was right to say yes to a marriage proposal?"

Realizing the sensitivity of the question, Samuel chose his words wisely. "I knew him, he knew me. He knew me. At that time, who I was was elusive to me. I was lost and dazed when I broke up with him. But throughout that year, I believed he did just what he told me. He spent the year solving problems I had obviously made up as excuses not to be with him out of childish fear. I am grateful he did not give up on us as quickly as I did. I wouldn't have the things in life that bring me the most pleasure now."

His daughter did not speak as he went on. "In that second when I was standing there in front of him, with him searching me for a response, I realized that I had missed something important. Your Papa had taken both my hands and placed a ring in each. I searched my soul for a directive. I noticed a ray of sunshine reflecting on the inside of my ring. It was an odd little twinkle. It felt like God was winking at me from inside the metal band. God returned to me; He was winking at me through the reflection of the sunlight. He wanted me to do this. I allowed my heart to be my compass at that moment. I said yes."

The story taxed Samuel's mind. These hidden truths had been locked away in his mental attic for decades and all but forgotten about. His daughter could see the struggle on his face from dredging up the dust-covered memories.

They hugged before Samuel continued his story. Eternity felt a connection to her father beyond anything she had felt before. His trust in her with his raw emotions tingled in her heart. She was uncertain where the story was going, but wherever it did go, she wanted to hear.

"Your father stayed true to his word." Samuel continued, "All senior year he spent every moment learning everything he could about advanced biology and genetics. He was convinced there was a way to biologically create life from two men's DNA. That is why he chose Harvard to study biogenetic research. To answer your question, after college we came back here because your father thought he had solved it. He was sure he had found a way to erase genetic material from an unfertilized egg and replace it with the genetic material from a second male donor. He knew the world was not ready for such a breakthrough, so he never shared his work.

He never revealed his findings, and never applied for FDA testing. Instead, he came back here and tested his theory privately, in nature. He inseminated male/male zygotes into mice, birds, dogs, cats, cows, goats, chickens, and any other animal he could get his hands on. Then, he studied their offspring. He observed their reproduction and studied how their babies turned out. The real reason we still come back here every year is so your father can check in on the animals from his research.

After watching multiple generations of offspring, your father concluded that the animals were unaffected by the genetic change. Finally, he felt confident enough in his work for us to try it ourselves. We moved to Atlanta and spent the next two years searching for the right birth mother for you. Then, your father used both our DNA to impregnate her with you.

Eternity was astonished. She had always been especially interested in biology. In all her studies, she had heard of scientists around the world contemplating something similar, but here she sat today as the living proof that her father had figured it out some twenty years ago in secret. She patted her skin to make sure her epidermis still felt real and normal.

Now it all makes sense, she thought.

Questions swirled around in her mind like a tornado, trying to decide where to hit. Her tornado was not ready to land. Eternity grasped into the abyss of her mind, trying to form a single question, anything to add to this conversation. As she opened her mouth to speak, the tornado escaped in silence. She searched her father's eyes for signs that she could revisit this conversation later with gathered thoughts. The portals to the past showed no signs of closing. There was no rush to answer everything tonight.

SEVEN

They both sat in silence, surrounded by the fields that used to hold up her Papa's childhood home, for a long time until Eternity was ready to speak. "I knew there was something different about me, but I never dreamed of this," Eternity said. "So, you're saying I am one of a kind?"

Samuel answered cautiously, slowly separating each word. "You were, until Tavia."

The obvious realization kicked in. "All four of us are the same?" Eternity half-asked.

"Yes, my love," Samuel replied.

She breathed quietly, not wanting to draw too much attention to herself. "Am I normal? Will I be able to have kids? Will *they* be normal?" The questions spat out quickly, faster than she had intended. As her brain began to catch up to her emotions, there was a sudden revelation of questions on her tongue, and she didn't want to forget to ask a single one.

Samuel answered as honestly as possible. It helped that he had already predicted some of her questions. "You know biology is not my forte. Your father has run every test that he could think of on you four. You are all identical to every other normal child of your age. There is no reason to doubt you can reproduce normally. I'd speculate that your kids will be just as amazing as you are."

Eternity's mind was racing, but now coherent thoughts bubbled up to the surface. The mental rollercoaster was frustrating. She was unique, even though she had three siblings with a similar genetic makeup, she was the first among them. This had happened to her before it happened to anyone else in the world. If anything bad did manifest eventually, it would affect her first. Looking at the pale-faced man who stood in front of her, she knew that this was not a line of thinking she could share with him. Her dad was a worrier, and he wouldn't really be the one with answers anyway. She would have to follow up with her Papa in private.

"Well, I can't imagine having any two people I am prouder to be genetically formed from," Eternity remarked. Though the statement was true - she was proud to be the offspring of her dads' genes—she had an ulterior motive for offering it up. The nervous look on her dad's face told her he was seconds away from shattering like webbed glass. She could not bear to do that to him. She could not do that to her siblings. Eternity could feel her expression tightening and becoming colder as she resumed her efforts to comfort him. She took control of her lips and bent them up at the corners toward her eyes.

Samuel was relieved to see a smile on Eternity's face. *She was more composed than he would be in her situation*, he thought. "I've always been worried this would freak you out, yet you appear very collected. I should have known better than to speculate your reactions. You are brilliant, like your Papa... Nothing phases him either."

Eternity smiled genuinely at the comparison. She was proud to be like her Papa. She had just learned her father had bent the rules of nature just to create her. That was the kind of person she was thrilled to be connected with. So many more thoughts zipped around inside her head, but she would need some time alone to collect and analyze them. First, she had to get her dad through this conversation. If she wanted to be left alone, she would have to shift his focus elsewhere.

"I never thought to ask who my biological father was. I always went back and forth. I could see characteristics of both of you in me. Turns out I was right," she beamed.

This much is true, she thought. *The shift in the conversation tone would hopefully be enough to get him to lower his guard*. She hoped her happy expression would be enough to satisfy Samuel, but he knew better. The news was a bombshell. He suspected she was hiding her thoughts from him.

Samuel probed softly, "Are you sure you're all right with this? It's OK to be freaked out."

"This does not change who I am," Eternity proclaimed confidently. "If anything, this *made* me who I am. That's the important part. My two dads wanted me so badly that they overcame all odds and worked for a decade to have me. It feels good to be wanted that badly."

That did it. Eternity could see Samuel's shoulders relax and his eyes soften. He was in awe. She had stroked the right part of his ego without him even knowing it. Now she was in charge of the show, and it was time to roll the credits.

"I'm sure I'll have more questions once this all sinks in. For now, it's getting late, and I have a blood type lab to watch everyone else do tomorrow." She hugged her Daddy and they seeped into one another.

As they turned to head home, Samuel closed the conversation. "Obviously you know you have to keep this between us. Your blood and cells are all normal as far as anyone can tell. But we can never tempt fate. Something might come up and draw attention to you." Eternity nodded in understanding, braided her fingers into her father's, and tried to lead the way home.

* * *

Eternity excused herself to bed early. Finally, she was alone with her thoughts. Tavia was still busy with the boys. She lay in bed, staring at the ceiling and reflecting on the night's revelations. There was so much information for her to take in. She had expected the knowledge about her origin would leave her flabbergasted, but somehow it just seemed right. She had never even imagined the possibility of genetically originating from both of her fathers before today. Now that she knew the truth, it felt correct. "I am original. I am a snowflake of the purest variety, start to finish. I am the first," she muttered to herself.

Of all the things that rattled around in her mind, the one that stood out the most was that her parents had broken up, twenty years ago. She had never imagined a world where they weren't together; they just seemed to fit.

That must be why it's so easy for me to accept who I am, she thought.

She tried to imagine her dads in such a serious fight. She had rarely seen them in a quarrel before and couldn't imagine them with so much time apart now. Eventually, she drifted off to sleep.

Meanwhile, Samuel drank his coffee and thought back on the rough memories he shared that night. They brought back thoughts he had long wished to forget. Matthew was always going to be the one to tell the kids how they came to be. The story would have been so much nobler from his side. He never once wavered in his feelings. Samuel allowed a lonely tear to creep down his cheek into his now cold coffee.

EIGHT

Samuel thought he was hearing things when a light knock sounded at his door. He tip-toed, trying to answer without waking the kids. It was Julia. Samuel motioned her inside quietly and directed her toward the small kitchen. Samuel put on a pot of coffee without asking. Instinct warned Samuel that this visit was a terrible thing. Nothing good ever came out of late-night visitors or phone calls. He turned to her and asked, "What is going on?"

Julia smiled her motherly smile and answered, "Nothing is going on, dear. You were so upset earlier, I had trouble getting to sleep thinking about you. I know this situation is awful. I pray for you and the kids every day. I cannot imagine the toll being with someone like Matthew takes on you."

Samuel was silent, trying to decide if he believed Julia's story. He had no reason to distrust her; she was his friend. But he couldn't help but think she was there for something more. Samuel poured Julia's coffee before responding. "Loving Matthew is easy. I mean, how could anyone not? You look at him and you can see that he cares about you with every fiber of his being. He would fight off space invaders if he had to protect you. Sometimes I wonder if that's not exactly what he's out there doing right now," he chuckled. Julia joined in.

"Well, he is a director who splits his time between NASA and the CDC. That's the hard part. It's hard not to be greedy with Matthew's time. When he looks at you with those rosy cheeks and those big blue eyes, you know nothing else in the world matters to him at that moment. You have his full attention. But his job is saving the world from things they do not know they need to be saved from. Hopefully, they never do. I know I must be strong and endure this for now. Matthew promised he would retire in six years. The one thing Matthew does beyond all else is keep his word, so I will try to be patient."

Samuel thought he saw Julia lower her eyes to her coffee mug as he made mention of Matthew's retirement. The corners of her lips dropped slightly. Her sudden preoccupation with her half-finished cup was an obvious distraction intended to give her time to collect her thoughts.

Is she seriously using the same tactics I use with the kids on me now? he considered. This was as much as he was going to get from her in the way of confirming his suspicion. The personal level of shame her movements gave away threw Samuel's mind into overdrive. He knew that it was time to act.

"Julia, would it be an imposition to ask you for a favor?" Samuel wasn't sure how he'd phrase his request. He was used to formulating his response on the spot in court.

"I've been consulting on a case back in Atlanta and I really need to put boots on the ground there. If I could get a flight out tomorrow, do you think you could check in with the kids for a couple of days? Eternity is very mature, and I do trust her to look after everyone, but we've never left them overnight before. It would help me travel with ease if you could check in on them while I'm gone since you're already in town." Julia's expression was a little suspicious. Samuel knew he needed to tug a bit more on his puppet's heartstrings. "I could really use a couple of days of fresh air to center myself. This move has been hard on us all."

Julia's knowing eyes told Samuel he had played the right card. Samuel lowered his head slightly to indicate embarrassment at his admission. Julia walked over and hugged him right on cue. "Sweetie, you have nothing to be ashamed of," she said. "I raised my three kids alone. I know exactly how hard it is. I would be proud to spend a couple of days helping this family. Matthew has done so much to change my life.

How could I refuse to help you out in his absence? You book your flight for tomorrow, and I'll be here with bells on to make breakfast for the kids before school."

Samuel thanked her and allowed himself a much-needed embrace with his friend. He found himself holding on to her a bit longer than expected. He hadn't realized how starved he was for human touch.

As Julia pulled out of the driveway again, her phone rang through the car speakers.

It was Matthew. "Did you plant the bug?" he asked.

"Of course, I did, honey. It's under the kitchen table just like you asked. I don't think you have anything to worry about though. Eternity is just a smart girl that misses her Daddy; nothing more than that." Julia didn't wait for Matthew's response. She knew that he felt this was necessary—he wouldn't have assigned her this mission otherwise.

"I do feel a little guilty coming back in the middle of the night to do this," she added.

Matthew's low, clear bass voice responded, "It had to happen right now. I knew Samuel wouldn't be as alert at this time of night. He's exhausted from the day. I figured he wouldn't notice you taping a listening device under the table. The kids are long asleep. No chance that Eternity would be around to notice you either."

Julia exhaled a little louder than necessary. "He asked me to watch the kids the next couple of days while he makes a trip back to Atlanta. I fear he's reaching his tipping point. I suspect he's in serious need of a day to himself; you've been gone for months now."

Matthew was softer as he answered. "I suppose he is exhausted. I appreciate you giving him a break. I'll owe you."

Julia interjected sternly before Matthew could finish his thought.

"You owe me nothing, love. You hired me for a job that changed my life forever. I am grateful to have been working in the right diner on the right day when you stopped by to think. Get some rest, boss. I have to rest too. I've got four kids waiting on me tomorrow." Matthew thanked her again and hung up.

Meanwhile, Samuel tiptoed into the girls' room with cotton-light steps. He knew his efforts at silence were useless; both girls could be awakened by as much as a mouse. He snuck his way over to Eternity's bed as quietly as possible. He stood over Eternity's bed for a moment, watching her sleep. He hoped that, by some miracle, he managed not to awaken her. His heart zoomed as he turned to observe Tavia. She was gone. She was no longer in bed.

He quickly spun around and screamed as both girls stood in front of him, smiling at their now-frightened Daddy.

Samuel reached out to steady himself on Eternity's shoulder as Tavia spoke.

"Daddy, you're not a ninja. You shouldn't try to sneak up on two future Dan belt holders with your peasant feet."

Samuel was used to this type of jab. Matthew had required the children to learn self-defense as they grew up, something that Samuel had never had. The children often teased Samuel about their skills. He struggled to catch his breath and slow his heartbeat as both girls chuckled at his expense. Fortunately, luck was by his side: the boys were not roused by his panicked scream. They must still be exhausted from the previous night's storm.

Samuel sat on Eternity's bed as he waited to regain speech. He patted the bed beside him to indicate for the girls to sit down. "I have to fly tomorrow for work. I have an important case I need to do some legwork on. I won't be gone for more than a couple of days. Julia will be checking in on you during the day. She still has work of her own to do for Papa, so I assume she'll leave you at night to work from her hotel room. You'll both have to help look after the boys."

Eternity looked at her father with searching eyes. She had been in charge for an afternoon plenty of times before. That didn't alarm her. But the timing of this trip seemed off. She wondered if he had shared too much with her earlier. Was he off for some damage control? She resolved to pursue the thought some more in private.

Eternity stood up and kissed her Daddy on the cheek as she responded. "Don't worry, Daddy. If anyone wants to break in here, they're safer doing it while you're here than when you're not. We can kick some serious butt." She smiled at him slyly. Tavia joined her in a fighting stance from the other side of the bed. Samuel opened his mouth to object, but she interjected.

"Relax, Dad, we're playing. Mostly. I know this routine well. We may not be in Atlanta anymore, but I do still know how to be in charge."

Samuel stood up and kissed both his girls. "Julia will be here to help with breakfast. I am catching the red-eye out of Omaha so I will be on the road early in the morning."

Tavia excused herself to get a glass of water. Samuel was grateful for the opportunity to have a moment alone with his eldest child. He spoke softly, making sure he wouldn't be overheard. "Eternity, I know there are a lot of questions brewing in your mind. I'll do my best to answer them. While I am gone, I need you to call me first if anything happens that may require medical attention. We must be extra cautious, as you are now aware. Papa has never noticed anything about you all that could be easily detected. But medical files create records, and records are searchable.

Someone may be able to accidentally discover something years from now. Remember, no one knows but Papa and me. I just need you to be extra alert now that you're aware of the situation. Not even Julia knows this secret." Samuel could hear Tavia making her way out of the kitchen and back to the bedroom. He addressed them both on his way out. "I will be back Saturday afternoon. Take care of each other. I love you both, goodnight."

The girls said their goodnights again as Samuel closed the door. He stopped to kiss Matswell and Lias but did not dare wake them to share what was going on. This was not their first rodeo either.

Matthew really planned this all out, Samuel thought as he walked into his makeshift office. *Thanks to him, the kids are strong and independent, despite their young age. Nothing ever happens by accident with that man.*

Samuel had to stop himself from going further down that path of thought. He could already feel his throat tightening and his eyes glossing. He had no time to allow himself to think about Matthew. The longer he allowed that, the harder it would be for him to focus.

"No time for that counselor, you have work to do," he muttered to himself.

Now he had to throw together a plan. He wasn't sure what needed to be done, but he hoped he could do it in Atlanta. He had already committed to the story. Lord knows that Matthew would be watching his every move until he got to the airport. Luckily, the TSA's authority could keep even NASA at bay. The thought triggered the beginning of a plan in his mind. The airport was key; Matthew was blind and deaf to anything that happened there. That would be the only viable starting point for Samuel's deception.

NINE

Samuel pulled up a travel site on his laptop to look for the perfect flight. He wasn't shopping for price; he needed a flight that accidentally had a long layover where he needed it to be. The odds were not in his favor, though. It was simple enough to find a flight from Omaha to Atlanta. There were pages and pages of flights leaving out on Thursday. None with a layover that was where he needed it to be. Not a surprise... Billings, MT was in the opposite direction.

Samuel resolved to figure out that part later. He booked his flight, then sat back with his work cellphone in hand. He would have to be careful not to catch Matthew's eye while making this call. It was already getting quite late. He had to call soon, or she would be sleeping. She may already be sleeping as is. He would have to take that risk.

Flying always made Samuel a nervous wreck. Taking a walk after booking a flight would not catch

Matthew's eagle eye. Samuel grabbed his keys, locked the house up, and headed for the clearing down the road.

He started to dial the phone number, then stopped himself as realization kicked in. If he called her this late at night, Matthew would wonder what was going on. But Samuel had to reach out now if he had any hope of contacting her tonight.

Then it struck him. *I'm always answering work emails as I'm reflecting out here... She has an email account as well.* His fingers were already typing as he thought.

Please, please be up and checking your email for some reason, Samuel begged the universe quietly. He read aloud the draft he had just composed.

I'm sorry for writing so late, but I need the hugest of favors. Please don't call me right now. The kids are asleep, and I don't want to wake them. I don't want to alarm you, but I need you. Is there any way you can meet me tomorrow at the Atlanta airport without telling ANYONE where you're going or what you're doing? I hate to sound so cryptic, but it's honestly a necessary precaution. I'll be landing at noon and will be waiting at Moon Dollar's coffee at Terminal B for you. I can't stay there long, but I hope you can make it. It's the only private place I can think of. Love you very much.

– *Samuel*

He knew better than to hope for a response as he locked his screen. After all, it was a middle-of-the-night email regarding some sketchy-sounding help. He just hoped that she wouldn't reach out to Matthew. If Matthew found out Samuel had called his mother, he would be mad. Even though Matthew was close to his family, his mother was unaware of the closely guarded secrets about her grandchildren.

Well, that was that. Now he needed to sell the illusion of getting ready for his work trip tomorrow. There was so much to do. He couldn't just hurry back and start now. Matthew was likely watching, or at least Samuel always secretly hoped he was. It would look off for Samuel to hurry back into the house so quickly. That was out of his routine.

For the next half hour or so, Samuel would have to sit on that weathered log and look out into the fields. He thought that he would use the time to focus on his plan for tomorrow, but that was a lost cause.

As soon as Samuel sat down on the numbing, drenched log, he was 16 again. Sitting on the ridged curb of the parking lot of his corn-fed high school. The smell of fresh-cut grass assaulted his sinuses and forced him to sneeze.

"Bless you," an unfamiliar voice said from behind. It was low and booming, yet friendly. Samuel quickly turned around to see an alien face. The stranger was taller than him and had short, well-cropped hair which faded into the sides of his long face. It formed into a small line of hair hugging the stranger's jawline from ear to ear. The foreign boy's hair was dark, with streaks of bleach running throughout.

He had impossibly blue eyes that were set against his cloudy, white face. The piercing sunlight seemed to make them sparkle, like two clear diamonds. Samuel was at a loss for words as he looked at the boy's lithe build. Something felt off. Samuel had never found himself noticing, admiring, or even lingering a look at anyone else's appearance before.

The boy's sudden appearance was magnetic. Samuel had never taken such detailed notes about anyone's unique features. But then again, there were no strangers in the small town of Verdigre. In ten years of schooling, Samuel had never come across a student he didn't know. He was not sure how to act in this situation. In fact, there had been a rumor going around about a new student coming to town, but Samuel hadn't expected him to arrive today.

"Thank you," Samuel replied to the blessing after an awkward amount of time. His face shifted, and his eyebrows furrowed towards his nose until they touched.

The stranger winked and smiled, but his smile didn't climb above the edge of his lips. "I'm Matthew," he said, and waved his hand half-heartedly toward Samuel. When the hand hit Samuel there was a blip of static behind it. "Today is my first day here," the stranger continued, "I realize that every place has its own way of doing things, but is it common for students here to sit on wet sidewalks instead of going home after school? If so, I'm going to have to rethink my school attire."

Samuel found himself both captivated and intimidated by the boy's courage. He staggered to his feet unsuccessfully but scraped his palm on the sidewalk as he tried to stand too quickly. Samuel fell forward and planted both palms and kneecaps on the soaked parking lot.

Matthew howled with laughter and extended his hand. "I don't mean to criticize, but this seems like it might be a two-person job."

Samuel's face filled with blood as it started to redden with embarrassment. He reluctantly accepted the boy's help standing up.

He tried to speak to dispel the awkwardness of the encounter. "I'm Samuel. And just so you know, I meant to fall like that." Both boys chuckled as they shook hands, and Samuel could feel the volcano releasing in his face.

"It isn't common among students here to sit on wet curbs after school. Well, at least not for any other student... I'm sitting here because I've locked my keys in my car and I have to wait for my parents to bring the spare."

Matthew nodded in acknowledgment. "How long do you have to wait for them?" he asked.

Samuel's smile was forced as he declared, "Well, it'll be a while. We don't have a phone at my house. My parents say Jesus never needed a phone to call you when he needs you, and no one else should be more important than he is. I have to wait for them to notice that I'm not there and realize that I need their help again. It's usually about an hour."

Matthew took note of the way Samuel said usually but figured he should not push any further. This was obviously some type of ritual. "I could give you a ride home, so you don't have to wait for them. It looks like it might rain some more."

"Oh no," stated Samuel, waving his head quickly from side to side. "I appreciate the offer, but they would be incredibly angry if I left the car here and rode off with a stranger."

Matthew wanted to ask Samuel more questions. Instead, he pulled his backpack from his shoulders and dropped it to the ground. He sat down on the sidewalk next to Samuel. "Well, then, I guess I'll wait around with you. They can't get mad that another student chooses to sit on the sidewalk at the same time as you are, can they?"

Samuel was enamored that this new boy would choose to sit on a wet sidewalk with a stranger instead of rushing home after school. He was also a little thrilled that this kid had found a way to outsmart his parents in a matter of moments. It was never something that he had dared to try.

"You don't have to wait here with me," Samuel offered as he began to sit down. "I will be OK here alone."

Matthew looked entertained as he responded. "I don't know that I believe that. I mean, you already lost one battle today with gravity. I think it would be irresponsible for me to leave you here. What if the wind decides to attack you next? You may need the backup."

Samuel scowled for a moment but then reconsidered. He really did appreciate the company. He thanked Matthew quietly as they sat together and stared at the parking lot in wait.

* * *

The heavy raindrops splattering on his head brought Samuel back to the present moment. He staggered up quickly, trying to use both hands to form an ineffective shield over his head. He trotted back to the house, careful not to get too carried away and start jogging. He was in loafers and the grass was getting wet. More importantly, he was a natural disaster. The cold Nebraska air did its best to hurry Samuel along, but he was determined to best it.

Samuel opened the door harder than he meant to and darted inside. He heard the loud ensuing creak and instantly regretted his action. He just knew that he had woken the boys. He froze in place just inside the house, the door still wide open to the wind. Water dripped off the ends of his untamed curls into his eyes, but he refused to mop it away. A moment later he realized that luck had been on his side for once. None of the kids were awake. He packed what he needed to maintain his ruse of going to work tomorrow. He knew that if he was going to sell this, appearance was everything. Samuel took a long hard look at himself in the bathroom mirror. The disaster he became would never convince anyone he was going away for business. He ogled the dirty image dripping with corn-filled rain in the mirror. Anyone who knew Samuel knew that he cared too much about his image, particularly at work, to be seen looking like he did now.

He needed to focus on the task at hand. He cupped and scrubbed his face with running water.

Doing so, he noticed that his nails had grown quite a bit and were accumulating debris underneath. This would never do; it was disgusting. Pulling on the side of the mirror, he revealed the hidden shelves behind it and reached for the nail clippers. This was a good place to start.

Next, he decided to shave away the mountain dweller who currently stared back at him from the mirror. It had been a while since he'd seen himself scruff-free. The familiarity of his polished look tipped his mood. He felt a little more like himself already. His eyebrows, nose, and ear hairs had gotten out of control. All the excess hair he had been carrying on his face made him shudder a bit. Samuel ran the trimmers down his face and tamed it.

Samuel suddenly felt dirtier than he had felt in a long time. He hopped into the shower and scrubbed himself thoroughly. He avoided thinking about how much dirt he had carried lately. He kept scrubbing himself until the scalding water turned gradually colder. Finally, the chill of ice-cold water triggered him to get out of the shower and towel off.

Samuel brushed his teeth, flossed, and patted some lotion on his face. He applied fresh deodorant and spritzed himself a bit with a sweet aftershave. The night was slipping away. He hurried himself along to get stuff going for the kids. There were lunches to be packed and backpacks to be filled.

Julia startled him as he stepped out of the bathroom. A mute screech left his lips. She was sitting there in the living room. Samuel calmed himself and pulled his soul back into his skin. He approached her with a confused look in his eyes, silently asking her what she was doing back so soon. Had he given something away during their previous conversation? Was his plan foiled before it even got started?

She answered before he could even speak. "I thought you could use a little help getting ready for your last-minute trip. I don't think you will find a barber at this hour," she teased.

She got up and walked toward the kitchen, motioning for Samuel to take a seat. She had already set up her station at the table. Samuel followed, grateful for the much-needed trim. He would need this to complete his façade. He knew that Julia had always worked multiple jobs while raising her family. Cutting hair was one of them. As Julia went to work eliminating his bushy curls, Samuel allowed himself to wonder if the gesture came from her or from Matthew. Had he noticed the need for an intervention? Either way, it was much appreciated.

Julia looked at him pleased after she finished with her work. "It's a bit of a drive to Omaha… You better get going," she said softly. "Don't worry about things here. I've dressed and fed many kids in my day. I assume you already told the girls I would be here?"

Samuel nodded in confirmation. "Then you get going and I'll handle everything here." Samuel gave her a quick hug and jetted off to grab his bags.

TEN

As **Samuel stepped** off the jetway in Atlanta, he felt like a stranger in a new land. The airport was somehow different than he remembered, though all the elements he expected to see were there. A massive crowd of people moved around as if in sync. Everyone had their eyes buried in their phones. An army of suitcases skated across the freshly waxed tile. Toddlers were towed along by their parents, who gripped tightly at their offspring's leashes. The smell of newspaper and body odor filled the air.

The last few hours were a blur. Everything had happened so quickly. Whoever sat in the seat next to him was unwillingly exposed to two hours of grandpa-style snoring. It didn't matter though; Samuel felt more rested than he had for a long time.

There was much to do. He began to mentally prepare for the deception ahead. The digital clock hanging above announced that the hour was just past noon. Samuel could not stay in the airport for too long. His shroud of protection was already fading.

"I need a reason to be here for a few hours without raising suspicion. What do you have for me?" Samuel muttered to himself, not caring who was around to hear him.

As if in answer to his query, Samuel noticed that the very next business along the hallway was a surf and turf restaurant. Matthew was allergic to seafood, so Samuel rarely had a chance to enjoy it. Matthew would expect Samuel to take advantage of the culinary opportunity. This would be normal. He passed the hostess' station and hurried along to the cashier. She stared at him in irritation when he asked her to open a tab and charge it for a whiskey and the surf and turf special.

"Charge this card, but please do not have the food prepared," Samuel instructed.

The young cashier cracked her knuckle, preparing to object. Samuel opened his mouth to explain, "My boss is making me travel today and it's my son's birthday. I'm charging anything I can think of to the business in revenge." It was shocking how easily the lie came to him. "Won't you please help me teach that jerk a lesson?"

The cashier nodded. It seemed like this was the right card to play. "You're in luck," she announced. "We are running a special today—buy two, get none," she laughed. "This will teach him. I charged you for a dessert too. I'll be here when you're ready to pay and get the receipt."

Samuel retrieved his card and read her name tag for the first time. "Thank you, Michelle. We gotta look out for each other, you know?"

She nodded subtly, already engaged with the next customer. Samuel picked his bags back up and then headed farther down the terminal. It was really a shame. The aroma from the surf and turf did smell amazing. Maybe he would ask Michelle to put in an order after he returned.

Samuel was still not sure that Mama Jene would make it. She hadn't responded to his email. Even if she did make it, Samuel had no idea what he was going to be able to share. He knew he was early to the meeting. He needed the extra time to figure out how to share what was going on. How could he explain the state of his affairs to her? Or what he needed? He was going off of nothing more than a gut feeling, but that feeling was urging him to act. Samuel lingered at the arrivals board. He ducked around each new traveler that decided to walk up and obscure his view. He had no idea where her connection would be from. Regardless, there were no more arrivals from anywhere for the next 17 minutes.

"It's time to grab a cup of coffee, find a seat, and try to calm down," he announced to the airport.

After paying for his coffee, Samuel sat down and opened the lid to let it vent. He decided to message the kids while the cup's sweet scent filled the air. The call-box's design was simple and utilitarian. Samuel sent a heart symbol to all four of his kids. It would be simple enough for the boys to understand. To the girls, he added, "I will be home tomorrow evening. Be good and look after your brothers - Dad." Tavia, always quick to respond, immediately sent back an emoji sticking its tongue out. Apparently, school was not holding her attention.

Samuel slowly sipped on his cup of still-boiling beans. Growing up, he never imagined he would become a coffee drinker. With time still to spare and no sign of Mama Jene, Samuel allowed the sweet taste to take him on a trip down memory lane.

* * *

The day after graduation, Matthew pulled up at the only gas station in town. Samuel had decided that now he was an adult, he would get his first cup of coffee to drink. It was the color of chalk, full of sugar and milk. Not exactly coffee as much as coffee-flavored sugar water. But to him, it was the same. He was about to drink coffee; the world was his oyster. He was proud of the fact he was about to be a true grown-up. Nothing was going to stop him now.

Samuel paid little attention to the fact that Matthew had been observing him preparing his witch's brew. He obviously realized exactly what was going on. Samuel marched out confidently into the humid May oven. He did not go into the car. Instead, he decided that a proper adult would loiter for a few moments while waiting for Matthew to finish inside.

Samuel rounded the corner, hiding from the stream of patrons packing into the small service station. He did his best to remain unseen. Graduated adult or not, the last thing he needed now was for his parents to get wind of the fact that he was spending time with Matthew again.

Samuel leaned back against the red-brick wall of the antiquated gas station. He took a big sip of the coffee-like beverage. He had no idea exactly how hot the coffee would be, having never been allowed to drink it at home. It scalded the roof of his mouth. He instinctively swallowed the tissue left from his gum, a mistake that filled him with instant regret. The knife of pain ripped flesh from his throat and continued all the way down to his toes. To make matters worse, the beverage was utterly disgusting. With impeccable timing, Matthew walked around the corner laughing boisterously. He had not missed a minute of the show. He was laughing so hard he had to hold his gut to gain control of his ill-received outburst.

Samuel turned beet-red, though he couldn't tell if it was more from anger or embarrassment. "Shut up!"

"May I?" Matthew asked, trying to contain his outburst. He gestured for Samuel to swap his cup for the one he held. "If you're going to be a coffee person, you should have a better start than that."

"I've had enough of this coffee. It's disgusting!" Samuel snapped, waving off the cup.

"This is a darker roast coffee. Nothing added. Plain black coffee, just the way nature intended. It will be stout, and you may only be able to stomach a few sips."

"No, thank you," Samuel reiterated.

"You'll get used to it the more you have it," Matthew extended the offering again.

"Just give it a few minutes to cool down, let the aromas seep in, and allow yourself time to anticipate the flavor," Matthew said, sounding like a salesman. His description sparked Samuel's interest.

"When you do drink it, start with small sips. Allow your mouth time to slowly acclimate to the hot temperature." Matthew's diamond eyes made it impossible to resist further.

Samuel took the drink reluctantly from Matthew without any intention of tasting it. He was so irritated at Matthew's condescending tone. He didn't need a lesson on how to consume a cup of coffee. This was supposed to be his moment to be an adult. He hated coffee at that moment.

Matthew drove off toward the vast nothingness their one-horse town had to offer, with no obvious destination in mind. Most of their youth was spent this way, aimlessly driving.

Samuel found the aroma from his cup inviting. He had smelled basic coffee before, but never so close. Never close enough that his nose wanted to go right into the cup to be closer to the scent. The aroma was inviting, tempting, and alluring. His sense of smell had never been so stimulated before. Samuel ignored it with all his might. Refusing the urge to allow more of his body to enjoy the magic cup. Finally, he decided to try just the smallest sip. No one needed to know if he timed it correctly.

He waited until Matthew was gazing off into the distance to sneak a sip from the cup. It was still hot. Samuel quickly moved the cup away from his mouth, spilling a little of the scalding liquid on his chest. He quickly patted himself down to cool the burn, but the damage was done. The incident had betrayed Samuel. The small brown drops created an obvious trail of evidence. He was not certain, but he thought Matthew was grinning out the driver's window.

That bastard, Samuel thought, *he probably planned this whole damn scenario*. Nevertheless,

Samuel enjoyed the caffeinated treat. He would try it again later when he was not so closely observed. No need for Matthew to get the satisfaction of being right.

* * *

Samuel found himself drifting to the present as his cup cooled in front of him. He was staring out the window when a cool palm touched his shoulder from behind. He jumped, spilling his coffee and knocking his phone to the floor. He reached down to retrieve it, bumping his head on the edge of the table on his way back up. He straightened and found himself standing eye to eye with Matthew's mother. Jene had made it to their rendezvous.

Samuel was overcome with a thrilling mixture of relief and fear. Jene's presence made his whole ordeal seem much more real than before. Her cropped hair was light and woven through with blonde streaks. It framed her bronze face perfectly. Jene was short, like Samuel, but she carried herself confidently. Her purple eyes were focused and ready to conquer whatever the day held.

Mama Jene was one of his favorite people in the world. She wasn't much for saying 'I love you', but her love was evident in everything she did. She always knew how to make someone feel special, even if they were on the butt end of one of her jokes. She often showed her love in non-traditional ways. If you were in a bar fight, she would roll up her sleeves and throw down.

"You might want to calm down there, Skippy, before you break the whole airport," it was clear where Matthew got his witty remarks from. Jene had already managed to find napkins and bent down to help him clean his mess.

"I'm so glad you made it," Samuel exclaimed, leaning in to hug her. "I wasn't sure you could come on such short notice."

Jene stepped back, allowing Samuel to see her fully. She placed her right hand on her hip and rolled her eyes as she addressed him. "Well, I figured whatever you were up to, you needed to keep it quiet from Matthew. Otherwise, you would have just called, like a normal person."

Samuel was shocked at how easily his intentions could be read. If Jene had figured things out, could Matthew also know? His face must have betrayed his fears. Jene flashed him a quick smile. "Don't forget, you've only been with him for twenty years. I raised him for nearly forty. I know his quirks as well as anyone, dear."

Of course she does, he thought. *But would this help or hurt my case?* "I don't know where to begin…"

Samuel scooted his chair tightly under the table but could not relax. His right leg was beginning to shake despite his attempts to portray calmness. His jaw clenched as if some force was keeping him from talking. Something was keeping him from spilling the beans along with the coffee.

Mama Jene noticed this apprehension and tried to help him to relax. She spoke in a low tone while her violet eyes scanned the room. It reminded Samuel of Matthew's eyes, always alert to everything going on around him. Watching Jene sift through faces as they walked by was an oddly calming experience for Samuel.

"I know that there are things I'm happy to not know. Matthew's lot in this world requires trust. Entrusting the wrong person with the right information can be a horrific thing, I assume."

She paused her radar-like scan and focused on Samuel. "That is why I never ask what's going on with your family. I trust Matthew knows how to best protect you all. I know that at times this protection means that I have to be left in the dark about certain details. But a mother does know when something is out of the ordinary."

Samuel had not considered that anyone would figure out there was a need for alarm. He assumed the world was blissfully ignorant of the inner workings of his little clan. Jene was scouring the room again while he collected his thoughts.

"How long have you known that something was off?" Samuel questioned.

She zeroed in her beaming eyes and glared at him as if he were an idiot. Perhaps he was. "Months ago. Ever since you brought the kids to live back in Nebraska."

Samuel was taken aback. He tried to repeat his well-worn cover story. But Jene stopped him before he could speak. "Spare me the excuses. I knew that awful pile was a cover story the last time I heard it." Samuel's throat clenched. He was not prepared to be confronted in this way. He had no rebuttal at hand.

"If there's one thing I know in this world, it's that Matthew hates Nebraska. His sights were set on leaving the state before we even unpacked," Mama Jene continued.

Samuel had not known this. Matthew encouraged them to come back to Nebraska every year. Samuel had always imagined that Matthew felt some connection to the place, a feeling of home perhaps.

"Why would Matthew drag the family year after year to a place he despised so much?" Samuel asked.

"He tolerated Nebraska because he knew you would always feel a connection to there. Even if you don't realize it, you need stability, a place to return to your roots," Jene replied.

Jene's information overwhelmed Samuel to the point of tears. He could feel the water resting at the corners of his eyes, awaiting its release. But as soon as she spoke, Samuel could sense that she was being truthful. Jene was right; he needed the place he should hate. He had no idea that such a need was even nestled inside him. *How could she know something about me that I didn't even know?* he asked himself. *More importantly, how could I not know this?*

Mama Jene reached across the table to grab his hand in hers. "Don't be upset now. Matthew has a way of knowing what people need, even if they themselves do not. He knew you needed your roots. That's why he never sold that old shack in Verdigre after all these years, so that you could recharge there. He knew that if you ever needed to take care of the family on your own, you'd feel the most capable over there. When you told me that you'd decided to bring the kids back to Nebraska, I knew something was going on."

She tightened her grip on his hand to focus his attention. "That is why when I got your email late last night, I was ready. I'd been waiting for a sign from you for months. I knew you might need some help with the house, with the kids, with something. I wasn't expecting it to be so cryptic, though. That leads me to believe we are here against Matthew's wishes. And if you're going against my son's will, it must involve his wellbeing."

Samuel was floored at all Mama Jene had pieced together by herself. He had barely even said a word. He had forgotten what an insightful and amazing woman she was. *I wish we could live closer to her*, he thought. *There is so much the kids could benefit from being around such a strong soul.*

Matthew's father was set on living in Montana. He did not function well alone. Mama Jene pretended to like the country for his benefit. Truth be told, she was far more suited to city life. The way things were, Matthew and Samuel had to settle for a visit once or twice a year.

"The truth is I don't know much more than what you've figured out already," Samuel said. His voice turned raspy as he tried to catch her up with the story.

Mama Jene locked eyes with him. He could feel their pull like tractor beams, extracting words out of his helpless body.

"A few months ago, Matthew told me that he was going to have to go no-contact for an indefinite length of time and that I needed to trust him." Samuel coughed the jumping frog from his throat.

A few sips of coffee gave him the courage he needed to continue. "Years ago, he made me promise that if I felt the family was in danger, I would bring them back to Nebraska. I had always assumed he felt it was safer there. Looks like he felt it was where I would be in my element the most. I guess I shouldn't be surprised that I failed to realize it sooner."

Samuel paused for a moment, fiddling with the lid of his cup. "When he told me he would be gone, with no idea if or when he would be back, I knew that danger was coming. So, I moved us back, as promised." "I am sure you did the right thing," Jene said with encouragement.

Samuel appreciated the much-needed confirmation. He glanced down at his watch reluctantly. "Time is going to be short. I only have a narrow window for my alibi." He pulled a sealed white envelope from his bag. Inside was a letter he had penned for her on the plane. "There is a security firm in Billings that I did some work for a few years back. The president's name is Kerrie Thompson." Mama Jene's eyes widened at the mention of the words "security firm." She collected herself quickly and focused again.

"Can you get this to her? I am calling in a favor. I have it all spelled out in this letter. I need you to see that it gets to her, please. The address and name are on the envelope." He slid the legal envelope across the table to her. She swiped it and stuffed it into her purse.

Mama Jene looked at Samuel intently before responding. "I will do what I can. I always have. I need you to know..." She paused as a well-dressed businessman walked by, apparently pretending to talk on the phone while interested in their conversation. They locked eyes for a moment before he decided it was best to keep moving.

After a momentary pause, Jene went on. "When Matthew was in high school, he was so focused on changing to be with you. I didn't know what he was trying to change, but a mother recognizes change. Dinner conversations were things he never seemed to be interested in before. His sudden interest in science was noteworthy. I didn't ask him for any details. I could tell it was important to him, so I did my part to encourage him. I kept him focused and motivated. Now it's your turn to stay focused and to bring him back to me."

Samuel nodded, holding back a new brigade of tears. He leaned over and hugged her with desperate need. She allowed the hug to last longer than needed.

"I hate to drag you all the way here and have to run so soon, but..." Jene placed a finger to his lips to silence him before he could finish the sentence.

"Stay focused on your part now," she reminded him. Having said her piece, she grabbed her purse, turned, and walked away.

ELEVEN

Samuel **thanked** his young rideshare driver as he stepped into the familiar driveway. He could barely recall the events of the last hour, after leaving Mama Jean: the crowded airport, the swarms of people waiting around the smelly baggage carousel, and the never-ending traffic on the 404.

He was home now, and it felt great. The few months he had been away from Atlanta now felt like years. The beloved home hadn't changed. The landscapers had done an amazing job as always; the house was as inviting as ever. It was the kind of house you couldn't just ignore when walking by. It beckoned you to stop and stare for a moment. Samuel took a deep breath, closed his eyes, and lost himself in the feeling of home.

His work phone rang as he reached for his luggage. "Hello," Samuel cleared his throat and tried again. "Hello."

"Hello," It was Julia, of course. "Just checking to make sure you arrived okay," as if she didn't already know exactly when he landed and where he was.

Samuel had to play along. "Yes, thank you. I slept the whole plane ride. I had no idea I was so tired until I had nothing to keep me awake. I stayed in the airport a little longer than I should, but there was this new surf and turf place that smelled too good to walk past, so I didn't." He tried to giggle and sound lighthearted. "How are the kids?" he asked, shifting the conversation away from the subject. He didn't want to be caught saying something he didn't mean to.

"They're all great," Julia offered. "Everyone seems a little stir-crazy, so we decided to go to the lake tomorrow after school. The girls are packing up day bags for the boys and the boys are...well, they're being boys. They've been awfully quiet for a while. I fully expect some chaos to strike any minute now." They laughed together.

"Thank you again so much, Julia," Samuel proclaimed. "I just got to the house. I'm going to change clothes, freshen up from the trip, and head into the office." *Wow, it felt good to say that again*, Samuel thought.

"Okay, dear," Julia replied. "Take care of yourself out there and try to recharge a bit. I'm sure you could use it." He thanked her again, then hung up the phone. She was right; Samuel was glad to be back where he belonged. He grabbed his bags and headed into his sanctuary.

Samuel had no work to do in town, but he had to make it look like he had a purpose for visiting. He ordered a ride-share to head downtown to the old office. It might be nice to check in on everyone; it had been a while since he was there in person. According to the ETA on the app, he had about 45 minutes to pass before his ride's arrival. That meant he had some time to wander around the house.

The memories of their arrival here were still crystal clear in his mind. They had not brought much with them from Nebraska, just the stuff neither of them could bear to part with. It was as if only yesterday he was fumbling at the front door and tripping over boxes of random junk while unpacking the pull-behind trailer. Samuel remembered they ate take-out on the floor for months.

Matthew insisted that they paint all the walls and put in the carpet/flooring throughout the whole house before buying any furniture. Samuel could never understand his Vulcan logic. Samuel wanted to fill the house with furniture the first day and be done with it. Looking around at their home, he could see that the care and caution they had paid off. In retrospect, it was all they had done back then that made this house so perfect now. He had no plans to admit that to Matthew ever.

The north-facing wall was the first thing you'd see when entering the house. It had a full-service home bar, with high-back stools facing a ceiling-to-floor wine hutch. The hutch was filled with corked bottles of wine gathered from every corner of the world.

Beautiful crystal wine goblets hung by their feet above the countertop, reflecting the sunlight that poured through the windows onto the Italian marble. Samuel brushed the back of his hand down the cold countertop. It felt as smooth as silk. The sweet scent of cherries and bourbon lingered in the air.

Before taking the family to Nebraska, Samuel hired a cleaning crew for the house's upkeep. They had done an amazing job maintaining the place. He made a mental note to write them a thank-you card before heading back to Nebraska.

Sitting in the parlor, he remembered just how irritated he was that Matthew saved this room for last. A whole month was spent creating a cobblestone fireplace against the western wall of the parlor. Matthew had taken his sweet time with the room. Now, the imperfectly matched stones created the most beautiful fire frame Samuel had ever seen.

No two stones of the hearth were the same shape, size, or color. But every single one was placed in exactly its perfect place. Once it was done, many beautiful Christmas mornings began by retrieving plump stockings that hung along the mahogany mantle. Samuel ran his fingers down the chimney, soaking in the vibrant smell which still lingered in the wood.

Matthew had stored the stones in secret for years. They came from the schoolyard parking lot where he first saw Samuel sitting on the curb in defeat. When the school decided to replace the cobblestone with concrete pavement, Matthew bought up a load of it.

The texture, the images, and the smell of the wood were too much joy for Samuel's senses. He loved this place and missed it dearly. Samuel had to focus hard on his breathing to stay collected. He took a long deep breath in, then closed his eyes and held his breath before exhaling. Over and over again, until he could feel himself relaxing.

Long slabs of solid rosewood ran across the eastern side of the room. A full-sized Steinway with velvet keypads was placed on a raised dais in the middle. Samuel recalled the many nights his family spent sitting by the fire, enjoying a glass of wine and hearing Matthew or Eternity breathe life into Chopin's melodies.

A floor-length black plush stage curtain was placed behind the piano. At night, anyone playing on this homemade Opry looked like they were ready to entertain the queen. During the day, the curtain pulled back to reveal a bay window with a reading nook large enough for any adult. Samuel had lost himself in a book there countless times.

Outside, a beautiful apple tree could be seen from the window. It was always filled with fresh lush fruit. The kids loved plucking an apple and eating it as they played. A tall maple tree framed the window from the right. Nestled into the lowest branches of the mighty tree was a clubhouse Matthew made for the boys. They loved spending their afternoons up there. The fresh scents of maple and apple always attracted birds and squirrels to the yard. The boys loved watching the different critters visit.

Matthew had asked Samuel to paint a giant tree that branched out over on the southern wall. The tree's arms were barely contained by the entrance door. The leaves were painted in metallic green and auburn gold. Over the years, more family photos bloomed in its branches, each photo safely nestled on it like a leaf. During the day, when the stage curtain was pulled back, the sunlight streaming from outside would bring the tree to life.

A subtle, yet elegant staircase lived between the bar and the Opry. It wrapped over the top of the bar and led up to the second-floor bedrooms. Samuel drew in a long breath and held it to steady himself.

Samuel loved this house to its core. Growing up with a disconnected family, he never knew what having a place to call home would feel like. But the manor (as Matthew liked to call it) felt like home. Samuel was ready to rush back to Nebraska and bring the kids over. He wanted to give them back the comfort of the house. He was ready to be home again, to be a family again. Alas, it was not time yet. He had to wait for... He wasn't sure what he had to wait for, but he knew he had to wait.

A small hallway to the left of the bar led to their indoor garden. Growing up in the country had left both Samuel and Tater with a taste for home-grown produce. They also wanted to make sure the kids all learned to appreciate the labor that went into growing their food. Samuel's heart swelled as soon as he walked into the condensed greenhouse. Looking around, he could just about see the kids pitching in to care for the crops. They were so tangible that he could almost touch them.

The western wall of the greenhouse was made out of sheer glass, allowing for plenty of light to cascade over their harvest. A variety of tomatoes, peppers, corn, cucumbers, onions, and squash ran in neat rows from east to west. The quantities were modest: just enough vegetables for their family, and a little bit extra for a rainy day. Samuel hired a gardener, Tony, to tend to the garden while they were away. He was paid to donate the produce to a local LGBT shelter until the family could return to enjoy it. The north and south walls of the greenhouse were filled with rows of cooking herbs. Food had to be flavored right to take proper care of your family.

As they built the home together, Samuel enjoyed everything they did. In this moment, he could see Matthew's blueprint. His design, his ability to make every inch of their home full of purpose, full of life. This was not something that Samuel could imagine anyone else capable of doing. This was not a house. This place was more than a home, it was... it was a legacy to pass down through generations. Something to ensure that their great-grandkids would still be able to see their ancestry alive around them. Samuel was completely lost in his realization. He had to remind himself to breathe.

Matthew's family moved around often. That was the nature of their business. Matthew's father was a roofer, so the family moved around following natural disasters. Making a living while helping others put their homes back together. Matthew was adamant that his own kids would never feel the stressful freedom of lifelong travel. He wanted them to be brought home from the hospital straight to shelter. As an adoptee, Samuel fully understood the need for safety in Matthew's mind. They shared this vision. Looking around and feeling every ounce of welcoming air, he knew their vision had finally come to life.

A sudden ding from his pocket startled Samuel and sent a shiver down his spine. He clumsily tried to retrieve his phone. TJ, his rideshare driver, was fast approaching. Samuel rushed to the bathroom and splashed water on his face. There was no time left to walk down memory lane. He patted down his hair and hustled out the door.

* * *

The ride downtown was peaceful compared to the morning's chaos. Samuel enjoyed the casual chit-chat young TJ provided, as well as the upbeat music on the radio. He allowed himself to get lost in a few songs and forget all about what he was doing and why he was back home in the first place. It felt good to relax in the familiarity of home.

Growing up in the country, Samuel never imagined himself enjoying the city. Yet here he was, totally in love with all the pleasures it had to offer. He felt pleased staring out the window. The closer he got to his old office, the more his excitement grew. *It was going to be nice to see everyone again*, he thought. It was a way to live in the shadows of his former life, however briefly.

* * *

Being back at the office proved to be exhilarating. Samuel could feel the hustle and bustle of life in every room. The energy flowed tangibly through the air. He walked down the hallway and recognized many familiar faces.

The glass partitions of the office reflected glimpses of himself back to him as he passed by. At first, his reflection showed him the rock-hard emotionless face he had been using for months. But soon, he noticed tiny dimples pulling at the edges of his lips, like the rolled-up corners of a carpet. Finally, his lips gave in to a huge smile. He could feel it in his whole body. Happiness was almost pulsing through the air. It was electrifying. He could feel his heart racing in an attempt to keep up with the energy a full-body smile required. The experience was renovating. No matter the lie that brought him here today, Samuel needed this.

TWELVE

It **was still** incredibly early by the time Samuel arrived home. However, he was exhausted from the day, the week, and hell, the year. He allowed himself a quick call to check in on the girls, who were not interested in his overprotectiveness. The call was short and sweet. Samuel collapsed in his well-missed bed, still fully clothed. Sleep caught up to him the minute his head hit the pillow. He woke at 4 AM after a string of incoherent dreams. Disoriented, it took him a moment to remember where he was and what he was doing. He had slept for almost 10 hours and woken up still feeling exhausted. He permitted himself a trip to the bathroom and a glass of water before getting a few more hours of much-needed rest.

Even though he fell asleep immediately, he felt awake. He was aware and focused on the imaginary world around him. He was in a parking lot of what he assumed to be a run-down business. There was nobody around him as far as he could see, not even any wildlife; just him and the occasional tumbleweed rolling past.

A building appeared in front of Samuel. It was a colonial-style two-story house with no distinguishing marks to indicate its purpose. Samuel felt drawn to the building for an unknown reason. He began to walk around its perimeter, trying each door he saw as he passed by. They were all locked. The windows he passed by were too high for him to peek into. The walls were all surrounded by shrubbery.

Samuel felt like he knew the building from somewhere, but he had no idea where from. Even though it was unfamiliar to him, his instincts told him he should be able to recognize it. He searched the back parking lot as he rounded the building, but it was just as empty as the front. The doors and windows on the back were just as elusive as their counterparts in the front.

Samuel was getting frustrated. His investigation was going nowhere. He decided to step out to the little two-lane highway next to the building and search for a street name. He looked as far as he could see but had no luck identifying the highway. There were no other houses or buildings in any direction. As he crossed the ditch back into the parking lot, his shoe caught on something, and he tumbled forward.

Heart now racing, Samuel rolled over to see a small piece of wood that was not there before. He turned the wood over and realized it was a dust-covered sign. Puffing mightily against the timber, Samuel let layers of dirt fly off and revealed the lettering underneath. The sign read "Dolton Funeral Home."

A loud beeping sound demanded Samuel's attention as soon as he read the sign and woke him from his slumber. He must have forgotten to turn off the alarm on his work phone. Now, it wanted him to get the kids ready for school. He fumbled with the blanket, sheets, and pillows to reveal his phone's hiding place. With the memory of this dream still fresh in his mind, Samuel tried to figure out where he knew the funeral home from. He was confused. The information felt like it was on the cusp of his consciousness, barely out of reach.

Phone still in hand, Samuel did a quick internet search for "Dolton Funeral Home + Atlanta GA". Nothing. Then he tried "Dolton Funeral Home + Verdigre, NE". Again, nothing, though that was expected. He felt confident that he still recalled every business around back home. A general search for "Dolton Funeral Home" spat out a few towns that Samuel was sure he had never been to. After a little scrolling, the intense feeling of the dream already started to fade away. His stomach called for his attention, begging him to refuel it.

He abandoned his self-appointed quest and decided to get breakfast at one of his favorite cafes. That would look completely normal to anyone who might be watching. He would do just that, right after he showered and changed from the clothes he had passed out in.

Samuel loved the scones at NoNo's. As he enjoyed them alongside an amazing fresh brew, he recounted his plan. The food was handled with such care, you could taste that in every bite. Love is an unmentioned ingredient many recipes tend to leave out. The gingerly set older woman who tended the counter hugged every customer before they left. Samuel never minded the flour-covered apron pressing against him. She had the best hugs. With a hug, a bag of scones, and a cup of coffee, Samuel felt re-energized.

With a little luck, Mama Jene had made it to Billing in time for Kerrie, president of a former security firm Samuel represented, to help him with his request. Samuel had asked her for a tracker, the smaller the better. He emphasized that he needed it immediately as a matter of high importance. Kerrie was aware of the role Samuel's husband played in the government. Hopefully, she would comply without any questions.

Samuel asked Kerrie to send the device back overnight to his home in Atlanta. Samuel needed an opportunity to receive the package without raising any suspicion. He didn't want any unintended eyes to peer at his plans. He had not shared with Mama Jene what the request was. He was worried that it would seem too dark or raise flags. In honesty, he hoped that they could get through this with as little involvement from her as possible.

* * *

Friday morning and afternoon passed in a blur for Samuel. He made another appearance at his old office after breakfast and had lunch with some former coworkers. After lunch, he made a trip to a few department stores around town. The house and grounds had been kept up so beautifully that Samuel wanted to get some small gifts for the gardener and the housekeeper to express his extreme appreciation. Then he hurried home to wait.

Now that his façade for the day was completed, all that was left to do was hope and wait. He hoped that Mama Jene found Kerrie. He hoped that Kerrie agreed to help, no questions asked. He hoped that Kerrie would mail the package in time for Samuel to receive it before he left. He hoped that he didn't miss the parcel carrier.

Samuel fought to hang on to his hat as he got his shopping bags out of his rideshare. The wind had been unusually active the entire weekend. Samuel headed through the tall wrought-iron gates, fighting Mother Nature the entire time. The waist-high hedges which lined the driveway offered no protection from his silent attacker.

At the end of the driveway, Samuel set down the bags to catch his breath. Everything was as breathtaking as it had always been. As he reached back down for his bounty, he realized something was missing. The yard was too quiet. The homemade windchime which had lived on the porch forever was missing. Samuel looked around to see if the heavy wind had blown it across the yard. His eyes scanned the perimeter to no avail. He could neither see nor hear the chime's music.

"Who would steal a windchime?" Samuel fumed aloud to no one. The good mood shopping had put him in was gone. He hurried inside to sulk on the parlor couch.

The wild wind whipped against Samuel's home like the big bad wolf who tried to flush out piglets in Aesop's children's fables. Inhale, huff, huff, puff, repeat. The rhythmic whooshing was hypnotizing. It took Samuel back to Eternity's fourth birthday party. Sinking back into the armrest, Samuel allowed himself to get transported back in memory.

* * *

Eternity wanted to learn to play the piano, and Matthew was thrilled. He had always wanted his kids to love music the way he did. Unfortunately, Matthew had to report to work that morning, so Samuel was instructed to go to Berkeley's Music Store and find a small upright piano that Eternity liked. Berkeley's motto was "Pick it by 8, play it by 8": Samuel trusted that they would be able to deliver, set up, and tune any piano from their showroom within a 12-hour window. Samuel hoped that the piano would arrive in time to be tuned during Eternity's birthday party. The kids would play outside, and the family would be able to enjoy the music when they returned home at the end of the day.

Back in Berkley's giant showroom, Samuel swam in a sea of grand pianos. Every piano here was beautiful; every one of them called out to him. His inexperience left him unsure about brands, size, and other crucial factors. The only instructions Matthew gave him were to make sure Eternity felt a connection to the instrument. That way, she would be willing to spend time learning to play it well. This was a very extravagant gift for such a small child, but Matthew really wanted a musical family. The first glimmer of interest had to be acted on while it still shone bright.

Matthew wanted to make sure she found a piano to love for years.

Almost immediately upon entering the showroom at Berkley's, Eternity all but ran to an older piano set back in the corner of the room. It was a hidden gem, past its prime. It was teal on all surfaces and was lined with a gold border where every piece of wood intersected. It had old, webbed feet, which Samuel found to be beautiful. The ottoman that came with it had a floral-and-gold pattern, set on a soft green velour cloth. The colors and webbed feet made Samuel think of the piano as a reincarnated mallard.

Eternity touched key after key, her face lighting up with excitement as she brought random notes to life. Samuel never heard such a unique sound from a piano.

He was sold on it even before Eternity said, "Daddy, I want this one!"

Samuel made no attempt to persuade her to look at other pianos. He wanted her to have this one. The piano's beautiful surfaces spoke to its rich history. The few keys his daughter played he often described later as sounding like God's tiny bow, drawing across the eyelashes of angels.

The showroom was particularly busy that day. *It's like Super Bowl Sunday here*, Samuel recalled thinking. The two teams on the field were guitars and pianos. The employees acted as referees, scurrying over the field and throwing flags down. All hands were on deck taking orders from customers.

Brandon, Mr. Berkley's teenage son, approached Samuel. "We will take this one," Samuel quickly announced. Another point for team piano. With no questions asked, Brandon placed a sign on the piano that read "Sold" and ushered Samuel to the counter for payment.

"You are all set, Sir," Brandon said. "The piano should be up and running at your place by 8 PM."

Matthew arrived home late that afternoon and rushed immediately to the backyard to help coordinate the day's celebrations. Matthew and Samuel had rented a bouncy castle and some water slides for the birthday party. All the kids in Eternity's daycare were invited over for the celebration. A client Samuel had helped a few weeks before even arranged for a few ponies to arrive as an added thank-you.

Samuel, as he often did for birthday parties, enjoyed painting joy on the excited faces of little kids. His yard was full of zebras, lions, monkeys, aliens, superheroes, and clowns running past him. The light of excitement on each child's, and some adults', faces as he held up a mirror for each to see their transformation, brought sheer happiness to him. Samuel loved to create.

Matthew was outside watching over the kids and guests until the yard returned to normal. The last ponies were taken away around 7:30 PM. It had been a long and exhausting day for Matthew. He was thrilled to spend some time that evening watching his daughter play her new instrument.

Samuel stared out the bay window as Matthew walked back up the driveway. He knew Matthew could make out his daughter sitting at her piano and striking keys through the bay window. He wondered if Matthew could see the level of excitement on Eternity's face from the distance.

To Samuel's surprise, Matthew's expression was not one of joy. Instead, his face flooded with confusion. Eternity's back was to the door, and she was too engulfed in her new toy to notice the subtle exchange between her dads.

"What is this?" Matthew questioned, gesturing towards the piano.

"This is the piano that she fell in love with, isn't it beautiful?" Samuel asked.

Matthew's eyes widened a bit. "That's not a piano, honey. That is a harpsichord. Did you not notice it had two sets of keys? Or that it sounded totally different than every other piano in the store?"

Samuel nodded. "I did notice that. I knew it was an older model, and I figured that maybe that's how they made them back in the day."

Matthew shook his head subtly. "Did the staff there not wonder why you were buying a harpsichord? It's not a common instrument."

"Not really," Samuel offered. "They were busy, one of Berkley's sons helped me out."

Eternity played a few more notes, causing Matthew to shiver in disgust. "It's so gross. It sounds like the devil picking out the hairs of crying babies."

Matthew had hated the harpsichord for years, but Eternity loved it from the first stroke. Matthew was forced to endure its sound, fearing that she would lose interest in music if he forced it away from her. It pained him to have to sit with Eternity and teach her to play daily. Samuel grinned in recollection of Matthew's daily string of insults about the instrument. For his part, Samuel found the harpsichord to be quite beautiful.

It was years before Matthew convinced Eternity to transition to a "real piano." She fell in love with playing music and wanted to do it well. Matthew was overjoyed with her willingness to evolve. He learned his lesson and did not allow Samuel to have a hand in selecting the instrument's replacement. Matthew bought the new piano himself while Eternity was at school and asked the movers to help move the harpsichord to the backyard to celebrate the transition.

Samuel watched through the upstairs window as Matthew took a sledgehammer over and over to the beautiful harpsichord as soon as the movers left. Samuel was sad to see the instrument be destroyed but was quite entertained at the spectacle Matthew was making. It was hilarious to know that the instrument bothered him so much that he needed to demolish it. Matthew was always so composed. It was funny to see him like this, so irrational, so normal. '

Once the harpsichord had been sufficiently crushed, Matthew rushed into his truck. "I'll be back," he yelled out to Samuel. "I have to go get some gasoline for the fire."

Fire? What fire? Samuel thought. The realization hit him almost immediately. He grabbed a box from the pantry and hurried downstairs. He was determined to save a little bit of the beloved instrument for himself. Filling the box with as many wooden pieces as he could fit, he hid the box inside the pantry before Matthew's return.

The next day, Samuel took the harpsichord's remnants to a local woodwork artist and asked for them to be made into something, anything. The artist commissioned a windchime. She strung together the windchime's bells using harpsichord strings and surrounded them with plastic guitar picks that thumped and ricocheted against the cords whenever the wind hit them. Samuel found the harpsichord to be even more beautiful in its afterlife as a harpsichime.

The first time Matthew came home and heard the chime he was not thrilled. "I do not remember there being any survivors of my war," he mentioned to Samuel.

"Well, just consider them a few POWs that'll stick with us over time," Samuel answered. Matthew was unamused by this response. He fell silent and stared at his sworn enemy intently. Samuel was certain that he had won the battle until he came home a few days later. He noticed that all the guitar picks had been replaced with plastic vehicle keys.

"What is this?" Samuel confronted Matthew the first chance he got.

"Well, I thought it was only fair that your POWs have friends for their stay," Matthew answered.

"I don't understand," Samuel admitted confusedly. Matthew was delighted. "The keys you see are not random. Those are replicas of the keys to your first car. The one that you were always locking yourself out of." This time it was Samuel's face that was not amused. "This way, the sound of cats being choked in the wind will always guide you back to your lost keys," Matthew concluded with a triumphant smile.

* * *

The sound of a shutter clapping against the house brought Samuel back to the present. It was 7 PM and the day was nearing its close. Still, there was no package from Kerrie, and Samuel could feel his heart plummeting in his chest. He hadn't counted on this setback.

Why had I thought that everything would just fall into place? Samuel thought. *What do I do now?* He contemplated calling the kids and delaying his flight, but he knew that wasn't really an option. He could already feel his paternal heartstrings tugging him to get back to his babies.

A knock at the door startled him. *Had the carrier made it in time?* Samuel allowed himself a moment of hope, but that too was crushed as soon as he saw a pizza delivery driver outside the door.

Samuel had not ordered a pizza. He opened the door, prepared to let the driver know that he was in the wrong place. But before Samuel could speak, the driver extended the pizza to him. "Delivery for Kerrie Thompson," he said. Samuel's heart began to beat fast in his chest. As confused as he was, he knew that the pizza guy would not have any answers for him.

"How much do I owe you?" Samuel murmured.

Checking his notes, the driver responded, "Prepaid online. Napkins, cheese, and peppers in the bag, sir." Samuel thanked the driver, collected the pizza bag, and quickly closed the door. He rushed back to the living room immediately.

Samuel carefully opened the grease-stained pizza box, unsure of what he would find inside. To his dismay, it was a large pepperoni pizza. Samuel studied the box lid and lifted the grease tray. He took in a calculating whiff, pressing his nose right against the box. But to no avail; he realized that the object in front of him was, in fact, a pizza. Kerrie must have been unwilling or unable to help, so she decided to send him dinner as a peace offering.

That hurt, but Samuel reminded himself that he shouldn't be surprised. What did he expect, with all the secret-agent-sounding requests he'd been throwing around lately? Regardless, the smell of fresh garlic, basil, and mozzarella was quite inviting. Samuel hadn't thought about dinner and saw no reason to let the gift go to waste. He decided to indulge. The pizza was piping hot, the cheese still gooey, the crust steaming and hard to hold, but he was hungry. He wolfed down a piece so quickly that he burned his tongue and the roof of his mouth in the process.

I'll still send Kerrie a thank-you email later for the pizza, he thought. He appreciated that she had responded to him, even if it wasn't in the way he was hoping for.

Now that his hunger had been slightly sated, Samuel took his time with the second slice. The pizza was good, but it was missing something. He fumbled around in the delivery bag and found Parmesan cheese and a pack of red crushed pepper. Now it hit the spot.

Samuel decided to call the kids and remind them that he would be home tomorrow as scheduled. The girls were just as interested in their conversation as they had been yesterday. He was obviously interrupting their busy day. As Samuel forced them to engage in a little small talk about their day, he reached into the bag to grab more red pepper.

As he fumbled around the bag, his fingers hit an unfamiliar object. It was not cheese, peppers, napkins, cutlery, or anything else he had expected to feel. It was cardstock. *Probably just a coupon for the next pizza order*, Samuel thought.

By now, Eternity was barely paying attention. Samuel gave her his love and released her from her vocal prison. He peeked into the bag and realized that the object his fingers had stumbled upon was not a flyer, but a greeting card envelope. His ears perked up like a Doberman's. He was now at full attention. Samuel slid out a small, folded note from the envelope and opened it. He read:

Samuel,

> *I hope this finds you in time. In time for what, I do not know, but in my line of work, it is rarely important to*

know all the details. Judging by the fact that this missive was hand-delivered to me in a sealed envelope, I assumed I should handle my reply with the utmost discretion. The private courier service I use is known for its secrecy. Personally, I also find their pizza facade delicious. Inside this envelope, you will find an ordinary-looking ink pen with two buttons. Do not touch the pen until you are ready to place the tracker. When you are ready, hold the tip of the pen onto the surface you want the tracker to stick to. It has its own adhesive. Once you put it in place, press the red button and hold the pen steady for a few seconds. You will not see the tracker with your eye. Wait until the pen's red button changes colors to blue. This will be your indicator that the tracker has adhered to the surface and the pen can be removed. Press the now-blue button again and it will flash, thus activating the tracker. Once the tracker has no movement for eight hours the second button on the pen will glow green. Make sure you are near a phone before you press it. A phone number will appear once you press the green button and turn over the pen. Make sure to have a writing pad nearby, since it will only appear for 15 seconds. You will have 30 seconds to call the number and retrieve the tracking data. Be ready to write everything down, because once the automated system gives you the information the call will drop, and the phone number will become inactive. The tracker will reset itself to make it untraceable if discovered. You can then use it again in the same way, as many times as you need. Hope this helps.

- Kerrie

A wave of relief flooded over Samuel as he folded the letter and tucked it back inside the envelope. He had a chance now. Sure, it was the smallest of possible chances, but it was a chance all the same. Samuel found himself wondering about the "pizza cover" mentioned in the letter. He closed the box and looked for the name of the pizza business. The box simply said "Pizza." How had he not noticed that before he started eating? There were red and green stripes going across the box and a little cartoon Italian guy in the corner, which made for a very convincing fake box.

Clever, he thought. He realized that he had been so focused on the box's contents that by the time he had finished his investigation, the driver was long gone. There was no traceable name or delivery address. Without a company name, there was no way to track the box left behind. Indeed, Kerrie's security was every bit as good as she advertised it to be.

Samuel made a big show out of cleaning up the mess he had made, just in case anyone had been watching him eat his dinner. He felt silly going through the motions but decided he would rather be safe than sorry. His suitcase was already packed and waiting by the door. He quickly tucked Kerrie's card into the suitcase's front pocket as he carried the scraps of his dinner outside to the trash. He would not want to attract insects into the house. That was normal, right? After dinner, he hurried himself to bed and slept a dreamless sleep for the first night in a while.

THIRTEEN

Dusk was coming on quickly when Samuel pulled up to his small first home in Verdigre. He already missed Atlanta, but he couldn't wait to see his children. He knew he had no hope of sneaking up on the kids. They were out of the house and into the driveway before the car even came to a complete stop. It had only been two days, but he hated being away from them. The idea of leaving his and Matthew's family unprotected scared him more than anything. But protecting them from afar was impossible. Logically, Samuel knew that Julia was more than capable of taking care of the children. But logic does not help a father feel at ease. The girls had to pull back Matswell and Lias as they barricaded Samuel in the Jeep. They were happily oblivious to the fact that Daddy couldn't open the door when they were standing in front of it.

The shock of his return had already passed for the boys by the time Samuel put his bags down in the office. They lingered outside with Tavia, trying to fill a mason jar with lightning bugs for the night. Samuel slid into his office chair and spun around to face Eternity, who was waiting for him. "How was everything while I was gone, sweetie?" Samuel asked.

Samuel was quick enough to register a brief eye roll on his daughter's face. "It's only been two days, Dad, not a decade. Plus, Julia almost lived here the entire time you were gone. I didn't have time to sell Tavia online or feed the boys to a pack of hungry wolves."

Samuel laughed boisterously, though he felt bad for doing so. Eternity's way with words had a knack for catching him off guard. "I'll try to remember you need more time the next time I'm away," Samuel retorted.

Samuel moved his eyes around the room, gradually registering a few small changes. All of the kids' nice shoes were lined up by the door; they were all clean, as if ready for inspection. Two genuinely nice outfits were folded neatly on the ironing board in the corner of the kitchen. A dress was hanging from the light fixture next to the ironing board.

Samuel was confused. The scene made no sense to him. It was Saturday night. They were obviously not going out to eat, so why prep all these junior black-tie clothes? Had Julia made plans for them to go somewhere nice and not told him about it? "Eternity, what are you up to? Are we having a dinner party you forgot to invite me to?"

He could tell that she wasn't ready to answer him. She turned away, something in the other room obviously needing her attention at the same moment. She started singing softly to herself, never a good sign. As mature as she was at times, Eternity was still childlike when she wanted to be. Samuel continued scanning the room, trying to piece together clues from the silence.

He gave her a moment before prying further. She turned back around and walked towards Samuel. Slowly and purposefully, she sat down next to him. *Well, this can't be good*, Samuel thought.

Her tone of voice was calm as she spoke to her father. "No, Daddy, there is no dinner party you were not invited to. But we will be attending a celebration tomorrow, and you are the guest of honor."

Samuel was certainly not expecting this turn of events. He paused, not sure how he should respond. "What celebration are we going to and where?" he queried.

He could hear Eternity's voice crack just a little bit as she replied. "Well, I'm not sure where exactly the celebration will be. To be honest, all I know is that it is happening tomorrow and that we are all going."

Samuel could still not fathom what his daughter was going on about. He felt tired from the trip and confused to be caught off guard. Once they locked eyes, Eternity could tell he was ready for answers. Instead, she offered her biggest smile. It was obviously fake, but Samuel would only realize that later. "We are going to celebrate Jesus, Dad. We are all going to church tomorrow."

The family had been to church before, but they were not an overly religious family. Matthew felt strongly about presenting all possible truths to the children and letting them decide for themselves what they believed in. He had always been honest with them that he believed in God, but also in science. Anytime that anyone in the family wanted to go to church, they all went to support each other. They always dressed and behaved respectfully, but never down to the letter. This was the norm; Samuel couldn't figure out why Eternity would feel so awkward about it. He knew there was something more going on here, but he couldn't put his finger on what it was.

Whatever Eternity was planning, he knew it was more than church. Samuel tried to probe her cautiously without sounding unsupportive. "Was there any particular reason you wanted to go to church and dress nicer than usual, honey?"

She returned his gaze steadily as she responded. "Well, to tell you the truth, I've been thinking a lot about the conversation that we had the night before you left. The one about where I came from."

Samuel immediately felt horrible. The conversation had completely slipped his mind. He had dropped a bombshell on his daughter and then left town. *She must have so many questions left unanswered*, he thought. *She feels like she needs God's wisdom.*

"Sweetie, I am so sorry," Samuel muttered. "I told you all of that, and you didn't get a chance to ask all your questions before I rushed off for work. I feel horrible. You must feel so lost... I'm sorry, baby."

Realizing that her father had come to the wrong conclusion, Eternity decided to be more forthcoming. "I'm fine with where I came from, Daddy. I know where I fit in the world. I know you and Papa wanted me so bad that you changed the rules of nature to have me. It's amazing to be one of a kind...ish. But that's not the part of your story that I've been thinking about."

Samuel had no idea what was going on. He felt like he was drowning in a sea of confused thoughts. Fortunately, Eternity picked up on his feelings and hurried to complete her explanation.

"I've been thinking about how much your parents hated Papa. They were glad when you stopped seeing him and they thought he was a bad person. You said they called him the devil," Eternity said.

The words stabbed Samuel in the chest. His parents did feel that way about Matthew. They hated him for no good reason. Now, their bile was somehow affecting his daughter.

"From what you've told me, Papa has always been amazing to you," Eternity continued. "He was always there for you, even when you didn't know you needed him."

Ouch—another needle. What is she getting at? Samuel wondered. *Is she trying to hurt me?* She was certainly hitting all the right cords.

"It makes me mad that they felt that way about Papa," Eternity confessed. "I've been thinking a lot about that since you've been gone. I have spent days dwelling on this, if I'm being honest. I don't understand disliking someone so strongly who has given you no reason to dislike them. They hated Papa and that infuriates me."

She fell silent after that. Samuel took a moment to try and find the right words to comfort his hurting baby. "Honey, my adoptive parents were raised in a different time and culture than we live in now. They fear the different. Anyone that behaved differently was a sinner to them. Your father never pretended to be anything he wasn't. As soon as he moved here, there was a target on his back for being different. But it never bothered him; he was always trying to help the rest of us see the world differently, even when we weren't ready to see the truth. Don't let these people's ignorance make you feel bad about our family. We kept them away from you children for a reason."

Eternity responded heatedly, with venom at the edges of her words. "I don't feel bad about our family, Daddy. Every day, I feel lucky for the life you and Papa have made for us. I always wondered why we only had two grandparents, but it never seemed right to discuss it. After hearing your story, the other day about your childhood, I'm proud to have only one set of grandparents. Your foster parents don't sound like they deserve kids, let alone grandkids."

Samuel was still struggling to connect the dots. Knowing he had no chance of following what was going on, he decided to simply ask. "But what does any of this have to do with us dressing up for church tomorrow?"

He could still hear the anger in Eternity's voice when she answered. "Well, based on the little that you shared, I assumed that your parents are the type of people who've lived in the same town their whole lives. They'll probably stay there until they die. I know that they don't live too far from here. Likely they are still going to the same church they always went to. I think they should see how well the devil's family turned out."

Samuel was flabbergasted. Never in his life had he thought he would see his parents again. He had no reason to believe that he and his parents would ever cross paths. Even when the family returned for visits, it always felt like they were living on a different planet.

Samuel winced. He should have known that Eternity would understand way more than he had intended from his story. *This was exactly why it had always been supposed to be Matthew that told the kids about their origins*, Samuel thought.

She was exactly right. Just as she had, Samuel assumed his former parents still lived in the same house he had grown up in. He imagined they still went to the same church house weekly. Never, never in his wildest of dreams did he ever dream of facing them again, especially not without Matthew.

Samuel felt fear rushing through him like he was a little boy again. He wanted to curl into a corner and hide behind the furniture. His heart was racing and sweat bubbled just under his skin. This was the most he had thought about his parents since leaving for college decades ago. He could feel all the old wounds opening again.

His tired eyes started to fill with tears, but he quickly faked a giant yawn to try and conceal it.

FOURTEEN

Samuel **woke** to the sound of the overstuffed yellow comforter hitting the floor of his bedroom. He couldn't stop tossing and turning all night. *I'll never get used to sleeping here*, he thought. He quickly dismissed the feeling and tried to wrap his mind around today's challenge. He wasn't sure how to handle arriving at church, a place he once thought of as a sacred worship ground.

"How did I let myself get talked into this?" he muttered in a cracked voice.

Eyes still half-shut, he fumbled around the floor in search of the comforter. Ironically, it was one of the few things he had hung onto from his childhood. It took more patting around than he had hoped to retrieve the old patchwork comforter.

Samuel lay hiding under the blanket, fervently hoping that the day would pass him by. He was not so lucky. The sounds of cartoons and tiny giggles rose from the living room. The kids always woke up at dawn on the weekends. He rolled to his side and forced one eye open just enough to see the time through squinted lashes. The clock smiled an annoying little smile at Samuel as it reported back the time. 6:14 AM. His ears picked up more conversation than he was accustomed to hearing from his platoon this early in the morning.

Samuel mustered up all his might and forced himself out of the bed. He tied his robe as tight as he could to trap in every single degree of warmth near his body, before venturing out to investigate the disturbance. The boys were sitting together, legs crossed in a tangle, watching a blur of cartoons that Samuel could not focus on till he had his coffee. He could see Tavia in the yard through the window, doing her morning Tai chi.

Turning to the kitchen, Samuel realized that the source of the racket was Eternity and Julia. They were in the kitchen making breakfast together. "Good morning, Julia, long time no see," Samuel made a limp attempt at humor. "What brings you by so early on a Sunday?"

Julia put down the mixing bowl and dried her hands on her apron. "Good morning, sunshine," she replied, her tone gently teasing him. She reminded Samuel of a mother talking to a grumpy child. Julia poured Samuel a cup of coffee and offered him the treat. "Well, I noticed all the nice clothes that were being prepped yesterday and assumed that you were headed off to church this morning. I figured you would be exhausted after your trip, so I thought I'd make you some breakfast. After all, we don't want any growling tummies to interrupt the preacher."

Samuel thanked her and sipped his coffee. He could feel the scent waking his body up with each new inhale. Though his exterior was cold and grumpy, the vibrant taste of the drink jump-started his body back to life. "Eternity told me you were starting on biscuits and gravy the other day when the tornado came through, and I know how much you love them so I thought I would surprise you with some." Those were the right words. By now the coffee had reached his ears. He was liking what he heard.

Samuel wore a sheepish smile. "Biscuits and gravy are my favorite!"

Like everything else he liked throughout his childhood, he kept this a secret as well. Only by doing so could he avoid whatever he liked being taken away. Samuel thought back on all the childhood toys that were taken away from him, never to be seen again. It seemed like as soon as it was obvious something was his favorite his adoptive parents would in the same moment decide he had committed some grave infraction which would only be appeased by removing the object of his attention. The pair thrived on the fact that they had complete control over their children's happiness. So easily they could display at any moment exactly how much control they had. They were vindictive to the core. As he sat at the table uselessly, he allowed his mind to drift back to his first birthday with them.

* * *

He had been so excited about the strawberry cake he had asked for. Shelia, his adoptive mother, had made a big gesture to draw attention to all the work she was doing just for him. The aromas seeped through the house for hours. "If I am going to be in the kitchen putting in all this work to make a cake you want, then you will need to help out with some extra chores around the house," Shelia instructed. Samuel could hardly contain his excitement.

He had been instructed to clean his room before the entire family came over. This seemed like a fair exchange for cake. He rushed happily into his room. He would do anything for the mouth-watering strawberry delight he could all but taste. He started picking up the stray clothes on the floor like he was supposed to, but the sweet smell of cake just kept calling to him. He found himself running to the door and peeking down the hallway towards the kitchen. It was impossible for him to focus on anything but the time he had to pass until he could enjoy the treat.

Time passed so slowly for a seven-year-old. He started playing with some of the toys he had retrieved, hoping they would take his mind off the cake. Instead, he forgot about cleaning his room. As his first cousins started to arrive, he rushed out to greet them and ran off into the yard. As he played, his mother finished the cake and walked into the hallway to retrieve matches for the candles. She could see his bedroom door open and the mess it still was. She shook her head in disgust as she wiped her hands off against her apron.

Sheila called the kids back inside. On the table was the most beautiful cake Samuel had ever laid eyes on. It smelled just as heavenly as it looked. Samuel could hardly contain himself and found himself jumping up and down in place at the edge of the table. The candles were not lit, and he shot his foster mother an annoyed look.

Shelia looked down on him both literally and figuratively.

"Young man, since you did not follow the simple instructions I gave you to help out today, you will not be making a wish. Idle and lazy hands do not get rewarded around this house."

Samuel was barely listening. The cake was still calling to him. His lack of understanding made Shelia angrier than ever. She slapped him across the face to re-focus his attention. "You will respect me in this house and listen to me when I speak to you," she commanded.

Samuel was forced to sit and watch everyone else enjoy the cake that he so desperately wanted with tear-filled eyes. He was not permitted to have any. Shelia forbade him from leaving the table until everyone was done eating. He watched mournfully as the cake dwindled down to a quarter of its full size. He begged and pleaded with Shelia to relent and give him a piece of cake, eyes filled with tears. After everyone left, Shelia asked, "Have you learned a lesson about doing as you're told?" Samuel nodded. "Well then, go and clean your room," she said.

Samuel hurried off to do as he was told. There was still plenty of cake left, and he knew if he could just clean his room fast enough and well enough, he would finally get to enjoy it. Samuel made sure the room looked perfect. His bed was made with childhood precision, every toy hidden away in a giant wooden chest. He swept the floor from corner to corner, even dusting the window seal. When he finished, his mother called him back to the table to sit down. They were joined by his father.

She took out a plate and a fork from the cupboard and cut the remaining cake in half. She gave one half to his father and reached for another fork as she addressed Samuel. "When you are told to do something, we expect you to do it when we tell you to, not whenever you get around to it." Samuel did not know what to say. He whimpered and watched his two foster parents eat every remaining bite of the cake in front of him.

Never again did his mother make, bring in, or allow a strawberry cake to be brought into their home. It wasn't enough for her that Samuel learnt his lesson once. She had to make sure he would remember it every day, for the rest of his life. The lesson stuck and Samuel found it impossible to enjoy strawberry cake to this day. His love for the smell and the flavor never outweighed his emotional trauma. He was grateful that so far none of his four children seemed to have any interest in strawberry-flavored treats.

* * *

Samuel was brought back to the present by the sound of Julia and Eternity giggling over a shared joke. He quickly tried to refocus before his tears escaped from within. *I can't believe that I'm about to expose my family to those—those demons,* he thought. No other words fit their description. Panicked thoughts began to race through his mind. *How am I supposed to see them? What am I supposed to say? Should I say anything? Will they recognize me? What will they think of the kids?*

Today's church visit was different in more than one way. Even though the family had been to churches together before, this one felt different. Samuel was conflicted. He wasn't sure whether he should set the children's expectations similar to those he had grown up with. Should he forbid them from going to the bathroom? Should he instruct them not to look at anyone but the pastor? Should he tell them not to put any money on the offering plate?

Samuel shuddered. The house of God should have been a place where he felt loved and accepted, but instead, his parents made it feel like an extension of their reign of terror. Even when his parents were horrible to him in public, no one batted an eye at their ways. They were upstanding pillars of their community, who had done the Lord's work by fostering him in their household. But to Samuel, they felt less like parents and more like wardens.

No, he decided; none of that is how my family attends church. He gave each child some money to put in the offering plate when it came around. He bent down on one knee to speak to the boys, face to face. "Boys, the preacher is there to help guide the flock closer to God," he reminded, tucking the folded cash into their tiny pockets. "The church is part of his house that everyone is invited into. Just like our house, it takes money to pay the bills. That is why we all must give to support the church. Salvation is not free." Both boys nodded solemnly, and Samuel kissed them on their cheeks.

Standing back up, he looked at his mini congregation, smiled, and addressed them all. "If anyone speaks to you, smile, nod, and be sure to speak back. It is polite to acknowledge that we are no better than anyone else." Samuel felt awkward and fidgety as if he were preparing his family for some great war. But it was he himself who was going to war, not them. Today he would face his greatest enemies. He must stay unwavering for his clan. Samuel exhaled and extended his hand towards the door, letting the kids know it was time to go.

The boys raced to the Jeep as soon as he ushered them out of the house. The girls were helping them buckle in when Samuel called out. "Boys, get out of the Jeep. Girls, come and help me." Samuel rolled back the cover on Gabriel, his sleek black BMW. The car was his pride and joy; a gift from himself to himself. "I'll be damned if I let them take anything else from me." The boys started to laugh as they rarely heard Daddy curse, and the girls just looked at each other in confusion.

The window tint was like smoke rising from the car, escaping into the sky. The rims were 360-degree mirrors as they rolled down the road. The glass packs roared as Gabriel awoke from his hiatus. It was as if he were clearing his throat, ready to scream at the world. The license plate frame was a metallic box with the colors of the pride flag surrounding his plate GA91221.

Samuel opened the sunroof and cranked the sound system up. He was in the mood to feel the car beat with the music as he soared down the highway. It was quite flashy for the corn-raised town, but it was very fitting for his line of work back home. The beat-up highways and old dirt roads were rough on Gabriel, so he hadn't moved since the family got here.

Today, Samuel wanted everyone to see whom he had become – not only his former parents but the entire town. This place would take nothing away from the man he had grown into. He tossed Gabriel's keys to Eternity. "I think you should drive us today." Eternity was a great driver, but Samuel never let her behind the wheel of Gabriel. She was excited and her face beamed as she rushed around the car to the driver's seat.

The family all felt at home flying down the highway. They sang along to the radio, just like they always did. But Samuel could not get out of his own head. He was grateful for not having to focus on driving this morning. He needed a few more minutes to just be. His heart pounded harder than the subwoofer's thumps. He feared that it would be so loud that the whole family would hear his fear.

Samuel didn't have to think twice about where to send Eternity. After all these years, it was still etched into his memory where the old church sat. From miles down the road, the family could spot the church atop the tallest hill in the area. The bell tower's long shadow engulfed the building beneath it.

"Well, there's no turning back now," Samuel muttered under his breath. *I guess this is really going to happen*, he thought, gripping the car's handle tightly. Regret washed over him as he remembered agreeing to this endeavor. Suddenly, a tiny voice rang out. Samuel turned down the radio to hear it better.

It was Matswell. "Daddy, is this where you went to church when you were my size?" Samuel adjusted himself in his seat and looked at his son as he answered.

"Yes, bubba, this is where I went to church when I was just your age."

That appeared to be the answer Matswell was hoping for. "Did Papa come here with you?" The question sent a sharp pang through Samuel's side. He was not ready to think about Matthew on top of everything else going on.

Eternity interjected before Samuel could reply. "Papa didn't live here when he was your age," she said, glancing up at her brother through the rearview mirror. "He went to a different church far away."

Samuel was relieved by the rescue. Eternity's answer satisfied all the little boy's questions for now.

Samuel adjusted himself once again and gritted his teeth. He was bracing himself to face the warzone ahead.

FIFTEEN

The parking lot wrapped around three of the four walls of the Lord's house. The north wall of the church faced incoming visitors. Samuel remembered that his parents always parked on the east side, so he instructed Eternity to park on the west side, placing the cathedral between his family and his former parents.

Samuel froze for a moment. He sat in the parked car and debated whether or not to instruct Eternity to drive back to the house. He had almost convinced himself to make a run for it when a sudden peck on the window startled him. He jumped as high up in his seat as his seatbelt would allow and clutched the door handle. He spun his head around and saw Julia waiting for him, dressed in her Sunday best.

"I thought I could be of some help today with the boys while you and the girls attended service,"

Julia said with a smile. Samuel was instantly relieved. He was not alone; he had backup.

Samuel smiled genuinely. "That really would be such an amazing help today, Julia. You are absolutely the best, as always!"

He couldn't help but wonder whether Julia had been acting on her own initiative or if she had been instructed to play defense for him and his team. Samuel was sure Matthew knew where he was and what he was up to. It would be exactly like him to ask her stand in for him when he couldn't. Either way, Samuel was thankful for the help. Today was going to be a complete disaster, so all help was appreciated, no matter from what source. He decided he wouldn't let himself dwell on insignificant details.

The boys scampered off towards the church house with Julia in tow. Samuel listened to their little giggles until they disappeared inside, out of sight. He turned to face his daughters. He struggled to interpret the callous expressions on their faces. "Are you guys okay?" he asked in a loving and labored voice.

Eternity had a scowl on her face and remained silent. Her sister was quick and brusque in her response. "We're fine."

Samuel was shocked at Tavia's harsh tone. It made sense for Eternity to have shared today's mission with her sister. But her reaction was uncompromising and unforgiving. His chest constricted as he wondered whether Eternity had overshared any other details with her twin.

165

No, he thought. *Eternity understands the importance of keeping my secret. For now...*

He exhaled with exhaustion and addressed the girls. "I know you are both upset over this. Remember, this is a church, and you were raised with manners. You cannot let anger or frustration get the best of you."

Tavia answered in a bitter, mocking tone once more. "Well, we're not in the church yet. We have about 40 yards to find those manners we were raised with." She raised an eyebrow and bobbed her chin down quickly as if to say that that would be the end of their conversation. Too exhausted to retort, Samuel swallowed the laughter building inside him and ushered them out of the car.

Once inside, Samuel led the girls to a pew near the back. With two angry ninjas by his side, he wanted to make sure to put as much distance as possible between himself and his former parents. If he could keep his offspring out of the spotlight, they might make it through the service unnoticed.

It was still quite early, and the church was completely empty except for a fragile-looking preacher with white hair, who was pacing frantically in front of the altar. Eternity was up on her feet and headed toward the man before Samuel even realized what was going on. "

"Hey, hey, what are you doing?" Samuel tried to whisper, grasping at Eternity's elbow as she strode away. The gesture didn't yield any result; she was clearly ignoring his pleas. *What is she up to?* he thought, squirming helplessly in his seat.

Eternity approached the preacher and started exchanging words with him quietly. Samuel wished he knew what they were talking about. He prepared himself to bolt at the first sign of trouble.

The preacher put one hand on each of Eternity's shoulders and smiled at her widely. He then motioned for her to head up a stairway behind the altar.

"What is happening?" Samuel huffed to himself.

He couldn't imagine how Eternity could have helped alleviate the preacher's worries so quickly. Eternity poked her head back out of the doorway and motioned for Tavia to join her inside. Tavia was up and headed towards her sister before Samuel had a chance to restrain her.

"Oh, this cannot be happening," Samuel muttered to himself a little loudly. He could feel himself beginning to hyperventilate. He glanced down at his watch. There was about half an hour until the start of service. He knew he needed to retrieve his two daughters and figure out their plan before they got more attention drawn to them.

Striding along the pews, the preacher locked eyes with Samuel.

Oh crap, Samuel thought, unsure of what was going on.

The room began to fill up with beautiful music as the preacher headed toward Samuel. The music reminded him of why he always wanted to get to church early. He loved to hear the organ being played. As a child, the organist would always arrive before the congregation and the organ's music would be playing as people started to make their way in. He loved to hear it play as much as possible before the sermon began.

Samuel cleared his throat and prepared his most charming smile for the quickly approaching preacher.

"I am Brother Samuel," he said, extending his hand towards the man.

He tried to keep his smile down at his little joke. "I hope my girls haven't caused some problem for you this morning, Father," he said.

The preacher quickly waved off Samuel's apology. "Quite the opposite, actually. I was stressing about today's service," the priest said, glancing back towards his pulpit.

"So many people are sick right now, and some key members of today's music aren't going to make it. I wasn't sure how I was going to keep the room's attention with just my old voice," the preacher chuckled.

"I am Father Rusty. I'm glad to see your family joining ours today," he continued.

Realization hit Samuel like a wall of bricks: Eternity had offered to play the organ. She had taken almost ten years of organ lessons back home. How could Samuel not have recognized her playing? By this point, the room was starting to come alive with sound. He recognized the traditional melodies of his church youth, but his ears now picked up the tunes' alterations. Eternity was taking artistic liberties with the music she was playing. He cringed, hoping Father Rusty couldn't tell.

"God knew that I needed two angels today, so he brought some just in time. Praise the Lord!" the preacher said.

Samuel smiled semi-sincerely. "Eternity loves to play. I'm sure she's enjoying being needed today. Thank you for indulging her."

"Thank you for helping God answer a prayer," Rusty said softly. "I had just finished sending off my prayer to Him when you and your beautiful family walked through the door. I do hope you will stick around after services. I would love to speak to you more. Unfortunately, right now I have to prepare a greeting for my flock."

Samuel nodded. He was honestly grateful that Father Rusty needed to be elsewhere. He was not ready to be "on" this morning. The preacher turned back to the altar. An angelic voice began to waft through the church, stopping him in his tracks.

It was Tavia. The priest held his Bible close to his heart as she started belting out a song: "Precious memories, unseen angels, sent from somewhere to my soul." The words vibrated as each left her lips.

This is not happening! Samuel staggered, gripping the pew in front of him tightly. *We were supposed to be hiding in the corner. Now the spotlight is directly on my kids!* His heart pumped heavily in his chest, warning him of the imminent attack.

Samuel took stock of the damage. *There's no way we're getting out of here unnoticed. The preacher is definitely going to give a special thank you to my family...*

Octavia's voice continued to bounce around the room. "How they linger, ever near me, and the sacred past unfolds," she sang.

Samuel tried to calm himself by closing his eyes and breathing in the words of the song. "How they linger, how they ever flood my soul," Octavia continued. He could feel her words grabbing hold of him and flooding through his entire body. It was too much to bear. Tavia had a beautiful voice, and Samuel loved to hear it. But it had been years since she would sing anything for her dads. Tavia simply didn't enjoy being the center of attention. Both dads figured that that was the reason she refused to sing more often, despite her captivating voice. A few proud tears snuck out of the corner of his eye.

He had forgotten how much he loved to feel Octavia singing. With Tavia, one wouldn't just hear the words, but feel them. Hearing her sing was always a full-body experience. Samuel could feel his soul cleanse as the song ran its course.

Samuel noticed a middle-aged couple had walked into the church while he was lost in the music. Samuel could only see their backs: the husband wore a nice blazer atop a freshly pressed pair of jeans, held up with a pair of snakeskin cowboy boots. His wife wore a simple knee-length blue dress with ruffled white lace. The couple stopped about halfway up the aisle, suspended in place. They were listening to - feeling - his daughter's voice.

"I remember Mother praying, Father too, on bended knee," Tavia sang. The couple obeyed her and sank to their knees to pray. The husband bowed his head as Tavia continued.

Samuel was flabbergasted. He had never seen this kind of behavior in church before. He glanced around the chapel and realized that Rusty had noticed it too. Even though the priest was thrilled, Samuel couldn't help but feel frightened. Today's spectacle promised to get bigger with each passing minute, and he dreaded it more and more.

As Tavia finished her song, the couple stood up and approached her. The husband offered her his hand and a smile, while his wife went in for a hug. Tavia smiled kindly at them both and offered them a few quiet words. Samuel couldn't overhear her from his vantage point. His mind raced wildly while he tried to figure out the possibilities. Did she tell them who she was, where she was from, who her dads were? The couple held hands as they walked away. Samuel's eyes followed them to their seat. He noticed he was staring. *What did they know now?*

Once Samuel allowed his eyes to wander away from the couple, he realized that a dozen more people had taken their seats in the meantime. There were still 20 minutes before the service was scheduled to start. *More than enough time to check in on Julia at the children's service center*, Samuel thought. *No doubt she had already obtained the blueprints of the place and kept them in her purse. Still, no harm in checking.*

Walking down the poorly lit hallway, Samuel couldn't help but feel some envy of his boys. He was never allowed to go to the children's services, even when he was too young to understand the adults. He was always forced to stand beside his family and try his best not to draw attention to himself. He was never sure why he was the only child present for service, but there was no convincing his adoptive parents of anything else. Whenever other parents offered to drop him off along with their own kids, they always politely declined. Samuel recalled them stating something like he had more important things to learn than how to color in shapes.

Samuel could hear the children's laughter and joy as he rounded the corner toward the room. The class must be a small one; he could easily distinguish the laughter of his two angel-adjacent boys.

The twins were sitting with their backs to the door. Samuel glanced through the glass and almost reached for the doorknob, but then decided not to go in. The boys hadn't seen him, but Julia had noticed his presence. She smiled and winked at him quickly, then gestured for him to get out. The boys were obviously enjoying themselves and there was no reason to disturb them. Samuel released the doorknob and headed back to his pew.

Crowds were filling in the empty pews closest to the altar. Samuel was relieved to find himself alone in the last row at the back. He found himself relaxing as the doors to the church closed. No one had found him interesting enough to approach. He could not see his former parents among the faces in the crowd. He tried to look for their features without drawing attention to himself.

Father Rusty approached his podium and the congregation settled down. Eternity's music trickled into silence.

"Welcome everyone, I am so thrilled that you all are here today and all in good health. Unfortunately, Sisters Edna and Alma are under the weather and will not be with us today. I pray for both to have speedy recoveries." There was some slight murmuring around the room that quickly dissipated.

Rusty continued. "This morning I was quite honestly worried about how I was going to deliver a great lesson without their amazing talents to support me. I asked God for advice on how I could do justice to His word today all by myself. And lo and behold, as soon as I raised my head, in walked two angels."

Samuel forced his eyes shut in dread. The intro made it clear what was on its way.

"Both angels had never been in this church before, but one angel approached me as soon as she entered God's house. She must have been eavesdropping on my prayers." Father Rusty allowed a moment for the congregation's chuckles. "

She offered to play the organ instead of Sister Alma and offered her sister's voice up to fill in for Sister Edna. I would like to introduce you all to these angels." He gestured behind him to the girls as he addressed the flock.

"Please help me in welcoming Eternity and Tavia Anderson."

Excited clapping rang around the room momentarily. The two girls nodded slightly and smiled at the room before returning to their stations.

"With the increase of the Covid epidemic, I had planned to speak to you all today about God's healing. But in light of today's events, I think I would like to start off by talking about the book of Mark. Let's turn to Chapter 4, Verse 25: 'For those who listen with open hearts will receive more revelation. But those who don't listen with open hearts will lose what little they think they have!'" Father Rusty paused for a moment to let the holy words sink in.

"These two angels walked into God's house today and listened with open hearts to my current struggle. They acted without hesitation and committed to doing whatever was in their power to do to help. Neither angel asked for an explanation. Nor did they ask for funding or for me to take a picture for their Instagram account. They opened their hearts and listened to my plea for God's help."

Without another word, Rusty turned his gaze upwards towards Eternity. As if on cue, she started to play her music in the loft.

The congregation all stood as one as Tavia began singing again. Samuel's heart melted as he heard his child sing words he had heard so many times before.

Typically, the congregation would join in the song after the first few lines - or at least that's the way he remembered from his youth. But today, no one joined in. Not one voice dared to sing along with his angel. Even though Samuel loved to sing - especially at church - he felt like he just couldn't do it. It was as if singing along with Tavia today would disturb the clarity of the message. The words she was singing were already perfect. *Was everyone feeling the same way?*

Samuel couldn't help but ask himself. Samuel scanned the room to try and register the congregation's reactions. By the third verse, everyone, including Father Rusty, had bowed their heads in prayer.

Samuel tried to recall any other instances where the entire congregation listened to music and allowed it to move them to uninstructed prayer, but he could not. "Children of the devil my ass," he muttered softly under his breath.

After services were over, the girls quickly made their way over to their Daddy. Samuel was counting the seconds before he could make a polite run for it with the girls, but just as he decided to make a dash for the door, the sweet young couple from before approached them to express how much Tavia had touched their hearts.

"It was like God was singing to us today," the wife beamed.

"We hope y'all will join us again next Sunday," her husband tacked on.

Samuel offered his hand to thank the couple for their kind words, scanning the room behind the couple. Samuel realized that there was a small line of people who appeared to be waiting for their chance to appreciate the girls. Panic and greed both flooded his veins. Panic, because he knew that if they were there, his parents would too be in this line. For showmanship's sake, they would appreciate the support given to the church. Greed, because he wanted to enjoy being the father of two such talented girls.

Some of the congregation seemed to love Eternity's music, but Tavia was the one who stole today's show. Samuel allowed himself to momentarily revert back to a proud Daddy as the girls were flooded with compliments.

He all but forgot what they were doing today when a familiar voice, shaky with age, called out to him. "Hello, son. When did you get into town?" The raspy-voiced man in front of him now was his adoptive father.

SIXTEEN

Samuel squeaked like a chipmunk as he tried to respond. "We haven't been here long, just passing through."

He wanted to say more, but his voice broke at the end of the sentence and his mind turned to mush.

Samuel's mother had her short, grey hair pulled back tight against the back of her head. So tight that Samuel imagined her skin must have been pulled back as well to hide the years she wore. She stepped forward, wearing the largest fake smile ever, and spoke to the girls.

"You girls both did such an amazing job today. Wherever did you learn that from? It must have been from your mother. Where is she?" she exclaimed, glancing at Samuel with a raised eyebrow.

Tavia interjected before Samuel had the opportunity to respond. "We learned it from our other dad. You know him as the devil."

Samuel extended his arm protectively across Tavia's chest as if slamming the brakes on his car with an unbuckled child in the seat next to him. Not that she needed his protection. He would be hard-pressed to find anyone in this church today that Tavia could not take down if she intended to.

Samuel's mother physically recoiled from Tavia, as if she had seen a snake preparing to strike. Her black eyes locked with Samuel's and narrowed in disapproval. "Let's get home before we catch something we can't pray away," she said to her still-shocked husband. "Looks like you haven't taught these kids the same manners we taught you," said Samuel's father as he took his wife's hand.

Samuel was completely frozen in his tracks. He tightened his fist, which was still stretched across his daughter's chest. But his father turned his back and began to walk away before he could respond any further.

Did all that just really happen? Looking back toward the pulpit, Samuel was relieved that at least his parents had the good sense to be the last of the worshippers to speak to the girls. *Of course, they don't want to draw attention to their true nature*, Samuel thought.

"Looks like you missed the whole point of today's service. Don't worry, I'm told Father Rusty is available for one-on-ones to help."

Samuel's mother 'pfft'ed at her and kept walking, while his father swatted the air in front of her as if she were a bothersome fly. Eternity couldn't bear not having the last word. "Have a blessed day," she said, before returning to her father's side.

Samuel stood stock-still, trying to process everything that had just happened in front of him. He knew he should do something, but all he could do was mindlessly look around. He was at a loss for words. What could he even say?

Staring at the pulpit, he said the only thing that came to his mind. "What did that other couple say to you?"

"You mean the Smiths?" Tavia responded. "They came up to tell me that they were finally in a spot in their lives where they felt ready to have kids. They were struggling with the idea of whether it's safe or selfish to bring a child into the world, what with the pandemic and the general state of everything."

Samuel met her eyes with surprise. She continued, "They told me that they had been struggling with the decision for a while and decided to ask God for guidance. Apparently, they felt like my song was God's way of answering their prayers."

Samuel could feel his legs wobble beneath him. "What did you say to them?" he questioned.

Tavia leaned in closer. "I told them that the only thing a baby needs is parents to love them, no matter what's going on in the world." She stepped back and smiled at her Daddy. "Apparently that was the message they were hoping to find today."

Samuel pulled his daughter in close and hugged her tightly. "You are an angel."

Samuel lingered a little longer than necessary with his daughters in the church to make sure that his parents had plenty of time to leave. He was hoping that any further contact between them could be avoided. He wanted to debrief his girls on the day's events but now was not the time.

He pulled Gabriel's keys from his pocket and handed them to Eternity, "I am going to go collect your brothers. I'll meet you two at the car. Please refrain from antagonizing anyone, whether they deserve it or not."

The girls both looked at him for a moment before turning together and walking away. Their silence was not acquiescence to Samuel's request. No sooner than they made it out of his sight, a set of tiny footsteps pattered on the floor. Lias was running down the aisle towards him, waving a piece of paper in his little hand.

"Daddy, Daddy, look what we made today!" Lias exclaimed. Samuel took to his knees, so he could be face-to-face with his son's excitement. Samuel looked down at the paper to see two sets of handprints. The handprints were colored deep brown, with tiny green strands surrounding them. They were surrounded by an orange sun, a bright blue sky, and some yellow grass.

Matswell slowly approached Lias and Samuel with his usual controlled swagger. Every step he took was strategic and intentional. *He truly was his Papa's son,* Samuel thought.

Lias was talking so fast that it was hard for Samuel to keep up with his words. He pointed to each part of the painting and explained it to his father. "That's me! Papa is the thumb, you're the little finger, and then Mats, Turn-t, and Tavia," he pointed at each finger in between. Matswell jumped in and pointed out his handprint as well. He handed his Daddy an index card with the teacher's explanation of today's lesson.

Samuel's dimples rose and made room for the biggest grin he could muster. "Well, boys, I think this is just great! Shall we put it on the fridge when we get home?" Both boys nodded ferociously and smiled as radiantly as their Daddy. Samuel scooped both of the boys up and lifted them off the ground. "Well, we better get home to get to that fridge!"

They made their way towards the car, where Julia was waiting. Samuel thanked her for all her help and gave her a mighty hug.

"It was my pleasure. They are great kids," Julia shared and turned to get into her own car.

Samuel noticed Eternity was missing. He asked Tavia, who was helping him buckle up the twins, where she was. "I'm not sure," Tavia replied. "She saw a kid from her class and went to say hello. They were walking around the parking lot together and disappeared behind the building. I'm sure she'll be back in a minute. She's just being polite."

Samuel felt unsatisfied with her explanation. "Watch your brothers and stay in the car, Tavia. I'll be right back." He was unsure why his legs picked up their pace, as if of their own accord. He found himself frantically cornering the building in an attempt to get hold of his daughter.

As soon as he rounded the corner, Samuel noticed his father talking to a stranger and his family. Samuel had not been seen; his father's back was turned to him. He circumvented the group stealthily and finally caught a glimpse of Eternity.

Samuel's heart dropped to his shoes and tripped over his laces. Eternity stood at the far end of the lot, next to her would-be grandmother. The pair were facing each other. He could not see what they were doing, but they were standing close to each other, far too close for his comfort. Neither of the two had noticed Samuel's approach. Samuel picked up his pace.

Two things became apparent as he approached Eternity and Shelia. The first was that Samuel's mother was giving Eternity some kind of tongue-lashing about being disrespectful to elders. The second was that his mother was gripping Eternity above her elbow. Samuel could remember that grip viscerally. He recalled the feeling of his mother's fingernails sinking into his own arm when she was giving him a similar lecture.

He skidded to a stop behind the two. "Get your damn hands off my daughter right now, Shelia!" Samuel roared. His tone was commanding and unshakeable. Shelia's hand obeyed instinctively, startled by his immediate presence and the confident demand.

In the same commanding voice, his attorney voice, his dad voice, Samuel turned to his daughter. "Go to the car now," he said. Eternity offered up no retort or hesitation. She simply obeyed, sprinting away from the scene while rubbing her arm.

Samuel positioned himself face to face with his mother, jaw firm and tone unwavering. "You may not know this, but she could have flattened you at any moment had she chosen to. Her inaction towards you was a sign of respect. Respect you do not deserve." Shelia glared back at him silently.

"I, on the other hand, was not raised better, so I will say this to you, Shelia." He spat at her. "If you ever touch one of my children again, it will be the last thing your hands ever feel, old woman!"

Shelia's eyes widened. Samuel's words had rattled her confidence. "You threaten your own mother?" No sooner than she said the words, Samuel responded: "No, Shelia, I am sharing a premonition with the true devil."

Samuel stared into her evil eyes. This was his courtroom and he owned it. After a moment he stepped away. He turned back to fire one final shot in a cool and calculated tone: "Have a blessed day."

SEVENTEEN

The **drive home** from church was deafeningly silent. The boys fell asleep in the car before Samuel returned with Eternity. Eternity abandoned the captain's chair and sat quietly, staring away from her father as he drove them home.

It's best she stays silent now, Samuel thought. He didn't want Tavia to become aware of what had happened with Shelia. If she got a whiff of what had happened to her sister, no power in the world would have been able to stop her from releasing her wrath then and there. Samuel wanted to make sure to put as much space between them and the church before she found out. Luckily, Tavia seemed to be engrossed in the boys' artwork. She was dipping her fingertip into the still-wet brown paint and using it to dot the back of her hand.

Samuel was sure that Tavia could sense that something bad had happened, but she had enough wisdom not to comment on it. Since the twins were sleeping soundly, he decided not to play any music on the drive, even though he felt an urgent need to. *They must have had a tiring day*, Samuel thought. *They deserve to rest in peace back there.*

Neither boy woke up as their sisters carried them inside. "Mind your brothers," Samuel instructed Tavia. "Your sister and I are going to head into town for groceries while things are calm here." Eternity had still not spoken a word since the church. Now, she headed back silently toward the car.

Knowing her Daddy, Tavia knew that the grocery trip was just an excuse for him to speak to Eternity alone. But Tavia decided she might as well get something out of his charade. "I want pizza rolls!" Tavia announced. "While you're at the store anyway," she grinned.

Samuel beamed at her wordlessly as he quietly pulled the door shut. Samuel and Eternity cruised down the highway, driving away from the town rather than towards it. They drove farther and farther into the Nebraska nothingness. Samuel was still reflecting, trying to piece together everything from the day. Quite a while passed before either of them knew where to begin.

Eternity cut the silence as Samuel was sorting his thoughts. "Daddy, I'm sorry," she admitted quickly and quietly. Samuel had to physically lean in to make sure he heard her correctly.

"I was headed to the car just like you told us to when I saw a boy from my class who waved at me. I only went over to say hi to him. He was so excited about how well Tavia had sung. He didn't realize that we were sisters. We talked a little bit and walked around to the parking lot on the other side of the building." She was staring off into the distance, away from her dad.

"His family came out and called him to their car. I saw your dad over there, so I tried to remove myself before there was a situation." Eternity stopped for a moment to take a quick deep breath in before continuing. "I don't think he saw me. I turned to walk back to the car, and she came out of nowhere and stood right in my way. She was so rude, she was disrespectful to Papa, and she was saying that we were all just wolves in sheep's clothing and that we should be ashamed of ourselves for how we acted in the Lord's house." Samuel began to slow the car without even thinking about it. If there were any local turtles around, he would have found himself losing the race against them.

"I tried to be the bigger person and walk away from her," Eternity continued. "But she grabbed me. I didn't know what to do. I have never had anyone attack me like that. She just kept taunting me and saying that if I didn't get some better manners, God was going to strike our family down."

By now Samuel had forfeited the race. He pulled off the road and stopped the car. He could feel his fury building up inside him. Hearing Eternity describe the scene and replaying the images of his wicked mother in his head made his blood boil.

Eternity took in a ragged breath and pushed on with the story. "Every time I tried to say something she would get louder and ruder. I wanted to pull away from her, but I didn't know how to do it without causing a scene. I knew that if I caused a scene then she would win and prove her point that we were evil. That Papa was evil. She was digging those long nasty nails of hers into my skin and being rude about our family."

Eternity lowered her eyes to the floorboard in embarrassment, in defeat, and let her words trail off.

Samuel reached across the car and lifted her chin with his finger. He made sure to meet her eyes with his. "I am so sorry it took me so long to get to you, baby."

Eternity tried to jump in. "It's not—"

But Samuel cut her off and kept on talking. "I grew up with that evil woman, and I should have known that she wouldn't leave you well enough alone when you and your sister antagonized her. That was a bad call on my part. Taking the trip to the church today was a bad call on my part. I don't know what I was thinking." Samuel paused allowing his daughter to respond.

"I don't think it was a bad call to go to church, Daddy," Eternity replied. "Aside from that incident the rest of the day was fun. It lifted my heart a little, to be honest. A lot of stuff has happened to us lately in life, but I kind of forgot about it all while playing my music."

A moment of silence passed before Samuel answered. "I promise that you won't have to interact with that awful family ever again. Let me see your arm," he reached down at her arm, but she shied away from him.

"My arm is fine. It will heal. I am stronger than some mean old woman," she said.

"I know you are, baby, but you shouldn't have to be. I am glad that you were so strong today, but I'm sad that you had to be," he admitted.

She leaned into her Daddy and allowed him to embrace her, laying her head on his shoulder. They both sought comfort in each other for a moment. After a while, the car resumed its movement.

Eternity directed the conversation away from the morning's events. "It might not be a bad idea to head into town and get groceries," she suggested.

Samuel agreed. He reached for his phone and selected a song to lift their mood. He cranked the volume on the car radio all the way up, rolled down the windows, and waited. The uplifting voice echoed into their souls. Samuel looked down at his smiling daughter. Together they joined their voices in song with the car's radio.

* * *

Samuel and Eternity found themselves blaring music, singing at the top of their lungs all the way home from the grocery store. Samuel rejoiced in the shared time with his daughter. He could really see himself in her; she may be smart like her Papa, but Eternity was also silly, like him.

By the time they returned home, the day's events had been forgotten. They carried in the groceries and sat them on the large oak table. Tavia disappeared out the front door as soon as her plate of pizza rolls heated from the microwave. Samuel asked Eternity to check in on the boys and cycle the laundry while he finished putting groceries away.

As Samuel busied himself with the groceries, the boys' Sunday school painting caught his eye. Tavia must have hung it there while he was out driving with Eternity.

Samuel thought back on the way his daughter dabbed at the wet paint in the car. He found himself unable to resist the temptation to do so too. The paint was nearly dry, but he managed to get a small dot on the tip of his finger. He transferred the paint to his thumb by pinching his fingers together. A sudden idea hit Samuel as he opened and closed his fingers, playing with the small blob of paint.

Samuel stumbled through the kitchen and into his bedroom. He knew he had to be quick; he had to complete his task before Tavia or Eternity returned to the room. He unzipped the front of his bag and jammed his hand in, feeling around for the pen that Kerrie sent him. He rushed to the kitchen, trying to recall the directions she had written down for him.

Think, Samuel, think, he chided himself. *It's only two buttons!* He could hear Eternity in the laundry room singing to herself. Samuel held the pen against the wet paint of the tree bark as still as he could and pressed the red button.

After a few seconds, the light changed to blue. Samuel breathed a sigh of relief. He knew that this was his only chance to apply the tracker without getting caught.

If there were any other steps to take to activate the pen, it was now too late. Tavia slammed the door to the kitchen shut behind her. Samuel was startled. He recoiled and reflexively let go of the pen, allowing it to drop to the floor. He quickly swooped down to grab it and slide it into his pocket before his daughter noticed.

Fat chance. Tavia was by his side at the speed of light, reminding him that he had the grace of a commoner. Samuel was embarrassed but allowed himself to play it up a bit, hoping that she would not ask any further questions about his actions.

Tavia studied him for a moment before she spoke. "You had to do it, didn't you?" Samuel's gut fell. He was busted. Thankfully, she continued before he had a chance to reply. "You had to touch the paint," she laughed, pointing with her eyes to the evidence still on his fingertips.

"You caught me," Samuel admitted in relief. "I couldn't let you be the only one having fun."

She shook her head and reached past him to pull a bottle of water from the fridge before heading back out the door. Samuel squatted on the floor and closed his eyes. Playing the double agent and potentially spying on his family was stressful, but it all seemed necessary. He had to protect the people he loved.

Samuel allowed himself a second to make sure the fall had not broken the pen. After a moment of rotating it between his fingers, he decided that as far as he could tell, it was still all right. The topmost button still glowed blue, assuring him that the tracker was working.

EIGHTEEN

A **quiet knock** at the door woke Samuel from his daze in front of the TV. Glancing at the clock, he realized it was 11 PM. The house was quiet. The girls must have put the boys to bed while he had dozed off.

The visitor was Julia. "I apologize for the late hour, but I wanted to say goodbye. I have to return to work. I hope you can give my love to the kids."

Samuel tried to smile through his groggy state, "You know I will. Won't you have a cup of tea before your travels? I'll put a fresh log on the fire, and it'll be toasty and warm in a moment."

Julia came in and sat by the wooden stove, as Samuel busied himself with the log and the tea. He thought, *she's always so put together*.

Julia wore a snug red coat with large coal buttons. The long flowing lines of her red and black scarf perfectly matched her outfit. It was chilly tonight, but Julia was dressed for a much colder climate. Samuel wondered where she was headed off to, dressed like that. *Was Matthew freezing tonight?* Samuel felt around the kitchen quietly, trying to find all the ingredients he needed without waking the kids.

As the water boiled, Samuel began hatching a plan. He knew he had to sway the conversation quickly to where he needed it to go.

"Thank you again," Samuel offered, "for sitting with the boys in Sunday school. They had a blast, and their artwork is so adorable."

Easy does it.

Julia turned around to face him as she responded. "My pleasure, dear. You know those boys are like my own."

"Do you think you can take it with you?" he asked, removing the boy's painting from the fridge. "I think Matthew would enjoy having it around. I know the boys would love to know that it's in his hands." Julia paused for a moment before answering. *This was it*, Samuel thought. He was certain that she was onto his plan. *This is my only move...* Julia interrupted his thoughts.

"It would be my pleasure. I know just the spot to hang it in his office."

Samuel hoped his plan was not obvious to Julia. He couldn't see any accusation in her eyes when he peeked at her face while handing her the tea. It did not look like she was fighting against him the way he had imagined. All he saw staring back at him were the same kind and loving eyes as always.

Samuel poked at the fire a few times before sitting down beside Julia. Julia sipped her hot tea. Her expression betrayed that something was on her mind.

Is this it? Is she on to me after all? Samuel worried. He felt his hand grip the cup's handle tighter than necessary while he waited for her words.

"Matthew told me what happened outside the church," Julia admitted. *Of course he would be watching*, Samuel thought. A small sense of relief rushed over Samuel, only to be immediately overpowered by the dread of his remembrance. *It really did all happen,* he thought.

"I knew it would be very hard for you to see your parents after all these years, unpacking all of that emotional baggage."

Samuel was not sure how to respond. He was still hung up on the mention of Matthew's name. But Julia was not done sharing yet. "Matthew told me he was so proud of the way you sprang into action, protecting Eternity against your own personal monster."

Samuel had something to share too. "It wasn't about who it was, you know? It was about Eternity. At that moment, anyone could have been holding her and it wouldn't have mattered."

Julia nodded. "Oh, indeed I do know. When your baby is in danger, you act first and think later."

"Exactly," Samuel agreed.

Samuel filled Julia in on the parts of the day Matthew wouldn't have been able to see.

"You two have an amazing family," Julia affirmed him. "Four kids that would do anything for anyone. How you managed to keep them so humble when they have never known struggle is beyond me."

Samuel paused and thought about it for a moment. "I think it's this place, to be honest. Every year Matthew would drag us back here despite my objections. We lived here just like we did before the kids were born." He took a hot gulp of tea before continuing. "The absence of cell phones has a lot to do with it as well. The kids are forced to find other things to do than stare at a screen for entertainment. I think that's a skill that so many people have lost over the years."

Julia nodded in agreement, her cup lingering at her lips. She knew this battle all too well. Her grandchildren loved their phones. It was hard to garner their attention from the screens and have some real quality time together, even on the too-rare occasions they got to spend time together. Focus was now a commodity, divided amongst vast social media sites. It was a different generation.

"Very wise of the two of you," Julia shared.

Julia excused herself to the bathroom before hitting the road. As soon as the door closed behind her, Samuel pulled the pen from his pocket and pressed the blue button again. The blue light flashed just in time for Samuel to shove the pen back into his pocket when Julia exited the bathroom.

"Oh, I almost forgot!" Julia exclaimed, reaching into her bag and digging around. "I got the family tickets for the zoo. I thought since today was a bit of a mess and there's no school on Monday, it might be fun for you all."

Samuel loved animals. He felt like a little kid for a moment, thinking about seeing them all. "Julia, that is so great of you! Thank you. As always, you do too much for us."

Julia waved off his nonsense with a brush of her hands. "Your family is my family. I do hate to run, but I need to get going." Samuel gave Julia a big hug and thanked her again for everything. He remained waving in the driveway until her taillights disappeared into the darkness.

Once Julia disappeared into the night, Samuel returned inside to sit in front of the fire. He was still partially asleep. He could feel an ache in his bones. He knew that the time to act was nearing. He needed to think through the different implications and consequences. He needed to figure out how to make sure his family was ready.

Samuel was not sure how long he would be away. Once he hit the road, he would transfer some extra money into Eternity's bank account for her to take care of the kids. He needed to make sure that it was enough. Once on the road, he would need to be smart about stopping for gas. He resolved to take some cash with him, to make it harder for Matthew to track him down—that is, if by chance he even figured out what Samuel was up to.

The kids would be alone once he's gone. He would have to leave his callbox watch at home and remove the battery from his work cellphone. The house had a landline phone. He could call them on that. The kids would have to make do in his absence.

Eternity was mature and could take care of things for a while. Samuel was sure of that. She was a safe driver for her age - in fact, she was a safe driver for any age. He worried about leaving them with the old Jeep. It ran just fine for now, but what would they do if it broke down?

No, he thought to himself, *I'll leave them with Gabriel*. He felt better as soon as he made the decision. It was smart to leave his family with the nicer car and make do with the old Jeep himself. While the Jeep had always been kept in decent shape, Samuel was not sure how well it would hold up to the unknown trip he was soon going to have to make. Still, it had never given him any cause for concern. Samuel decided that they would take two cars tomorrow to the zoo. He would drop the Jeep off at a shop for a tune-up and make sure all of its systems were intact. Meanwhile, he and his family would enjoy the zoo and decompress for the day.

Samuel went to his computer and found a shop just a few blocks from the zoo. He was able to book an appointment for the following day at 8 AM. It was about a 3-hour drive to the zoo. The family would have to get up early to make it in time.

It was late, but Samuel decided to wake Eternity and give her a heads-up about the plan for tomorrow. She opened her eyes just enough to show that she had heard him and went back to sleep without uttering a word.

Samuel packed a backpack for the following day with some toys for the boys, a change of clothes—just in case—sunscreen, a few bottles of water, some road snacks, and a printed schedule of the zoo's events from their website. Samuel wanted to make sure his family wouldn't miss any of the exciting shows they had advertised. After all was done, he allowed himself to catch what few hours of sleep he had left.

* * *

The next morning, Samuel drove the Jeep in silence. There were no sounds but the Jeep's thuds, from hitting every missing chunk of the road below. It was peaceful, lethargic. He was shocked but thankful that all the kids wanted to ride together with Eternity. At least when the time came for him to leave them and find Matthew, he knew they would stick together.

The house had been filled with giddy laughter and excitement that morning, as his early risers were informed of the plans for the day. All four of the kids loved animals and nature, and they also loved the chance to escape their small-town life, even if just for a day. If he were honest with himself, Samuel was excited about the reprieve as well.

They found a charming mom-and-pop bistro right around the corner from the car shop. Eternity ordered a Denver omelet, while Tavia selected French toast to get her morning started. Each boy asked for a stack of pancakes with fruit.

Samuel could not bring himself to enjoy anything but a cup of coffee. He found himself lost in thought as he listened to the small talk that filled the room. It was exactly the kind of morning that he needed after everything that happened yesterday. *Was it just yesterday?* he thought. To him, it seemed like weeks had passed already.

With Tavia's help, each of the boys decorated their pancakes with faces made of fruit before eating them one by one. Each pancake person was given a name and the boys pretended to be cannibals as they devoured them. They christened the pancake with blueberry eyes and a banana-sliced smile as Jake.

William had raspberry peepers and chocolate chip teeth. Kathy sported cherry eyes, a strawberry nose, an awkward cantaloupe smile, along with the freckles Tavia gave her using powdered sugar. Samuel found himself unable to contain a chuckle as he watched this interaction unfold. He was thankful that his children had the chance to be children and enjoy the small moments of levity in their lives.

NINETEEN

There **was** a light chill in the morning air when they got to the zoo. Samuel did not trust the breeze to stay. They were in the Midwest, after all. He insisted the family put on hats and protect themselves from the sun that would certainly appear any second now. Once they got through the turnstiles, both girls stood under a weeping willow and applied sunscreen to their brothers. Meanwhile, Samuel stared at a giant map of the grounds in an effort to plot out the perfect route for the day. He did not want the kids to miss even a single exhibit or show. They deserved all the enjoyment they could get that day.

"I want to go see the elephants, Daddy!" Lias interrupted. His little face was full of life and his eyes exploded with excitement. Samuel couldn't possibly say no to that.

"Well, then, let's go see those elephants!" Samuel replied. They quickly found the elephant enclosure on the map. Samuel took each boy by the hand and began walking off with them at his side. The girls scooted along trying to hide their mutual excitement. Samuel knew very well that both girls adored animals just as much as the boys did. Teenager rules just forbid them from showing it.

The elephant enclosure appeared empty when they arrived, but the breeze drifting over told a different tale. The smells of fresh-cut grass, stale water, and manure lingered right beyond the fence. After a moment of focused search, a single elephant was spotted standing as far away as possible from the visitors. He showed no interest in coming over.

The boys whistled and smacked their lips together trying to find the right call to summon an elephant. It was still a bit early, and Samuel was trying to tell the boys that the other elephants might be sleeping. Lias stretched his small hands as far as he could through the fence, trying to grab the large-eared creature's attention.

Tavia was rifling through the family's carry bag while Samuel watched his son reach for the elephant unsuccessfully. He wasn't paying much attention to his daughter until it was too late. She climbed up on the wooden fence surrounding the elephants, holding a small object in her hand. Samuel couldn't figure out what it was. Tavia then threw the object toward the single elephant.

"What are you doing?" Samuel yelled in a frantic tone.

"I will not have these animals ignore us. I came prepared," Tavia answered as she threw again.

Now Samuel could see that she was holding a small pile of apples in her hand. She must have added them to their go-bag when he was distracted. Samuel took a quick look around to make sure they were alone. He didn't want any bystanders interjecting in the already-fraught situation. But he very quickly decided that he did not care if they were, as the single elephant was now walking toward them.

Other elephants were beginning to emerge from the distance now. Lias moved to his sister's side and tried to throw an apple as far as his sister. Matswell was peering around their surroundings, no doubt trying to plan how to mount the beast. Eternity had a camera in hand, as she always did on such outings. She was getting pictures of the boys with the elephants in the background.

The next few animal encounters went about the same way. Tavia had brought carrots for the giraffes, pumpkin seeds for the orangutans, and bananas for the apes. The zoo was almost completely empty that morning. Only rarely did they spot any other patrons or staff around the exhibits.

The boys were running full speed toward the reptile house when Samuel heard an unfamiliar chime flutter around him. He paused for a moment to listen for the source of the confusing sound. It took him a second to realize that it was coming from his pocket. He reached in and felt an icy waterfall run down his chest. The sound was coming from the tracker pen.

Panic, desire, and fear roared through his clammy veins. Samuel's immediate impulse was to press the flashing green button, but he reined himself, remembering Kerrie's instructions. Once he pressed the button, he would only have 15 seconds to write down the phone number he needed to call. After that, he only had 30 seconds to dial the number before his time was up. He grabbed his work phone to call immediately.

His throat tightened and his eyes welled up in frustration. This was it: he was about to find out where Matthew was. Samuel was not ready. The sour scents wafting by reminded him that this was a bad idea. If he acted now, he would leave a trail of breadcrumbs behind him. Any rash action that he would take could give away his plan before it came to fruition.

Samuel stumbled towards the reptile house and yelled for the children. "I'll be right back. Eternity, watch the boys, and stay close by. I need to find the restroom."

"Ok," one of the girls answered. The children were only half-listening, but Samuel departed anyway. He broke into a jog as he followed the signs back toward the main entrance. He vaguely recalled seeing a row of pay phones there when they first arrived. *God only knows if they work*, Samuel thought. They may just be relics of a different age that have never been removed, like dinosaur fossils.

By the time he got to the zoo's entrance, Samuel was panting and out of breath. He grabbed a map of the zoo and flipped it on its back so he could have some space to write on. He had to act quickly. Kerrie's instructions warned him that he only had 15 seconds to retrieve the phone number once he pressed the green button. From there on, he had 30 seconds to make the call before the phone number would disconnect forever. He needed to make sure he was ready to move swiftly. His palms were wet and clammy as he fumbled around in his pocket looking for change. He had none.

Samuel had not expected this today, so he was not ready. He fed dollar after dollar into a vending machine buying packs of gum so that he could get enough change back to make a call. With a pocket full of gum, enough change to make a call, and makeshift stationery he was ready to call the number.

Samuel scanned the area before picking up the phone. He was not sure what he was looking for or whom he thought he was trying to avoid, but he suddenly felt like he was under observation. It had to be the guilt. Samuel was rarely dishonest. He hated being sneaky about things, especially when it came to Matthew. But this was necessary. Samuel was not going to let fear talk him off of the ledge for now.

His excitement was premature. The first quarter he fed the machine would not go in. He pushed and jiggled the coin but only the rim would fit. There was obviously some change or other obstruction stuck in the coin receiver.

"Fuck!" Samuel muttered, pounding the phone handset against the phone again and again.

After the third or fourth collision, Samuel heard change falling down with a soft *clink*. It worked! The change had broken loose, allowing Samuel to pay the annoying machine.

Samuel fed three dollars into the payphone before turning over the pen and pressing the green button. He felt his heart stop as a number appeared before him. He echoed the numbers into the phone keypad as quickly as possible, hoping he hadn't messed up. The 999-area code was unfamiliar, but he couldn't dwell on the thought. He didn't have time.

After dialing the last number, he gripped his pen so tight it pushed a hole through the map. He had to force himself to relax and listen to the telephone ring.

A computer-generated male voice spoke with a low monotonous pitch. "Your destination is 811 Spruce Willow Street, Alexandria, South Dakota." The robotic voice bade him goodbye as soon as it delivered the address. Samuel heard the conversation disconnect with a high-pitched *beep* and then a dial tone. He traced over the address with his pen, darkening each character with every pass. The phone receiver still rested on his tense shoulder. He was burning the address deeper and deeper into the paper, ensuring it would never disappear. He couldn't help thinking that Matthew was not that far away. *Had he been so close this whole time?* Samuel couldn't allow the question to keep on hammering in his mind.

He still felt like someone was watching him. He had to get back to looking normal, on the off chance that his hunch was right. Samuel closed his eyes and took a series of deep breaths to force the color back into his skin. The cool morning breeze was helpful and calming. The air was cleaner this close to the park entrance, and less contaminated with the smells of animal life.

Samuel spent the slow, sticky walk back to the reptile house thinking through his next steps. He resolved to enjoy the day with his kids and then make up an excuse to sneak away tomorrow. Hopefully, he could do that without raising too much suspicion.

What can I tell the kids? Samuel thought. He needed a story that wouldn't look out of place, in case anyone—especially Julia—noticed that something was out of the ordinary.

A realization hit Samuel as the reptile house came back into view. *I'm already living the perfect excuse!* Julia had left tickets for the family to be at the zoo for the entire day. It was not even lunch yet. He had hours before she would even check in. The Jeep would surely be ready for him shortly. He could leave right then and there. The thought of leaving the kids again so soon tugged at his heart, but something stronger lingered within him. Something in his core told him it was time for action. He could not ignore that.

Samuel called ahead for Eternity to come meet him. He led her to a frosty concrete bench just out of earshot from the rest of his gang. He needed to talk to his oldest daughter first. Eternity jogged over to him. "What's up? You look like you've seen a ghost."

Samuel didn't meet her eyes as he responded. "Well, honey, I kind of have. I just got a call about a case that I thought was closed a long time ago. My clients, a super sweet LGBT youth center, are being summoned back to court in a few days. There's a possibility they'll have to be shut down." It wasn't completely a lie; he did get this exact call a few days ago, and he would need to return to court in a few months. He felt awful using the client's true story to lie to his daughter, but he would deal with that guilt another time.

Samuel paused to match her gaze and see if he was selling it. The soft, innocent look in her eyes told him that she did not suspect a thing.

Samuel continued, "I hate the idea of leaving you kids alone again, but it would be selfish of me to not help so many LGBT youngsters if Brian and Javier end up losing everything. Do you think you can hold down the fort for a couple of days while I am gone? Keep the house cleaned up and get everyone to school on time?" "

"Of course I can, Dad," she responded matter-of-factly. "It's not rocket science."

Samuel smiled at her. "I know I just got back, but I need to leave right now. I have to grab a red-eye out in time to be helpful."

Eternity looked a little surprised, but not suspicious. "Well, it's perfect timing. Good thing that God decided we need to bring two cars to the zoo today. Things always seem to work out the way they are supposed to."

Samuel nodded at his daughter. "You are right," he said. And she was; he had not realized how perfectly timed his excursion turned out to be.

"I will send some extra money to your account once I get on the plane," Samuel continued. "Take everyone out for a nice dinner and ice cream before you go home today."

"I will," Eternity replied. "It'll be like a family slumber party while you are gone."

Samuel chuckled. "Will you be okay driving back home so late? I assume it will be dark before you guys head back."

Eternity waved off his concern. "We don't all need 8 hours of sleep to function, you know?"

Samuel called the rest of his crew over and let them know what was going on. He made sure to emphasize that Eternity would be in charge in his absence. The boys immediately requested playhouse pizza for dinner and the girls reluctantly agreed.

Samuel felt relieved that none of his family was suspicious of what he was doing. He was a better liar than he thought he was. "I will be back before the weekend, and I expect you all to be on your best behavior for Eternity while I am gone," Samuel instructed.

The boys shook their little heads. "As long as she doesn't ask me to do anything stupid," Tavia said. Samuel knew that that was the best he could hope to get from his children. He hugged them all tight.

"Don't rush today, guys." Samuel reached into the backpack to pull out the itinerary he put together the night before. "The shows are all listed here. The last one starts at 3 PM. Enjoy all that you can before going back to school tomorrow."

Luck was on Samuel's side. The Jeep was ready to go by the time his ride-share driver dropped him off at the shop. He was gassed up and ready to hit the road within thirty minutes.

Samuel had one last task to do before leaving town. He drove back by the zoo and put his callbox in Gabriel's glove compartment. He didn't want to leave it on and alert Matthew to his plans. Removing the battery would likewise be problematic for his purposes.

Next, Samuel removed the battery from his work cellphone. He needed as much of a head start as possible. This would leave the kids with no way to reach him until they were home. He could call, but they would have to make do for now. They would be okay, he reassured himself. Eternity was mature and Omaha was a peaceful town. He would call the house landline later and let them know he had accidentally left his call box behind. His hurry to leave would convince the kids that the error wasn't intentional.

TWENTY

The trip up the I-29 flew by. Samuel wasn't paying any particular attention to his driving speed. It was a Monday afternoon in the middle of nowhere and he was alone on the road. The urge to get to his destination was strong. Samuel couldn't believe that all this time, Matthew had been just over the state line.

His mind was filled with questions. What was Matthew doing there? What was causing him to stay away so long? What was Samuel about to walk into? There were so many unknown factors, so many unplanned complications he couldn't even begin to imagine. The rumble stripe drew back his focus before his thoughts could overwhelm him. He quieted the questions for now while he took the exit headed towards Alexandria.

Samuel turned down the radio as he merged onto the I-90. He wanted to fully focus on what was ahead. He was less than two miles from his destination, and he had no idea what he was about to find. The GPS offered no clues: he wasn't headed towards a restricted area or a toll road, and there wasn't any road work or traffic delays ahead. Nothing. Samuel had absolutely no idea what he was about to see.

The GPS announced that they had arrived once the Jeep turned on Spruce Willow Street. Samuel did not stop. He drove slowly past the address, taking note of a single large building to his left. The building's burnt-orange trim ran along its edges and across a small awning like a lit flame running the length of a fuse. The afternoon's sun cast tall shadows off the neatly trimmed trees along the roadside. White cursive letters set on top of a green awning announced to the world that this was the Sunrise Hotel. There were knee-high shrubs planted in front of the building. A small white picket fence ran down the length of the sidewalk in front of the shrubs.

A white wooden trellis crisscrossed the walls of the giant hotel. Weaving in and out of the trellis was a mixture of ivy and colorful roses. Faux charcoal shutters at the sides of every window finished the hotel's cozy and welcoming look.

Samuel had never seen such a sight before. A hotel that beckoned, nay, *begged* for people to come and stay a while. Strangely enough, despite the inviting décor, no cars were parked in its parking lot.

Samuel glanced down at the clock on his dashboard. The time was just past 2 PM. Any former guests would likely have departed the hotel by now, leaving ma and pa to wait on the next set of visitors to their home.

Samuel lost all focus as he stared at the hotel. "That was it." He pulled into the parking lot. He could feel a panic attack coming on.

This is where Julia had been just hours before. *She must have spent the night here on her way back to Matthew*, Samuel thought. He realized that he had made a mistake. This place was just over the state line. This was not where Matthew was. This was just how far Julia made it after she left late last night. She must have needed to pull off and get some rest before driving on to God knows where.

Samuel palmed his forehead in frustration. "How could I have been so stupid?" he asked aloud. "So naive of me to think that my first and only attempt at being a detective would work out perfectly. What made me think that Matthew would be working out here in the middle of nowhere? He has no reason to be in South Dakota." Samuel felt his tear ducts heat up like a tea kettle when suddenly, three pecks against the window glass shocked him into focus.

"Y'all all right in there?" asked a white-haired gentleman in blue jean overalls. Tired dark eyes and a kind face stared at Samuel. The top right button of his overalls was not fastened, allowing the corner to drape down like a bib over his sturdy frame.

The sweet scent of rose petals and fresh honey wafted over Samuel as he rolled down his window. "Yes sir, I am okay. I've just been driving for a while and decided to pull off the road for a minute."

The stranger nodded in understanding. "Those highway eyes will sneak up on you if you're not careful. Y'all need a place to stay the night?"

"No, thank you," Samuel replied. "I only have a few hours of driving left till I am home."

"Well, if you change your mind come on back by and I'll give you a great deal for the night. I'm Jedd, by the by," the old man said. "Long as you're in town and not driving already, just up the road there on the left is Millie's place. It's got some of the best fixin's 'round."

"That sounds great," Samuel admitted reluctantly. "I haven't eaten since breakfast and a good old-fashioned Okey supper does sound mighty nice." Samuel winced as soon as he heard himself speaking the words. They left a bad taste in his mouth, as if he were cursing at a nun. He had not thought, let alone spoken the term 'Okey' in decades, but at that moment, it felt necessary to match Jedd's hospitality.

Jedd tipped his hat at Samuel before turning to walk back to the hotel.

Samuel dawdled in the parking lot for a few minutes talking to himself. "Well, this is all on you Samuel. Accept your defeat, pick up the pieces, go home, and try something else," he said out loud. His stomach rumbled as he was pulling out of the hotel driveway. He decided to take Jedd's advice and head over to Millie's.

He found Millie's café easily enough. Just like the hotel, the parking lot for the restaurant was pretty much empty. Samuel chalked it up to being between dinner and supper time. At least he would not have to wait long for food.

Samuel was greeted by a woman in her fifties or sixties. "Hi there, welcome in," she said as she looked up from wiping the counter. Her sandy hair was streaked with pelts of gray and pulled up in a messy ponytail, exposing her glowing forehead. Samuel couldn't tell if the shine all over the woman's face was from sweat or from grease. She was wearing a white short-sleeve button-up shirt, black slacks, and a red apron hanging down from her waist. The plastic jalapenos across her heart were engraved with the name Millie.

"Good afternoon," Samuel returned. "Jedd at the Sunrise said I would be doing a disservice to myself if I did not stop by for lunch before I left town."

Millie smiled a warm smile at the words. "Well, it's good to know that old Jedd still remembers how to speak the truth," she chuckled heartily to let Samuel know she was just teasing.

They are about the same age, Samuel thought. *More likely than not, they grew up together.*

Millie grabbed a menu and motioned for Samuel to follow her. "Come on, darling, let's get you seated before that wind blows you away."

Samuel followed her to a cozy corner booth. "It's certainly been doing its best to blow me off the road all day," he countered.

Millie stepped away and returned momentarily with a mug and some coffee. She poured it full in front of Samuel before unfolding his menu and pointing out the specials.

"I'll be back in a minute to get your order. You pick out anything you want, breakfast or supper, and I'll have Johnny whip it up for you," Millie directed.

"Thank you," Samuel called out, but Millie was already gone.

Samuel snickered to himself as he looked over the menu. Did he, in fact, have a choice? Millie had not waited for him to select a beverage. Maybe she had been doing this job so long that she knew a coffee drinker when she saw one. Or maybe she gave coffee to everyone. Maybe coffee was just the easiest for her to pour, so that was what he got.

Grinning to himself, Samuel thought, *it doesn't matter why, really. I was going to order coffee anyway.* The point was moot. Millie was sweet. She reminded Samuel of what so many of his friends' grandmothers were like growing up.

A younger server came back to take his order. School must be out by now, and her shift was just starting. She was nice, but in a tired and confused way, as if she was still trying to mentally shift gears. Samuel was not feeling particularly hungry, he just wanted to sit and think for a while as he licked his wounds. He ordered toast with some local homemade jellies.

Samuel sat there inhaling the aroma of fresh butter and orange juice that lingered around the diner. The joyful atmosphere was not enough to distract him from recent events. He considered his defeat; he had lost. Matthew was not here. That much was clear.

He told the kids he would be out till the weekend. How could he explain his early return? He would not have had time to fly to Atlanta and back yet. He would have to stay the night. *The Sunrise Hotel does seem awfully inviting...* Samuel thought. Maybe there were some local attractions around for him to see. He could tour the area for a day or so and then return to the kids on schedule. He may have to extend his lie to Julia if she happened to check in on them. But he would worry about that when it happened.

A few other kids were eating at the small diner. The room filled with laughter, teasing, and friendly horseplay. Samuel was so entranced in watching them that Millie's return caught him off-guard. As she started placing food on the table she confessed, "Now I know that this is not what you ordered, dear, but you didn't come in here to try my toast. I had Johnny upgrade your meal for you."

Millie winked as she put down an oval plate. On it was bacon, sausage, scrambled eggs, two biscuits smothered with white gravy, a generous portion of fried potatoes, and a second plate with three flapjacks.

Samuel looked up at Millie from under his overwhelmed eyelashes as he spoke. "I don't think this is just an upgrade. This falls into the category of a presidential spread." Samuel's stomach growled as he took in the feast. He really was hungrier than he thought. It did not matter; even if he wasn't, Millie's expression told him that he was going to eat this whether he wanted to or not.

"I can't have you going back to Old Jedd's bragging about how well I can stick bread in a toaster now can I? Don't you worry, honey, whatever you don't finish I will bag up. But I'm guessing you won't need a box, sweetie. I'll be right back with some jam and jellies for ya."

Millie hurried off before Samuel could respond. More questions popped into his head. Samuel couldn't help but wonder how Millie knew to order him exactly the foods he liked best. Was this an extreme upselling technique? Somehow, he didn't think so.

When she returned with the spreads and syrup, Samuel thanked Millie with an honest nod. His mouth was already crammed full of his feast. Everything was so good. It all worked magic on his body, filling a void he had not realized he had. Samuel was not much for cooking Good Ole Boy food. He wasn't allowed to cook when he lived at home, and when he left, he learned to cook other things. But everything here on the table magically hit the spot. Millie was right, he did not need a box for leftovers.

Samuel fit every ounce of food in his stretched stomach. He pushed the last pieces of flapjacks with his fork around the platter, making sure to soak up the last of the breakfast broth. He was content. There was no other word to describe his feelings at that point in time. Samuel looked around for Millie to ask for his check. He found her beelining straight to him. She walked quickly past everyone else. He knew this was not going to be good.

"I can't have you on your way without dessert," she said as she placed a hefty slice of warm apple pie in front of him. It was accompanied by a scoop of what he was sure was homemade vanilla ice cream. Samuel took in a mighty gust of air to object, but the smell of apples wafted through his body. They smelled as if Mille had just walked out the back door and picked them from the orchard herself. His mouth was already watering, and his resistance faded. Millie hadn't waited for Samuel's response. She scampered off as soon as she dropped off the pie and refilled his coffee.

Samuel was stuffed. He scanned the room quickly as he finished the last bites of his dessert. He resolved not to be caught off guard again if Millie decided he needed to eat something else. The other server was at the cash register helping a young father out. Samuel hustled in behind the family, hoping for a smooth getaway.

The server seemed to know the man and was not exactly rushing him out. *Working up that tip*, Samuel thought. He noticed the counter was littered with brochures advertising things to do in South Dakota. He grabbed a few and stuffed them into the back pocket of his jeans. Now that he had some time to kill, he might as well see what was around.

As soon as the young man stepped aside, Samuel offered up his card and asked that a $20 tip be added to his bill for Millie. The server smiled at him, did as she was instructed, and said, "Granny is the best, isn't she?"

"She sure is a gem," Samuel agreed with a grin. "She knew what I needed even when I didn't." Millie's granddaughter handed Samuel back his card and a receipt.

"She does that all the time. The locals rarely order anymore because Granny always knows what they need. I've tried it a few times myself, but it was always a disaster."

Samuel's cheeks tightened into a fatherly smile as he offered, "Well then, it's a good thing you still have her around to teach you. You have a wonderful day and thank Millie for me."

TWENTY-ONE

Samuel fought his way back to his mobile sanctuary against the wind. Now that his stomach was full, he decided to head back to the charming hotel, just for the night. He had some time to kill before the kids would be expecting him back home.

A little privacy to sulk would be helpful, Samuel thought.

Jedd gave him an excellent rate for the night, as promised. "I noticed you did not bring any luggage in with you," Jedd remarked as he was checking Samuel in. "I have a few just-in-case articles here." Jedd pulled a basket from under the counter and offered it to Samuel.

"Thank you," Samuel said sincerely. He took Jedd up on a few complimentary hygiene items.

Leaving on the spot meant that Samuel was missing everything he needed for an overnight trip.

Jedd escorted Samuel all the way to his door, not content with just giving him directions to the room. Samuel collapsed face-first on the bed as soon as he minutes, he rolled over onto his back, pulled the brochure from his back pocket, and opened it up to browse the entertainment options.

There were some nice restaurants with dinner shows listed in the city, though none were terribly close to the hotel. The area also boasted an assortment of nature trails and rock formations to look at, but nothing really called to Samuel.

Don't expect too much, Samuel reminded himself. He knew what Midwest living was like. The towns around here just didn't have much to offer. Looking at the names of the surrounding towns, he began imagining the histories that came with each unique name.

Samuel spoke aloud to the room as if he was leading a tour group. "Welcome to wonderful Winfred, founded in 1801 by the Winfred family. Throughout the years the town has stuck remarkably close to its roots. Billy's salon is still the place to be on a weekend. Come on in and sample the many malts he has on tap. James Graham is our local apothecary—he keeps herbs in stock from around the world that will cure anything that ails ya."

Samuel was enthralled by the game as he continued. "It is a wonderful day here in Colton, SD! We are known 'round these parts for two things: guns and horses. Head on down to Mac's Ranch just outside of town and you can spend the day doing both. For just a few bucks, Mac will let you experience a day of shooting at his top-notch range. Then you can spend the afternoon horseback riding on one of his beautiful thoroughbred stallions."

"Thank you for stopping by the wonderful town of Dolton, where..." Try as he might Samuel could not think of anything witty to say about the town of Dolton. He was enjoying the game though, so he did not let that discourage him. He quickly moved on to the next town while the iron was still hot.

"Good day to you all and welcome to Scotland! As you can tell from my attire our founding families were from Scotland. They wanted to bring that rich culture to the heart of the US. Downtown any day of the week at Emily MacMurray's you can hear the wondrous sounds of enthusiasts of all ages learning to play the bagpipes. Our town drink of course is Guinness. Finley's pub is where you will find the best price round for a pint. If you have a sweet tooth Smith's bakery has the best Scottish shortbread this side of the Mississippi."

To end his game Samuel decided on a tour of Alexandria. "Alexandria was the first of many towns nearby to be purchased and renamed after the children of wealthy families from around the world. Once the tradition began here nonrelated rich siblings of Alexandria quickly started to sprout up. Just to name a few: Dante, Tripp, Ethan, Howard, Spencer, Emery, Madison, Trent, Brandon, Chester, Wentworth, Lane, Marty," and since he still was upset at himself for coming up blank "one of the most unusual names around is of course, Dolton."

Samuel could feel himself getting tired. After getting up so early with the kids and driving all the way here it was no wonder that he found it difficult to keep his eyes open any longer. He listened to the whooshing of the wind against the building before quickly passing out.

Samuel's dream led him into a familiar parking lot. He looked around, taking in the scene. The place was deserted. Yes, he had certainly been here before. The landscape, the hedges, the building, even the eerie feeling of the place… it was all familiar. But he had no recollection of ever visiting the place in his waking life. The fog cleared his mind. *It's true*, he thought. *I've never been here before in my waking life*. But he had previously dreamed of this place.

Samuel remembered that the building in front of him was a funeral home. He didn't need to approach the doors to know that they were locked. He knew that no cars would be driving by. There would be nothing here but emptiness for as far as the eye could see. After wandering around for a while, he finally noticed something different. There was a sign on the ground, just like in the last dream, but this time it was damaged worse than before. All that the sign now said was "Funeral Home."

This was frightening for some reason. Samuel wanted to wake up but was unable to force himself awake. He headed towards the funeral home again. To his surprise, this time the door opened, and he could enter. But Samuel did not want to be in this place; everything about it gave him goosebumps. Once he crossed the threshold, he felt like he was leaving the plane of the living. His lungs struggled to absorb the stale, dead air around him. He could smell sage in each breath he took, the dust and ash in the air landing on his skin, clogging up his body, dying. He shivered as he walked down a long hallway and turned to enter a viewing room.

Samuel used the edges of the pews in the observatory to steady himself as he moved forward. The wood beneath his fingertips felt soaked with tears. Shots of empathetic lightning shot up his arms. His bare feet sloshed on the carpet. His eyes would not show it to him, but his mind knew that the carpet was soaked in blood. He could feel it rushing between his toes. Each crunch was a pile of rotted bones he had stepped on.

The room was barren. There were no attendees, no receptionists, no staff, and no coffins. It was just a room. But it housed every feeling Samuel feared most in the world. All his fears were crammed into one space. Still aware that he was dreaming, Samuel tried to shift his dream to something pleasant without success. He wanted to escape but was unable to find the spell to wake him up and run away.

Even the window, which usually made Samuel feel warm, safe, and full of love, offered him no refuge at this time. The rays of light that found their way into the room felt cold and empty. The sunlight that illuminated this place was somehow just as dead as everything else in the room. If anything, Samuel felt like the rays of light were funneling what little life could be found here out of the room. It was like they were taking life away to fill the rest of the world.

* * *

An obnoxious ringing sound startled Samuel from his dream prison. He picked up the outdated receiver.

"Everything all right with your room?" Jedd's voice crackled from the other side of the line.

"Yes, thank you. Everything is perfect," Samuel checked the clock after hanging up. He had only napped for a couple of minutes really.

A dull ringing began to sound in Samuel's ears. Adrenaline coursed through his veins. His heart was still racing with fear. The room was spinning around him. Samuel tried to recenter himself and slow down his heart rate. He closed his eyes and began counting slowly aloud, enunciating each number clearly as he did. "One. Two. Three," he said. He focused on fully recharging his lungs between each breath. "Four. Five. Six." By the time he made it to twenty, his brain had caught up to his body. He could focus and hear again in real-time.

Now that he was in the present again, it was time to lick his wounds and wash away the day's disappointments. He turned on the shower and let it run for a few minutes before getting in, making sure the temperature was nice and hot.

Samuel felt his tension drain with each blast of wet steam against his skin. The water seemed to wash away his fears into the drain. He slowly spun round and round, leaning in and out of the stream so the jet could hit every inch of his body.

Once his stress was all gone, he stood still in the hot stream, letting the heat burrow into his skin and recharge the hidden cells of energy just below its surface. As his skin recharged, so did his body.

Samuel began to replay the repeated dream in his head. This was the second time he had dreamed of that place he had never seen before. There was something about it; it was a place he couldn't forget about. Something was scratching at the corners of his mind, lingering just out of reach, like a tiny itch in his back, just past where his fingertips could reach.

"What was the name of that funeral home?" Samuel muttered to himself through the shower fall.

The memory was right there. Just beyond his fingertips. He felt like a cat with a toy held dangling from a string, just out of reach. He swiped and swiped at the memory with no luck.

Samuel lathered in his conditioner as the heat began to leave the stream. He washed off his hands, shut off the water, and reached for his towel. Once he finished drying off, he wrapped the towel over his head to help stimulate the conditioner. It seemed like it had been forever since the last time he had done this simple routine. He hadn't realized how much he missed its comfort until this very moment.

Now that he was feeling back on track, Samuel shaved and trimmed his eyebrows, nose, and ears. He finally unwrapped the towel from his head, drenched it in hot water from the sink, and then wrapped it over his face. Now blind, Samuel felt around for his way back to the bed while letting the steam from the hot towel soak against his face.

With his face covered and the routine of everything kicking in, Samuel felt like he was home again in his warm Georgia bed. The machine-like pattern triggered memories of Samuel staring at the ceiling in his slice of paradise. Eyes shut and mind all but turned off, the dream's puzzle came back to him.

The funeral home sign from his original dream appeared: *Dolton's Funeral Home*. The taste of the words was familiar on his lips. The words felt fresh in his mouth. He brought a finger to his lips to better reminisce. Where did the familiar feeling come from? As he tossed the towel beside the bed, the tourist brochure he had just been looking at fell to the ground. Now he knew why the name felt so familiar; he had just been talking about Dolton, SD.

I thought the name of the funeral home was a surname, but what if it was the name of a town? Samuel wondered. *What if Matthew was here after all?*

Samuel had taken enough psychology courses in law school to realize that, at some point, Matthew must have mentioned the town and his subconscious was trying to bring it back up to him all along, trying to guide him. Samuel began getting dressed and grabbed his car keys to storm out.

His hand was on the doorknob to leave when reality hit him. *My subconscious wanted to remind me of this town where Matthew may be. My subconscious had been processing everything this whole time, unbeknownst to me. But my subconscious chose to share this information with me in the form of a funeral home. My subconscious knows that Matthew is dead.* Samuel's knees gave out and he tumbled to the floor. As soon as he spoke the words, he knew them to be true.

Samuel began sobbing and shaking uncontrollably on the floor in front of the door.

"He's been gone...the whole time, he's been gone," Samuel cried out. "It all adds up. Matthew has not come home because there is no Matthew to come home. I've just been too blind to see it..."

His brain continued to connect the dots. *This must be why Julia avoided talking about Matthew. I bet she had shown up to check if I was strong enough to handle the truth.* He recalled her hesitation about taking the twins' painting to their father. *That explained it too. She knew he would never get it.*

Samuel lay on the floor, whimpering in pain, for what seemed like hours. Eventually, the physical exhaustion of his wailing wore him out. Once his heaving stopped and his sobs ran dry, Samuel forced himself back to his feet. It was time to go. With everything he had learned, there was no reason for him to stay away from his family any longer.

TWENTY-TWO

As Samuel hurried out the front door of the hotel, he heard a familiar voice behind him. "Hey darling, you rushed out of dinner faster than a toupee in a hurricane." It was Millie. Samuel was happy to see her again, though his eyes were still red from crying and his soul was still crushed.

Samuel turned around to see the woman setting bags out of her car onto the ground. "My apologies, ma'am. If I stayed any longer, you would have me fatter than the grease pit at the bacon booth at the county fair," Samuel answered.

Millie smiled. "Well, bless your heart. I didn't mean to get you in such a way. Here, come help me with these bags and we'll see if we can't work off some of that fat."

Samuel hurried over to help grab her bags. There were so many. "Whoever is eating all this will be fatter than me for sure," Samuel chuckled. He was glad for the distraction right now.

Grabbing the last bags and leading the way, Millie responded, "It's Monday night."

She continued moving in silence for moments before sharing more.

"On Mondays, Jedd and his wife let the Boy Scouts use their meeting room. After work, I always bring in the snacks."

The two carried bags past the front desk, where Jedd was greeting a guest. Jedd tipped his hat at Millie as she led the way right past him, acting as if she owned the place.

"It's our grandson's troop," Millie added. "I thought I was rid of old Jedd after graduation, but then my son went and married his daughter. Now I have to see that old fool every week."

Samuel sat down his bags in the meeting room. Millie started instructing him on how to lay everything out. She kept herself busy rummaging through the bags as she kept the conversation going.

"Pardon my intrusion, sweetie," Millie gently pried, "but I noticed you seem a little troubled."

Samuel kept himself busy arranging plates per Millie's instructions. The reality of the situation hit him once again, but it seemed more bearable to think and talk about it with Millie.

"I came to town for someone very close to me, and I just found out they had passed away," Samuel kept his eyes away from Millie's.

"Oh, sugar, I'm so sorry," Millie said. Samuel nodded in acknowledgment. "Where are the services being held?" she asked.

Samuel rattled off his response without hesitation, "At the Dalton Funeral Home."

Millie stopped scanning through her bags and met Samuel's face. "Sweetie, I think you might be confused. I've lived here in these parts my whole life. I know every hole in the road from here to the falls. Dolton doesn't have a funeral home." Samuel was still processing that as she continued, "In fact, that old town barely has a hook to hang a hat on. There are no stores there, no reason for anyone to go there. That's the first time in a long while I've even heard it mentioned."

"You may be right," Samuel nodded. "I was looking over a brochure earlier when I got the news, and I must have gotten my wires crossed. Thanks for letting me know before I head out there."

Samuel was more thankful than Millie could know. Her response helped him regain the smallest bit of hope. *Maybe my subconscious isn't psychic after all*, he thought. When the first scout flew into the room, Samuel thanked Millie again and hugged her without even realizing what he was doing. She hugged him back and turned away to address the swift scout, whom Samuel assumed to be her grandson.

* * *

When Samuel climbed into the jeep this time, he felt uneasy, but no longer lost. He had already given himself the space to think through the worst possible outcome.

"Nothing you find in this town could be worse than what you already thought," Samuel spoke out loud.

That was true, his mind had already put him through so much confusion.

What could be worse? he thought. *Not finding Matthew, finding he was already dead, not knowing anything at all?*

After grieving for Matthew today, nothing Samuel encountered would be as much of a shock. He felt prepared and ready to face the certainty of truth.

The sun was low and dropping fast as Samuel headed south toward Dolton. According to the GPS, he could make it there before sunset if he didn't dawdle on the road. From the way Millie described the town, he wasn't sure if there would be any public lighting there after dark, so he rushed to make the best use of the little daylight he had.

The drive offered little in terms of sightseeing. Fields stretched across the horizon for as far as his eyes could see. Tall stalks of corn surrounded him with outstretched hands. A heavy cloud of dust blew around him, and the smell of stale water puddled on the ground zipped through Samuel's open window. The rumble of his tired thudding over potholes in the poorly paved road created a hypnotic soundtrack to his drive.

* * *

Suddenly he was sixteen again, sitting in the passenger seat of Matthew's car, speeding down the old Nebraska highway away from the poorly run schoolhouse. The warm September sun hit his skin through the glass window and the unmistakable beat of some 90's classic pop tune was turned down low on the radio. Matthew was chattering about something too fast for Samuel to focus on. There were so many distractions around him at that moment, but luckily Matthew was driving and whatever he was yammering about did not need any input from Samuel.

A *pop* sounded, followed by a sudden dip in the car. Samuel was startled by the vehicle's heavy shaking. "Oh my God, it's an earthquake!" he bellowed in fear.

Matthew quickly snapped his neck towards Samuel. "We don't live in California. Relax, it's just a flat tire." But Samuel couldn't follow Matthew's instruction. His heart raced: the car was broken, and he would be stranded in the middle of nowhere with Matthew. Whoever discovered their corpses would tell his parents they were spending time together and the world would end.

"What are we going to do?" Samuel asked hysterically.

Calmly Matthew answered. "*We* are going to do nothing. *You* are going to sit there and continue to hyperventilate, while I get out and change this tire so we can get back on the road."

Once again, Samuel found himself unable to do as he was told. He fumbled out of his seatbelt and trotted around to Matthew's side of the car. He could see no sign of fear or confusion on Matthew's face. If anything, Samuel was certain he saw a slight lift in the corners of his lips, like a secret smile.

The jerk thinks this is funny, Samuel thought to himself. *Stranded in the middle of nowhere and bound to be caught—what's so funny about that?!*"

Samuel stared into the driver's side mirror at the crazy man as Matthew moved about the car methodically, like it was a routine he had done a thousand times before. Matthew used an L-shaped metal rod to spin each bolt on the tire just enough to break the seal. Samuel did not understand this.

"How do you know what you are doing? You're not a mechanic," he remarked.

Without taking focus away from sliding some flat device on wheels under the car, Matthew responded, "It's not mechanic-level knowledge. Everyone knows how to change a flat tire. It's part of learning how to drive. Didn't your parents teach you what to do if you got a flat tire when you were out driving by yourself?"

Samuel looked at him irritated, "Of course they did. They taught me to pull off the road and call home."

Matthew stopped pumping the handle of the foreign device to look at Samuel. "They don't even want you able to change a car tire on your own. They want you to be dependent on their rescue from the most basic of situations?" Matthew asked.

Samuel felt anger building in him at the accusation but wasn't completely sure what he was angry about. Was he angry that his parents hadn't taught him how to change a tire? Was he angry that Matthew was teasing him? Was he angry that he felt inadequate at this moment?

"I am not helpless!" he slowly spat the words out. Matthew was unphased. He turned back to his work, removing the old tire from its axle.

"Of course not," Matthew replied. "You know exactly what to do in the event of an earthquake."

There was no mistaking it now. Samuel could see Matthew's vicious lips perking back to meet his ears in profile. Matthew was taunting him.

Samuel felt his skin redden as Matthew started tightening bolts against the new tire, spinning it as he put each bolt on.

What an odd ritual, Samuel considered as he stood watching Matthew in silence. Matthew lowered the car, tightened the bolts one last time, and put his mobile workshop away.

"Let's go," Matthew declared as he motioned for Samuel to get back into the car.

"Are you sure it's safe?" Samuel questioned, moving hesitantly.

"Of course it is," Matthew answered with a little irritation. "This isn't the first time I've changed a tire." Samuel was not reassured.

How can I trust him if he has a history of allowing his tires to go flat? Samuel asked himself.

As Matthew started driving again, confusion crossed Samuel's mind. "Where are you going?"

Equally uncertain about the question, Matthew answered, "We are going out for Chinese food. Wasn't that the plan?"

Samuel's voice was shacky and shrill. "No! We have to go home! What if something else happens to the car? What if we don't make it?"

Matthew shook his head as he caught up to Samuel's concern. "I carry a full-sized tire as a spare, not a donut. The car is just as safe as it has been every other time you have ridden in it without worry."

Samuel was not relieved to hear this. His whole life he had never been in a car that had gotten a flat tire. "I think we should go home, something else could be wrong with the car," Samuel babbled.

Matthew pulled over and stopped the car to look Samuel in the eye as he responded. "Cars get flat tires. That is part of driving. People do not just throw away cars and get new ones because they have a flat. They change the tire and move on. If you want to go home, I will take you back to your safe and sturdy tireless car, but I am going out for Chinese because I am hungry."

Samuel did not agree with this. Something about the way Matthew said the words made him feel embarrassed. Matthew spoke the words so matter-of-factly. Although he did not understand the confidence behind Matthew's logic about the now-damaged-for-life car, Samuel was hungry too.

"No, I am hungry too," admitted Samuel. "Just drive more carefully." Matthew rolled his eyes and did not reply to Samuel's ridiculous request. He pulled back on the road and continued driving.

For months after that, every time they spent time together, Samuel tried without luck to offer to take his car. He was certain that at any moment Matthew's car would leave them stranded somewhere. Every time though, Matthew's response was the same. "No. If you want to hang out with me, you will just have to risk getting another flat tire."

Each successful trip made Samuel feel increasingly ridiculous. Eventually, he no longer tried to protest. That was the beginning of Samuel's trust in Matthew. Getting into a car with him that was sure to explode at any moment and trusting Matthew's judgment to drive anyway, despite all sound reasoning and every objection.

* * *

A small blackbird dove towards the windshield, causing Samuel to slam on the brakes. The bird's feathers grazed against the windshield, interrupting his trip down memory lane. Luck was with the bird; it flew away unscathed. Samuel remained parked on the road, allowing his heart rate to slow down from the adrenaline rush kicking in. He lowered his eyelashes in embarrassment as he reflected on his previous level of worldly inexperience. He could still vividly recall the honest fear that festered inside him over a silly flat tire.

Samuel stopped again just a few miles outside Dolton and turned off his GPS. He knew where he was going but didn't know what he was looking for inside the town. The GPS would be more of a distraction than a benefit now. He practiced some silent breathing exercises, just like he always did before court, not knowing exactly what would be in store ahead.

It was darker as he drove past the city limits sign for Dolton. The sun had finally collapsed for the day. The Jeep's old headlights were the only guide he had now. Though a few of the homes in Dolton did have porch lights, they were mostly just enough to keep someone from drunkenly tripping over steps while going in and out at night.

This is a retirement town, not a place to start a family, Samuel thought as he drove past the city. From his estimation, it looked like each farmhouse was no more than one or two bedrooms in size.

Each dwelling had a patch of lawn out front. A few of the lawns were nicely manicured, most likely those belonging to the freshly retired townsfolk in residence. But most lawns contained broken machinery resting in mounds of overgrown grass. Old cars, washing machines, tires, and mattress box springs were among the abandoned articles Samuel could make out as he drove past.

Samuel counted no more than a couple of dozen homes as he drove through for the second time. By this time, it was already completely dark outside. He knew his headlights would attract attention if he kept looping through town. So, Samuel pulled off the road just outside of town, leaving the old jeep parked along the roadside. He decided to walk back through for a more private search party.

This will attract less attention, he conceded to the empty air. Or so he hoped, as he tried to find... whatever it was that he hoped he would find. A clue.

Samuel walked to town, trusting the few distant porch lights to act as his guiding star. The heavy wind blew piles of dust-filled air against his battered face.

"Anemoi, I surrender," Samuel yelled out, but the Greek gods of the winds refused to let up.

He tried to keep the sand clear of his eyes. He was able to keep his sight unobstructed as the second attacker flanked him. A gang of mosquitoes swarmed around him, apparently finding him to be quite the delicacy.

"Go away!" he shouted. He swatted, waved, and spun around like a crazy man in an effort to keep them off him.

This pack must be next-level mosquitos— Mosquitos 2.0, Samuel considered. *The wind didn't seem to faze them at all*. It appeared that the two attackers were in alliance.

Samuel tried to calm his crazy dance with the mosquitos down. The first outlying house he approached had all its lights off. Samuel was confident that there would be no security systems on the houses here apart from an aged dog or two.

As long as he didn't trigger any porch lights, he was safe to snoop around the small town. Samuel was not sure what he hoped to find there, but he trusted that he would be smart enough to know it when he saw it.

Samuel tried to focus on house after house in the pitch dark. He looked for any clues that Matthew might have been in the area. He tried to imagine links between Matthew and the everyday objects around him.

Here was a light fixture that was exactly Matthew's style. There in the driveway was a car that looked like his. But no matter how many connections Samuel tried to make, his analytical side quickly forced him to admit that the evidence was circumstantial at best. It was hopeless; if he was in court, he would never win a case like this. He would have to keep searching for something more substantial.

The wind grew more boisterous, breaking the night's relative silence. Samuel could hear empty tin cans rattling around in a faraway playground. Coyotes were howling faintly in the distance. The sound sent a shiver up his spine. The wind swung an unlatched screen door down the street and slammed it mockingly. The brisk wind screeched through the high corn stalks around.

Yet an angelic voice called to Samuel amidst all the other nightly sounds. It begged him to come closer. Samuel strode up and down a few streets, trying to locate the source of the noise. It sounded vaguely familiar, like a celebrity's voice he couldn't quite place. Samuel strolled down a cul-de-sac with a lone house faintly visible on its end.

He was sure this is where the angelic sound was coming from. It got louder and more recognizable the closer Samuel got to the house. When he was just a few yards away from the driveway, Samuel finally realized what it was that sounded so familiar. It was like the ringing tap of ice against a soda bottle or the bright tinkle of rocks against a glass. It was the sharp pluck of renewed life. His windchime was here.

"I am coming, keys!" Samuel yelled into the wind. The clinking keys Matthew added to the windchime for spite all those years ago were now guiding Samuel. He slowed his steps as he moved closer to the house, certain he would find something to trip on. He knew that sound vividly. It was unique, it was familiar, it was his. There was only one reason his windchime would be here. Matthew brought it here.

He could see his former car keys glimmering in the night. Matthew was right. Samuel would never lose his keys again. He knew right where they were. And if they were here, so was Matthew.

There was no porch light at this house. No car in the driveway. The house was dark. This is where Matthew had been hiding; Samuel was sure of it. But he was not here now. Samuel couldn't help but feel a bit relieved. If Matthew wasn't here, it meant that he was free to leave the house from time to time and move around. It was a tiny hint, an indicator that Matthew must be fine. Relieved by this realization, Samuel approached the small house. It did not emit any sounds. Or rather, if it did, they were too faint for Samuel to pick up over the howling din of the wind.

The house's front door was not protected by a screen. It was a mighty red oak door. There was no hole for a key, only a numerical keypad beside it. This door screamed Matthew. He hated carrying keys around, and always felt more secure with numbers that he could change on a whim if needed. If not for the kids, this is the exact lock Matthew would have picked to protect their house back in Atlanta.

It was obvious that no one was home. Samuel was not turning back now. He decided to let himself in while he waited for Matthew to return. Samuel didn't need to guess the code. He knew exactly what it would be before he pressed the first number. There would only be one set of numbers that Matthew would use for such a passcode. Samuel pressed each digit with purpose and intent: Nine-One-Two-Two-One, and then enter. A little green bulb flashed at the top of the lock. A mechanical clicking sounded from within. Samuel pressed on the door's handle plate and pushed it open.

TWENTY-THREE

The hinges of the solid oak door creaked as Samuel pushed it closed against the wind behind him. He was now standing in an entryway with nothing more than a mat and a box to clean his shoes on. The entryway opened up into a ranch-style living room. The room was paneled from ceiling to floor with faux wood stripes.

"Hello?" Samuel called up from the hallway. Silence echoed in response, confirming what Samuel already knew. No one was home.

A gray leather sectional wrapped the center of the room in a mighty L. Two small tables flanked it on either end, facing a red brick fireplace. Now that he was certain that he was alone, Samuel sauntered to his left and studied the stack of freshly cut firewood nestled next to the fireplace, just out of reach of any dangerous flames. There were no embers in the fireplace, but the heat-soaked bricks still emanated a tiny breath of life. Samuel could only conclude that a fire had been burning here earlier that day.

A giant sliding-glass door overlooked a nice backyard beyond the fireplace. Samuel peeked out. The light from the house allowed him to make out the outline of a wooden deck in the yard. He imagined it was decorated with lounge chairs and most likely a grill.

A green and black marbled bar countertop was installed beside the sliding doors. Three high-back stools were tucked snugly underneath it. The countertop was bare, except for a freshly read newspaper. Samuel immediately recognized the perfectly folded crease in the paper. He had seen Matthew fold his paper the same way every day of their life together.

The kitchen was basic and humble, with no fancy appliances in sight. The only piece of machinery around was a very worn ten-cup coffee maker. A large tin of coffee was placed beside a basic fridge. The walls above the counter surface were lined with maple wood cupboards. The smell of pine lingered in the air from the freshly mopped floors.

Samuel followed the wall along the room down to a small hallway. The first room on the left was a bathroom with a shower but no tub. Next up on the right was a bedroom. It housed a rusted gold-framed twin bed. The head and foot of the bed had giant warm bulbs of gold illuminating them. A homemade patchwork quilt covered the bed, telling a story of generations of fabric remnants stitched together to create it. A black footlocker trunk sat at the edge of the bed.

The last room sat at the very end of the pictureless hallway. This room was empty except for a curved, blue-tinted writing desk with a black leather-trimmed chair. Goosebumps ran down his neck as he crossed the room's threshold. The air here was different. It was eerier somehow. The near emptiness of it bothered Samuel. There was nothing in the closet except for a few unused coat hangers and the lingering smell of dry mothballs.

Samuel ran his finger against the wall as he turned away from the empty closet and walked toward the desk. He pulled out the rolling desk chair to sit down. Samuel tried to imagine Matthew sitting at this desk in this unsettling room. His mind was still reeling from the lack of sleep and the emotional whiplash of his adventures so far that day.

Matthew sat here recently, said a voice in Samuel's mind.

It was nothing he could pinpoint down exactly, but the feeling of Matthew being around was still fresh in the house. Samuel knew that. He felt it. Now he would have to wait for Matthew to come back so he could get some answers.

The stale air and dour mood in the room made it impossible for him to relax. The tension was palpable all around him. Samuel's childish instincts took over. He used his legs to crabwalk the chair to the center of the room, then spun around in aimless circles over and over again until he had to close his eyes to keep from getting sick.

Once his brain caught up to the chair's stillness, he scooted up to the nearby wall. Samuel then pushed himself off the wall, sending the chair flying across the room in the opposite direction.

"*Wee!*" Samuel yelled in playful ignorance. Eventually, he grew weary from the effort. His small reserve of energy was gone by now; exhaustion was setting in. He used his feet again to pull the chair back to its parking spot under the Victorian-style desk. Samuel rocked back and forth in place for a bit, trying to stay awake. He felt antsy as he awaited Matthew's return. Looking back at his breakdown at the hotel, he couldn't help but feel a bit silly.

Of course, Matthew was alive, Samuel told himself. His mind always seemed to be working against him, dragging him from one extreme emotional pole to the other. It was a constant roller-coaster ride. Samuel leaned back a little too far and felt the chair getting close to tipping on his back. He reached his fumbling hands forward but there was nothing for him to grab. Luckily, his knees caught on the bottom of the desk drawer as the chair teetered back and saved him from the otherwise inevitable fall.

With the chair safely back on all four wheels, Samuel noticed his knee had slightly opened a desk drawer which he had missed thus far. The drawer had no handle. It was the kind of drawer that could only be pulled out from the bottom. Samuel's curiosity was piqued.

As he scooted back and pulled the drawer open all the way, a small stack of papers revealed itself. It was a few pages of ruled paper stacked on top of each other and folded in half. The outermost paper had one word written on it: Sammy.

Samuel immediately recognized the handwriting on the paper. The exaggerated S and the artificial curvy tail on the Y gave away Matthew. It was his habit to randomly write letters exaggeratedly, allowing the ink from his pen to pool in odd places. He would write some letters quickly, while others would be slow and deliberate. The unique thing was that he never emphasized the same letter twice.

When they were in college, Matthew and Samuel had watched a few too many crime shows with investigative handwriting analysis. From then on, Matthew would have fun crafting a fake handwriting style for an imaginary analyst to try to decode. It was his way of being funny.

Samuel was not ready to read the letter. He had been searching for answers for a long time. What if his wish could finally be fulfilled? The potential for that to happen lay on the other side of this sheaf of paper. Something told him to wait before diving into the abyss. He took the note and laid it on the couch in the living room. He poked at the freshest embers in the fireplace and managed to revive a little life in them. He placed four pieces of cut wood over the coal, forming a low triangular structure. Then, he took a few pieces of the newspaper from the counter and twisted them over and over into long wicks. He took the handmade wicks and weaved them into the tiny hut he had built in the fireplace. Samuel started a pot of coffee and headed into the bathroom. He washed his face to help him gain focus. By the time Samuel was finished, the coffee was done, and he could hear the crackling of a fire igniting in the living room.

Samuel took a sip of coffee. The steaming liquid warmed him up, and he felt better prepared for what he was about to read as the nectar traveled through his body. Samuel set the coffee mug on an end table, pulled his feet onto the couch, and unfurled the note.

There were only a few sentences written on the first page.

Sammy,

Before you read the rest of this letter, I must remind you that my work is sensitive. There is some information you will read about on these pages that you cannot share with anyone. I have been permitted to share these details with you due to my position. You are safe to do so as long as you sign the next page first.

The next page contained a standard Non-Disclosure Agreement, something Samuel was all too familiar with. It had today's date printed on it, and Matthew's chicken scratch rested at the bottom of the page, along with an embossed notary seal. Realization hit Samuel like a truck: *Matthew knew he was coming today. He was prepared. Typical…*

The NDA reassured Samuel. Somehow, it made it seem like he had less to lose, less to be afraid of, so he signed the NDA and walked over to the kitchen counter. He left the paper there before returning to his previous position on the couch.

Sammy,

Pardon the length and dryness of this letter, but the details are important. As you know, I was recruited for a dual director role at NASA and the CDC in 2013. The goal, which you do not know, was to advance the colonization efforts of other planets. I was brought on in conjunction with Dr. Simon Brown.

Dr. Brown's focus was to push colonization forward. My focus was to make sure this push was made with the safety of Americans – and Earth as a whole – in mind. We first began working on a supply chain network in space. To colonize space, we must first find a way to shuttle supplies and information back and forth consistently.

The US launched the Probe Station Project shortly thereafter. Backed by heavy amounts of private sector funding, the project's goal was to build and launch ten probe stations into space.

A probe station is a self-sustaining shuttle with no human life on board. The plant life onboard was genetically engineered to generate O_2

while surviving on mere drops of water per day. These plants are offset by specially modified plants called Revophiliacs, which also survive on water droplets.

Revophiliacs breathe O_2 and produce CO_2, allowing for a basic level of homeostasis to remain in the probe. Each plant station in the probe is 100% hydroponic, with 5000+ gallons of water to hydrate the flora. The station's upkeep is completely automated. Commands to each automation unit are sent via radio waves from NASA's home base.

Each station housed around one hundred probes which could carry various items from the space station to the planet's surface.

The goal of the project was to place probe stations on the outer edges of Pluto and Mercury, as well as between each planet. We numbered each probe station according to its location. Probe Station One was placed between the Sun and Mercury, and Probe Station Ten was placed past Pluto.

Between each probe station and planet is a solar farm station (named alphabetically A-S). Solar Farm A was placed between the Sun and Probe Station One. Solar Farm B was placed between Probe Station One and Mercury. 38 shuttle stations connected each solar farm.

Thus, the system was designed to produce a continuous loop of charged energy cells. The cells would transport energy from Solar Farm A, the closest to the sun, to Solar Farm T, all the way past Pluto. Once a new cell is fully charged at Solar Farm A, it travels to Probe Station One and replaces a partially used cell there. The replaced cell is routed to Solar Farm B to recharge before continuing down the path of probe stations and solar farms until it reaches Solar Farm T. After its final exchange, the cells are shuffled back toward the sun to be fully recharged.

The shuttles were designed to carry water, supplies, and energy. Each shuttle was designed to hold six stasis tubes for future use.

Solar Farms S and T, Probe Station Ten, and two Shuttles were launched in 2014. The last set was launched in 2019, thus completing the project.

Once the project was completed in Jan 2019, it was renamed the GSC (Galactic Supply Chain). The GSC was the first true building block on the road toward achievable colonization of other planets. I am including an extremely basic visual below of the GSC.

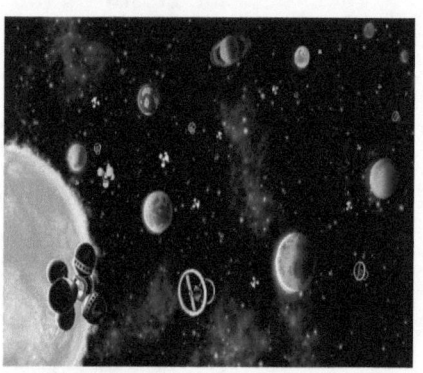

Immediately upon completion, I proposed a simple rule to moderate the GSC's operation. Ruling GSC-129C decreed that nothing should be removed from the GSC and returned to Earth. It was put into practice immediately,

though it would take years for an official decision to be made through NASA's existing bureaucratic procedures.

The network was designed to be a self-sustaining system for us to gain knowledge of space much quicker than ever believed possible. Anything that needs to be repaired or introduced to the chain is done so by the ISS, International Space Station, closest to Probe Station Three. Anything of consequence that needs to be analyzed in space is done there as well and is to remain in space. This process prevents anything potentially dangerous from hitting Earth's surface.

One of the first obstacles I focused on in the GSC was water replenishment. The initial model was set up so that replenishment supplies would regularly leave Earth to keep the chain hydrated. I knew that the strain on the Earth's water resources would eventually be detrimental to the planet.

My solution was to create autonomous drilling stations and surface-to-probe (STP) shuttles. We would add these on the surfaces of planetary moons as well as on Pluto. From my time at MIT, I had a thriving network of space engineers that were able to quickly make this dream a reality. They designed drilling stations that were powered by the same energy cells used by the GSC. Additional power cells were introduced into the supply chain to keep all solar farms, probe stations, shuttle transporters, and ADS running smoothly.

With the addition of ADS to the GSC, all probe stations were equipped with water-filtration systems to prepare for any potential findings on each moon. As the scientists were uncertain of what they would encounter, they felt it important to have the capability to convert saline water into drinking water.

We could finally see things that were previously impossible to perceive. We could observe temperature fluctuations on moon surfaces and measure their different impacts on living plants. We could see the plants dying or thriving on different planets.

The project's biggest discovery was the existence of previously unobserved moons around several planets. In the first 6 months of 2019, we identified 60+ new moons. With the GSC's help, we were able to quickly direct probes to the new moons' surfaces. We made amazing discoveries, some of which I will detail below.

We found 15 moons with atmospheric conditions nearly identical to Earth's. We discovered water bodies on ten of these moons. Dr. Simon Brown was extremely aggressive with his research and discovery efforts. As soon as the data was confirmed, we gathered ten teams of volunteers and launched them to their individually assigned moons. It would take years for any team to reach their destination.

What I was unaware of at the time was that Simon had already been violating GSC-129C. As soon as the data suggested there were suitable living conditions on the moons, he collected surface samples through the GSC and routed them back to the

International Space Station. The samples were shipped back to Earth from the ISS at the end of 2019.

By this time, the Earth was under attack from COVID-19. It was a perfect storm, which allowed for Dr. Brown's actions to go unnoticed. I admit I focused much of my time and effort on controlling the spread of COVID-19.

Unauthorized labs were set up with top-of-the-line equipment to analyze the alien soil. Simon used all known precautions and PPE with anyone who came into contact with the soil, as we know from combing through his notes in retrospect.

In March 2020, Simon shared with me what he had done. His confession included a disturbing revelation: more than 20 astronauts who had come into contact with the soil had fallen ill, including Simon himself. I took swift and immediate action to try and contain the outbreak. I ordered the soil samples to be sent back into space as quickly as possible. That was the only common denominator I could see at the time. Everyone who became sick had been near the soil in one way or another.

I ordered all of Brown's data to be uploaded to a backup server and the research facility to be completely sealed, with nothing but the soil physically leaving the building. Then, in accordance with safety protocols, everything contained in the building was burned at 4000 degrees. The ash was collected and shipped off-planet just to make sure no further contamination would occur.

From observations of the infected, we discovered that the alien virus did not pass from person to person. Only those who came in direct contact with the soil contracted the virus. The virus died with the host. What Brown's team failed to realize was that even our best PPE could not prevent the passage of the virus from the soil to the host.

Once the samples left Earth, only one new case of the virus was reported. In May 2020, Dr. Simon Brown fell into a coma. I had been closely monitoring him personally for months and I was the first person at his side, checking on him every morning.

I thought he was in a hard slumber until I noticed a sealed envelope in his hand with my name written on it. I took the envelope and flipped it over and over again. The edges were yellowed and stained as if the envelope had been written a while ago and had been touched over and over again. He must have known he was close to losing his consciousness and that it was time to deliver his prewritten message. This is what the letter said:

Matthew,

In all my years in this field, I have known very few people as honest and determined as you. You are a visionary. You see solutions to problems before most people even realize a problem exists. Your leadership will be what drives us further into space than we have ever been before.

Your compassion for people is your greatest asset.

In my professional career, I have found that there is no stronger or faster motivation for progress than fear. You will figure this out and save us all. Now you have to.

I am so sorry, my friend.

- *Simon Brown*

After reading Brown's letter, I dropped the envelope back on his chest as I pondered his words. Brown had said nicer things about me in that letter than he had ever said during our time together. I agreed with him about fear— it was indeed an extreme motivator. I also agreed that whatever was happening, it was now my responsibility to figure it all out. It all seemed like a very expected goodbye to a colleague.

But the "I am sorry, my friend" seemed off. We were colleagues but never close friends. I certainly never encountered him outside of work. I heard the final line over and over in my head in Simon's thick Middle Eastern accent. What I heard in the sentence was not an apology, but a veiled taunt. No, more than that—it was a threat.

As I replayed the voice over and over in my head, I realized the threat he was taunting me with. I had been rubbing my fingers against the palm of my hand all the while reading Brown's letter. The edges of the letter were covered in dust. He had intentionally infected me with the last remnants of the galactic soil that remained on Earth. Now, I had to make sure to find a cure for my own health's sake. It was a twisted kind of collateral, I suppose.

Shortly afterward, I returned home to see you and the kids for what I assume is the last time. I had no strong hope that we could cure this before my time was up, and as I am writing this, I am even more certain that I was right.

I did not want my family to watch me slowly decay. I did not want the kids and you to have lifelong memories of months of torture as I slowly faded away. The only hope I had was to make sure that my passing would be as quick as possible for you when it finally happened. I never wanted to be the source of trauma for the kids as they looked back on their Papa slowly fading away.

When I was a young boy about 4 or 5, my paternal great-great-grandmother was on her deathbed for weeks at my grandmother's house. I remember vividly to this day how fragile and small she was. Her skin just sagged off her bones, and it was almost translucent. Her body had no muscle mass. She had only strands of hair. Her eyes were glossed over, and her face was almost completely purple.

As the only great-great-grandchild, my family wanted to make sure we saw each other before she passed. She understood the gravity of the moment and reached out to touch me. I was too young to understand, and no one even bothered to warn me about what I was about to see.

The room was very dim, and when she touched me, it felt like ice cubes wrapping around my forearm. I was petrified in place. After what seemed like hours of staring in the face of death itself, she released me and fell back against the bed.

I have never asked anyone since, but I am certain that as I stood there at that moment, I watched the life leave her body. As I grew up, I often remembered that interaction. Anytime I walk into a poorly lit bedroom alone, I see her there. No matter how old I get, I am never able to walk into that room again. The bedroom was right next to the bathroom, and I am never even able to walk past that room to use the bathroom again without feeling the icy touch wrap around my arm and death's breath running down my spine.

After that day, I never used the bathroom again. I would go outside and pee against the house when no one was looking. I would never stay the night there, no matter how much my family asked me to. The thought scared me too much. Even as a young adult, when I would visit that house, I could still feel the fear lingering in the air as soon as I walked in.

I can recall everything about that experience so vividly all these decades later, but I can only remember the fear it left me with. I refuse to make my kids' last thoughts of me be like that. They should never be fearful of walking around their own home because I was too selfish to stay away.

So, to protect my family, and in case I don't beat this virus, I have exiled myself here, to work and pass in peace if need be. All the remaining infected who didn't want to go home to their families have been given sanctuary in houses like this around the US owned by NASA. They are left in peace there, for the most part.

Our bloodwork and vitals are monitored regularly, but we are not prisoners trapped under lock and key. We pose no risk to our families or the public. I chose this safehouse as it was the closest one to our Nebraska home.

When I step outside here, I smell the same corn-husked air that you and the kids are smelling. It helps me feel closer to you, closer than I will ever allow myself to physically be.

- *Matthew*

TWENTY-FOUR

Samuel's eyes welled up as he finished the letter for the first time. Mute tears streamed down his face as he read the last five pages for a second, then a third time. He was right today, but wrong today. Matthew was alive, but only for now. Samuel choked back a groan deep in his chest as he forced himself to read the letter a fourth time.

Simon Brown is such an ass, Samuel thought. *How could you do that to someone else?*

When he finished reading for the fifth time, he found himself crying over Matthew's secret traumatic past. Samuel had no idea that Matthew had endured such a traumatic event. He had never shared it before this day.

Mulling over the letter, again and again, a frightening realization hit him. He whispered it aloud to the room. "Matthew doesn't think he will beat this." Matthew, the most determined and stubborn man Samuel knew, did not believe he could survive. Matthew, who could alter the laws of physics and biology, believed he was at a dead end. *If he had no hope, there was no hope.* He was going to die, Samuel concluded.

The realization felt different than before. Just a few hours ago, the idea of Matthew being dead had scorched Samuel's soul. Now, his eyes were sore from rubbing out tears, but he was different on the inside. He had answers. He knew why this had happened. He knew that Matthew had not left him willingly. An outsider had forced this on him. Matthew, as always, was doing everything he could to protect his family. He was still the same man Samuel had loved and married.

Samuel's mind began to plan ahead as his tears ran dry. Obviously, Matthew would be back at the house at some point. Matthew had been struggling through his ordeal all alone. The last thing that he needed to add to his plate was an emotionally wrecked husband. After all, that was exactly the kind of hardship Matthew was hoping his exile would minimize. Samuel folded up the letter. He had already committed it to heart. *No need to ever read it again*, he thought.

Samuel crinkled the letter up into a ball and tossed it into the fire. He finished his cup of coffee and got up. It was getting late; Matthew might not be returning here tonight. All Samuel felt in his gut was that Matthew would return eventually. Samuel decided on another shower. He needed to wash away the evidence of his long day. He wanted to relax and center himself before anything else was added to his plate.

Once the last drops of hot water ran out and the shower ran cold, Samuel wrapped his head in a towel and headed off into the kitchen. His stomach reminded him that he hadn't eaten in a while. His hearty lunch at Millie's had been fully absorbed into his system. Matthew's fridge was not well stocked. *Typical*, Samuel thought. He assumed that Matthew was on another work bender where he was so focused that he forgot to eat. *With everything that was at stake, no wonder…* Samuel made a mental note to restock the fridge tomorrow. *Matthew needs to eat. He…* Samuel stopped himself before allowing his thoughts to go any further down that rabbit hole of Matthew not being healthy enough to eat well.

He was able to put together a decent charcuterie board from remnants he found in the fridge.

It was getting late. Samuel guessed that the kids would be getting home any minute now. He dipped a piece of cauliflower into the salad dressing as he dialed the home landline from Matthew's kitchen. Tavia answered on the second ring.

"Hello baby, it's Daddy, how was your day? Where's your sister?" Samuel inquired.

"It was fun, Dad," she answered. "The boys loved all the games at the restaurant, but the food was definitely less than stellar. Eternity just ran to the bathroom and I'm checking in on the boys. How was your flight? How's the house?" Samuel almost forgot his cover story.

"It was okay," Samuel offered. He knew Tavia would need more to be convinced. "It was a puddle-jumper, but the winds were so fierce it felt like they were trying to blow us out of the sky," he added. They both laughed. "Baby, before I forget, I left my call box in Gabriel, what with all the rush to get here. My work phone is acting up. You'll have to wait for me to call when I get back to our Georgia home."

He knew it was a lie, but he needed to make sure no calls could catch him off-guard. "I've got to call you right back, Daddy. Eternity is in the bathroom, and I can hear one of the boys crying." Tavia hung up quickly. She was gone before Samuel could stop her.

What was he going to say to her when he called back? Samuel worried. Gathering his thoughts, the kitchen phone rang. "Holy crap," he muttered. As he reached for the phone, he noticed that the caller ID box displayed a familiar Nebraska number he knew all too well.

"Hello," Samuel said shyly as he answered the phone.

"Hi, Dad," Eternity responded. "Tavia said you called. She's singing the boys back to sleep."

"How did you know where to call, baby?" Samuel asked before he could stop himself.

His daughter's voice took on the cadence of an irritated teenager. "I've been calling this number since I was five years old, Dad," Samuel paused for a beat before realization kicked in. *Matthew must have forwarded the house's phone calls here. Of course, he did...* he thought.

Trying to keep up with the conversation's pace, Samuel responded, "No, I meant how did you know not to reach me on the callbox?"

"Tavia told me." There was his sassy daughter again.

"Of course she did," Samuel chuckled. "I know it's late, baby, and you have school tomorrow. I just wanted to make sure you all got home okay. If you need to reach me, call the house. I love you."

"I love you too," Eternity echoed before hanging up.

Samuel walked back to the fireplace and added a few more logs to the fire. He went into the tiny bedroom and retrieved a pillow and quilt from the footlocker at the edge of the bed. He dragged the items back to the couch and poured himself one more cup of coffee before dumping the pot into the sink. He took his drink back to the couch and stared off into the fire, watching the ember children hop around until his eyes closed in sleep.

* * *

Samuel was unsure how much time had passed when the creak of the front door startled him awake. He stilled for a moment, trying to remember where and when he was.

A deep voice directed his attention to the entryway. "Well, aren't you a sight for sore eyes," it was Matthew.

"Matthew!" Instinct kicked in. Samuel ran across the room and leaped against Matthew, wrapping his legs around him like a kid.

Matthew was at the top of the entryway when they collided. The momentum caused them both to tumble down the steps into the vestibule. During the tumble, Samuel thought about letting go, but all he could manage was relaxing the grip his legs had around Matthew. As Matthew hit the wall, so did Samuel's head. Ignoring his wounds, Samuel buried his head and sobbed into Matthew's shoulder. Samuel thought he would have a thousand things to say at this moment, but his brain was mindless putty now.

Matthew rubbed Samuel's hair as he spoke softly. "It's okay, it's okay. I tried to come back before you got here, but you have horrible timing."

"You knew I was coming?" Samuel asked, still tucked into his husband's shoulder.

"Of course I did. I've known you were coming for a while now. You are not exactly James Bond," Matthew teased.

"How... when?" Samuel started.

Matthew cut him off before he could finish formulating his sentence. "I've known it ever since you had to 'rush out of town,' when Julia showed up. Booking a flight in the middle of the night? Leaving the kids without notice? You were acting way out of character. I'll give you props for creativity, though. The Surf and Turf ploy at the airport would have worked if you hadn't simultaneously bought coffee at another shop down the terminal.

Samuel wanted to interject and defend his actions, but he was too engrossed in Matthew's recount to interrupt him. Matthew kept caressing him as he continued. "I always told you: computers are not a safe way to hide your agenda. Your computer's IP history showed you looking for flights with layovers at Billings. I was confused until I realized you recruited yourself a sidekick. Mom's phone GPS showed her driving to Billings the next day. You two would not make for the cleverest spies," he chuckled.

Samuel winced. He thought he had been so careful. Only now did he discover that he had been leaving a trail of breadcrumbs right to his actions. "Well, if you knew what I was up to, why didn't you stop me?" Samuel asked.

"Is it not obvious?"

Samuel shook his head from side to side wordlessly. "I didn't stop you because I missed you too," Matthew admitted. "I have burned to hold you, kiss you, and be near you ever since the day I had to leave."

Samuel whimpered as soon as he heard Matthew's words. "I didn't tell you because you're not a good secret keeper for emotional things," Matthew continued. "If I had told you back in May, the kids would have known everything by now. Any attempt to shield them would have been rendered pointless."

Even though he knew the accusation was accurate, Samuel was still stung by it.

Matthew cleared his throat and went on. "Julia requested permission for me to tell you what was going on. I hadn't thought of it myself. She would make a great spy. Her networking skills are incredible. She sent the request all the way up to NASA's Head Administrator. It didn't take much to convince them that there was no risk in allowing clearance to a consummate professional such as yourself. As soon as I knew you would be here today, I had Julia draft up the NDA and get it notarized in advance."

Samuel stared into his husband's shoulder. His commitment to his clients made this moment possible. It didn't often happen, but right now he felt proud of himself.

"How did you get the NDA notarized in advance? You know that's not legal," Samuel asked.

Matthew snorted a bit. "Again, that would be attributed to Julia's networking skills. She assured the notary that it was necessary and that you wouldn't push back on the legalities. You don't plan on making Julia a liar, do you?"

"Of course not," Samuel answered.

"Good. The notary will come by tomorrow to complete the legal loop. Can we get up now?" Matthew queried. "I have been poked and prodded by needles all day and I'm sure you are exhausted as well."

Samuel's knees were wobbly as he tried to stand up. He ended up falling flat on his behind. Matthew couldn't contain his laughter. "Hush, you!" Samuel hissed as he staggered to his feet. He offered Matthew a hand to help him up.

Matthew struggled to get up and maintain his balance as well. Samuel noticed that Matthew's weight had drastically dropped. His jaw almost protruded through his skin. His skin was much paler than he had ever been. His stature was not as strong. Samuel realized that moments ago he had attacked this very sick man with the full force of his healthy body.

"Can we get some rest and pick this back up tomorrow?" Matthew asked in a winded breath. He could sense that something was building inside his spouse.

Samuel was not ready to sleep, but one look at Matthew made it clear that he needed to. *I've gone months without answers, what're a few more hours on top of that?* Samuel thought. He nodded and reached for Matthew's familiar and comforting hand.

TWENTY-FIVE

Snuggled in bed with her hands tucked behind her head, Eternity reflected back on the last few hours. The car ride home was peaceful. The night sky bounced off of the windshield like a mirror. The twins had passed out before they even left the ice cream parlor's parking lot. Matswell's nose and cheeks were covered in dried chocolate, and Lias had cherry and whipped cream dripping down his neck.

Tavia had wanted to clean them up, but neither girl wanted to wake the boys. School would start early for them all tomorrow, so they would just clean up the boys beforehand. Tavia leaned against the car window and passed out, leaving Eternity alone with her thoughts. Anytime Eternity had time to herself lately, her mind drifted to how she came into being. Even though Tavia lay only seven feet away, Eternity knew she was safe and alone with her thoughts. Her Daddy hadn't had the knowledge to explain any of the science, but he had mentioned that her Papa had experimented on the wildlife around their Nebraskan home.

Now that Daddy's away and Julia's no longer watching us, I can look for Papa's notes, Eternity thought.

She was certain his notes would be hidden somewhere. Her mind raced forward, trying to deduce where that would be. *He would hide them somewhere he could access once a year when we arrived here. But it has to be a place that's safe from prying eyes the rest of the year,* she concluded.

That night, Eternity's dreams featured highlights from every mystery movie she had ever watched. She found secret rooms by turning random light fixtures in the house. She discovered secret levers behind fake bricks that led to bomb-sheltered labs. She felt rope burn her hands as she hoisted up a bucket containing Papa's airtight journals from the depths of a hidden well in the overgrowth. She cracked the six-digit code of a briefcase she found hidden inside the walls. A secret keypad behind a wall painting opened up a wall safe.

Tavia roused Eternity from her dreams hurriedly; they had all overslept. The girls barely had time to get the boys dressed. Eternity grabbed them a few granola bars on her way out the door. Tavia climbed into the car's backseat and did her best to rid the boys of their ice cream extravaganza with hand wipes. They both protested, but Tavia knew that if her Daddy caught wind of the boys arriving dirty to school, she would never hear the end of it. They would never be left home alone again. She was sure as hell not about to let ice cream and some childish moans take that hope away from her. By the time all four arrived at school, the boys' faces were red but clean. *Crisis averted, for now*, Eternity thought.

The school day went by uneventfully. Eternity sat through classes she had already mastered, reflecting on her naïve dreams from the night before.

As if Papa would hide his work in such common ways; the thought amused her. *He was nothing if not original*. If she wanted to best him, Eternity realized she would have to be just as original herself.

Eternity began running through various scenarios. She was sure the notes must be somewhere on the Nebraska house's grounds. The weather here was so unpredictable, it seemed unlikely the notes would be hidden outdoors.

He wouldn't risk burying the notes, Eternity thought. It was *too likely that an animal would uncover them*.

The obvious conclusion was that her answers lay within the six rooms of the house. She initially thought the notes would be on her dad's computer, but she quickly ruled that out. Papa didn't trust technology, especially computers. That's why their family had no cell phones. The computer would be a dead end. It was more than likely that Papa never even touched Daddy's work computer.

The only interesting class that day for Eternity was health class. Each student was told they were being prepped for an experiment. They had gel rubbed on their hands and were sent to wash it off. When the last student returned, Mr. Gibson turned off the overhead light.

He said, "Considering the growing spread of COVID-19, today's lesson is about proper handwashing. You each washed your hands, I am sure, as you always do. Let us see what you left behind, shall we?"

He went one by one around the room, showing them all that not one of them had thoroughly cleaned their hands, even though they each had the same assignment. With everyone's full attention, Mr. Gibson gave a very enthusiastic lesson about the importance of proper hand washing, now more than ever.

Each student was given a blacklight pen and challenged to do the same experiment at home with their parents and siblings. Eternity was excited to share this later. She knew the boys would find the experiment fun.

* * *

Tavia jumped into the shower as soon as they got home from school. The boys were hungry for a snack, so Eternity parked them in front of the TV with a few carrots and pretzels each. She retrieved her notebook from her backpack while the boys enjoyed cartoons and sketched out a basic floorplan of the house on an empty page.

Next, she walked around the edge of each room in the house and measured their length by footsteps. She was grateful that Tavia took long showers and that the boys' eyes never left the TV, giving her time to work through her thoughts in private. Once the interior of every room was mapped, she snuck outside and quickly documented the house's perimeter the same way.

Eternity was sitting at the kitchen table with her notes when Tavia came through, a towel wrapped on her head and another around her body. She mindlessly headed off to retrieve clean clothes and yelled to the twins, "15 minutes then karate outside!" before closing the door behind her. The boys' reply sounded about as enthusiastic as the air being let out of a bike tire.

Eternity was happy to continue her research in peace. *Finally, a useful application for my geometry classes!* she thought. Before long, she had confirmed that the house's interior dimensions matched its exterior. *No hidden room behind any of the walls.*

Now that she had crossed off that possibility, Eternity went on to the second item on her mental checklist. She grabbed a flashlight from the kitchen drawer and hurried out to the crawlspace near their porch. It was a tiny space, designed for easy access to the house's plumbing. Eternity struggled to open the door, which seemed to have not been opened in years. She crawled inside and fanned the bright light from end to end, looking for signs of a secret basement. There was nothing but spiderwebs around her.

Eternity hustled out of the crawlspace and jogged back into the house. She decided to let the crockpot do dinner, so she could have more time to hunt around for clues. She retrieved the crockpot and placed it on the warped kitchen counter. She halved then quartered four potatoes, diced a small onion, and chopped up three carrots into sections, tossing everything into the crockpot as she finished with it. A few big spoonfuls of minced garlic and some soy sauce, and then she squeezed in a generous helping of honey. She added in a few shakes of oregano, basil, a can of tomato sauce, and two chicken breasts, chunked up. She added in some salt and pepper then gave everything a few giant stirs, set the timer for three hours, and walked away.

"Shower is free! Plenty of hot water left," Tavia called over to Eternity as she rustled up the boys for their lesson. "Thanks," Eternity said with a smile.

Once her siblings were all outside at a safe distance, Eternity allowed herself an additional pass through the house. She flipped over everything that hung on the wall: pictures, posters, calendars, wall hangings. It only took her a few moments to realize that there were no wall safes or hidden compartments on the other side.

You win round two, Eternity called out to her father. She turned on the shower, hoping that the hot water would clear her mind. Once she was freshly washed and clean, Eternity started on her next idea. She searched every piece of furniture for clues. She started with the living room, running her fingers under the couch and feeling for any holes or ill-fitting fabric on the recliner. Once again, her search was met with no results.

Eternity moved on to the kitchen next. She felt behind every cabinet and peeked behind the fridge. She ran her fingers along every chair before moving on to the table. It was there that she discovered something out of place. It was wedged tight in a corner, just out of sight: two tiny wires that came out of a flat circular battery.

She recognized the minute device. She had seen too many spy movies not to. It was a bug that must belong to her Papa. *Who else would care what was said here?* She asked herself why it would be here.

The answer was obvious. *This is here for a purpose.*

The kitchen table offered a likely spot for family members to discuss their findings or the day's events. *Papa was listening in.* Eternity's patience was wearing thin. She was angry that Papa had been listening in on every conversation they had but was unwilling to reach out and talk back to them.

Well, there'll be no more of that, she declared to herself. Eternity plucked the listening device from its place and attached it to the back of a radio she had found in the boys' room. She brushed the palms of her hands together and spoke to the wind, "If he wants something to listen to, that should give him his money's worth."

Eternity checked the furnishings in the boys' rooms, the bathroom, and her room with the same poor luck. She went into her parents' bedroom to check the furnishings next. The bureau was clean, the closet offered nothing, and the bed was a waste of time.

She gave dinner a quick stir and hollered out to her sister, "Do you mind giving the boys their bath when you guys get done outside?"

Tavia did not break her instruction to reply; she just raised her right thumb up to signal she had heard her sister.

Eternity sighed. Detective work was exhausting. She had searched every room of the house with no luck. Eternity climbed up onto her father's bed and lay on her side in irritation. She started tracing the long lines of the wooden wall in an effort to forget about her failure and relax. Her eyes moved from the ceiling to the floor and back again, over and over.

She never noticed it before, but the floorboards here were different from the ones in their Atlanta home. Back home, the boards were lined up in one continuous strip. Here, they were broken up into 8-inch-long blocks.

The longer Eternity played her game, the more curious she became. She moved closer to the blocks and began tracing her fingertips around them. She realized that even the application of the boards to the wall was different. It appeared that they were glued to the wall, piece by piece. *That's a lot of work*, she thought. *Papa must have really wanted these to stay on*. She knew that nothing, but intentional force would cause these boards to move.

Her stomach fluttered as she realized there was only one reason Papa would glue the boards so well: they had to be hiding something. Her heart began to race. She had figured it out!

Eternity raced to the kitchen and retrieved a putty knife, a flashlight, and a hammer. Filled with Christmas-morning excitement, she wedged the putty knife at the top of the base brick and tapped on it gently with the hammer. She couldn't contain her grin as she thought about the overly guarded secrets she was about to unearth.

Eternity's hands shook in anticipation. She moved the putty knife along the top of the wooden bricks and gently tapped until she felt the glue give way. She repeated the motion until the brick tipped free and fell away.

Eternity turned on her flashlight and scoffed in disbelief. After all of her sneaking and searching, the single brick revealed nothing more than a simple wall behind it. All the effort prying the single baseboard brick free had been for naught. There was nothing out of the ordinary here. No gap or hidden space to hide journals between the wall and the floor. There was nothing there but the wall. She flipped the single wooden brick over and over in her hand to make sure that nothing was hiding on the board itself. Of course, nothing was there.

Strike three, Papa. He had bested her yet again.

Eternity carried her tools and the brick back into the kitchen, placing them on the counter by the sink. She then began the final additions for dinner, crushing a few cloves of garlic in a bowl, adding some melted butter, and sprinkling in some chopped oregano, mixing it all well. She spread the paste onto some slices of ciabatta bread and added some fresh mozzarella cheese on top, before tossing them in the oven.

Eternity set the table for everyone just as Matswell and Lias came jogging through the house in their onesie pajamas. Matswell climbed up into his chair, put his curious nose right against the rim of his plate, took in a big breath, grabbed his little belly with both hands, and announced, "Smells yum yum yummy!"

"Well, hopefully, it tastes 'yum yum yummy,'" Eternity giggled.

Lias was just getting settled in when he asked, "Can we talk to Grace?"

Tavia passed napkins to both boys and answered, "Do you mean can we *say grace*? Of course, we can if you want to. Do you want to be the one to say it?"

Lias nodded fervently and stretched his hands out to his siblings. The children all joined hands and closed their eyes as the little preacher blessed the food. "Thank you for all this great food, Turn-T made. Let me eat it to grow tall and strong and make my hands strong. A man."

"*Amen*," Eternity corrected, trying not to giggle at her brother 'talking to Grace.'

After supper, the boys were released to watch some TV before bed. Tavia helped Eternity wash the dishes. "What's this?" Tavia asked as she picked up the single baseboard.

"It's just a baseboard that fell off in Dad's room today that I have to put back up," Eternity answered.

"Leave it to Papa to paint both sides of a board that no one's ever going to see," exclaimed Tavia as she flipped the board over for a minute. The girls laughed together at their OCD Papa as they put away the last of the dishes and swept the kitchen clean.

Once everything was clean, Tavia excused herself to finish up some homework. "Mats, Lias, turn off the TV and come in here," Eternity instructed. "I want to show you two something I learned in school today."

The boys turned off the TV and trotted into the kitchen. Eternity dug the blacklight pen from her backpack and turned off the kitchen light. "Hold your hands out," she ordered her brothers. She slowly fanned the blacklight on their hands and repeated the lesson she had learned that day. "All those glowing spots on your hands are dirt that you can't see with your eyes."

"Gross," Matswell announced.

"With COVID-19 spreading right now, it's more important than ever that we clean our hands really well," Eternity shared. She shone the blacklight on the crock pot, the drying rack, and the sink, showing the boys the germs in each area. "See," Eternity offered. "There are germs everywhere that we have to clean up. This light helps us to see them." She shone the light on the counter and noticed a glowing scribble on the baseboard brick. *Clever*, she thought, *hidden within hidden*. That was exactly how her Papa thought. She quickly skipped over it and drew the boys' attention to the stove. They both were interested in how gross the cleaning sponge for the stove was.

"Enough for the day," Eternity proclaimed. "Go pick out a book to read before bed and I'll be in there in a minute." The boys raced off. Before long, Eternity could hear them jumping onto their beds. She checked over her shoulder to make sure she was alone. She shone the light over the brick again and attempted to read the scratched-up cipher. "S-R1 Gen. 3 No Dev. S-R2 Gen. 3 No Dev, S-R3 Gen 3 No Dev." She memorized it quickly, clicked off the light, and flipped over the brick just in case Tavia walked in.

Turning the kitchen light back on, Eternity mulled over what she had learned so far. Just as she had suspected, the answers to her questions were indeed hidden inside the house.

But there are hundreds, maybe thousands, of bricks in the house. I'll never have enough time to read them all—and even if I did, I don't know what codes

Papa used to hide the information. The thought irritated her to no end. Here she was, answers literally in hand, yet simultaneously still so far away from cracking the code.

She wanted an answer immediately but knew that the best way forward was to wait for Papa to tell her everything when he returned. As much as she didn't want to, she would have to wait for him to arrive. Eternity turned off the kitchen light and headed off to tuck the twins into bed.

TWENTY-SIX

The **bright lights** of oncoming cars against the pitch-black sky blinded Samuel. A lifetime had passed since he had last driven like this. The city's well-lit streets had been a comfortable crutch. The Jeep veered further off the road to overcompensate for the oncoming cars on the road. Its tires grumbled and shook against the rocky terrain.

Don't crack the eggs, don't smash canned goods into the bread, Samuel hoped.

Samuel found himself drifting back to thoughts about the day as his eyes readjusted to the darkness around him. Not even 24 hours since he had found Matthew, and familiar routines already felt comforting. Matthew had woken up early, as he always did; something Samuel was always annoyed by. It made it impossible to sleep in, even on vacation.

Samuel lay in bed and pretended to sleep. *Apparently, there are never enough hours in the day for Matthew to get everything done.* He reflected on how true those words now were for his husband. Samuel squeezed his eyes shut and hung on tight to the swirl of emotions inside him at the thought.

By the time he re-opened his eyes, Matthew was walking towards the shower. The early rays of the sun shining through the high window in the room allowed Samuel to see details he had missed the night before. Matthew's once-flowing dark hair was now extremely thin, with patches of gray and white appearing like weeds in a rose bush.

Samuel could see the faint outline of Matthew's ribs through his loose skin. Deep purple and black patches were scattered across Matthew's alabaster skin. Samuel winced at the fragility of the man he had always thought of as indestructible. He wondered how many of the bruises were caused by their tumble down the stairs the night before.

Samuel blinked rapidly in an effort to force down any errant tears. *Not now*, he thought.

Matthew paused in the bathroom doorway, taking in a deep breath to steady himself. He leaned against the doorframe with his right hand, and a deep, throaty cough echoed down the hallway. It was a thing of its own, a beast that wanted to be free of his body, and Matthew struggled to contain it back into his lungs.

I've heard this before, Samuel thought to himself. *Anyone who has ever visited a family member in the hospital would recognize that cough; it was the cough of death, the sound of life slowly rattling its way out of a human body.*

Samuel pulled the blanket up over his nose and right to the bottom of his eyes. He readied himself to hide completely under the covers if the view got any worse. The guilt of adding to the wheezing man's pain was too much for him to consider now. A few minutes passed before Matthew was able to get control of himself. Samuel watched his husband from behind his shielded perch. Matthew was so weak he had to lean his head and shoulder against the doorframe for support. Samuel wanted to jump up and help, but he remained paralyzed and unable to move. At this moment, Samuel struggled to see the man he loved. The man he loved never needed help and never struggled to move around. The realization that Matthew was actually deteriorating hit Samuel like a Mack truck. He tightened his lips to not let his agony escape his lips now.

"I have to head into the city early this morning for follow-up tests. It may be late when I get back, but I'll save some time for you," Matthew announced to the hallway.

The words were stuck right on the tip of Samuel's tongue: *I'll go with you.* But he figured that the tests may be above his security clearance. Instead, he managed, "I'll make you some breakfast to take with you."

"Thank you," Matthew nodded without turning around.

Samuel forgot how bare the fridge was when he volunteered to take on the assignment. He realized he would have to go to the store while Matthew was out. He poured a little oil into a pan and then turned the burner to medium-low as he rummaged through the cabinets. Samuel wasn't a confident cook. He could make a basic breakfast quite fine, but he needed a recipe to follow for anything other than that. He opened drawer after drawer in search of a stray cookbook. Matthew rarely used them, but Samuel thought there might be one left behind by the house's previous occupants.

Luck was with him. He opened the drawer below the coffee pot to find three different cookbooks. He thumbed through each, but none seemed to have any rhyme or reason for their organization.

Samuel cracked two eggs into the heated skillet and guided them to opposite sides of the pan with a spatula. Instinct kicked in and Samuel found himself in the hallway outside the bathroom. "I thought I'd make us meatloaf for dinner. Do you know if any of the cookbooks in the kitchen have a recipe that you like?" Samuel asked.

Matthew slid open the shower door to answer, "I'm sure there are a few good recipes in one of them."

"The fridge is bare. What do you think I should get? Are there any herbs that can really make it stand out? Any particular cut of meat you recommend for the best flavor?" Samuel queried.

"Check the appendix," Matthew answered. "You're likely to find answers to all those questions in there."

Of course, Samuel thought. He knew that just as well as Matthew did. However, he was still not fully aware. So many things going on around him were causing him to miss basic things he already knew.

Back in the kitchen, Samuel started a pot of coffee. He dropped four pieces of bread into the toaster he found hiding under the sink. Matthew would want coffee for sure. In their decades together that was one constant that never changed.

Samuel added a few thin slices of ham from the fridge to each egg and topped them off with cheese. The shower stopped just as the toaster popped. Samuel could hear Matthew rifling through the dresser as he undoubtedly picked out his clothes for the day. The kitchen was filled with the smell of ham, cheese, and coffee. Samuel's stomach gurgled, reminding him that he too was hungry this morning.

Matthew appeared around the corner just as Samuel finished preparing his sandwich. Samuel stared in shock at his partner's attire for the day. He rarely saw Matthew preparing to leave the house on a workday in anything less than a two-piece, neatly pressed suit. Today he sported long dark jeans, tennis shoes, and a t-shirt.

"What?" Matthew asked as he saw Samuel staring.

"Nothing, I'm just not used to seeing you dressed like a local," Samuel replied.

"Well," Matthew started, "I don't see the point in getting all dressed up just to be treated like a lab rat." Matthew smiled at his own joke, but Samuel lowered his eyes slowly to the floor. He found that the coffee pot needed his attention immediately.

* * *

The obnoxious roar of the rumble stripe brought Samuel's attention back to the task at hand. It was too dark outside for his mind to wander far from the road. Samuel was disappointed that shopping for dinner didn't take as much focus as he had hoped it would. He wanted his mind to stay busy so he wouldn't have to remember the reality of his situation.

The love of his life was dying and there was nothing he could do about it. Samuel wasn't sure how much time he had left with Matthew. Just from reading between the lines in yesterday's letter, it seemed like their time was nearing its end. Samuel knew he would have to say goodbye to the love of his life and rear four children alone sooner than he thought. The fear of it all started to creep up his throat, but Samuel quickly flung it off.

Don't fall apart now, Samuel ordered himself. *If Matthew can survive this without falling apart, then the least I can do is be supportive of him. If you fall apart, you'll just make things more difficult for him.*

After all, Samuel thought, *this is exactly why Matthew exiled himself in the first place. If I break down, I'll just be showing him that he was right to leave. What if he disappears again and ensures I never find him this time?*

Losing Matthew again was not an option. Samuel resolved to enjoy every second he had left with his husband without adding any extra burdens.

* * *

Samuel called Eternity to check in, but she seemed too busy to be bothered with him at the moment. He didn't press her for details. The children were fine; there was no need for him to add more worries to his plate. Samuel allowed himself a long, tearful shower before starting dinner. He hoped to get all the crying out of the way while he was alone. He wanted to make sure the evidence was safely washed away before Detective Matthew showed up to sleuth around.

The front door screeched, and Samuel offered, "Welcome home. I wasn't sure what time you'd be back, but I kept a plate for you in the oven whenever you're ready."

Matthew stood in the entryway catching his breath before answering. "Thank you," he said. "Maybe in a little while." Matthew scooted his way over and joined Samuel on the couch.

The two sat there for a while in silence.

It was Matthew who ended the standoff. "I know you must have a ton of questions. I will answer as many of them as I can."

Samuel did not lift his eyes from the book he had been reading. He knew that avoiding Matthew's eyes would make it easier to keep his composure. Even though the conversation was deathly serious, he wanted to keep things seemingly casual.

"What is the prognosis? How fast is the disease's progression?" Samuel asked as drily as he could.

"Getting right to the point, I see." Matthew attempted to lighten his tone to soften the reality of it all. Samuel kept his eyes firmly fixed on the quickly blurring pages instead of on his partner.

"Well," Matthew offered. "We've seen a similar overall pattern in patients so far. It looks like— over time—the virus slows down the patient's heart rate and raises their body temperature. The changes are gradual but consistent."

Samuel thought back to how warm Matthew felt against his skin the night before.

"The disease affects hair and skin pigmentation." Matthew spoke as if he were talking about an abstract and distant figure. "Blood spotting and bruising riddle the body. Eventually, the patient drifts into a coma."

Matthew paused for a breath. He searched Samuel's profile for any alterations. Seeing none, he decided it was safe to continue.

Matthew spoke softly in hope of maintaining calm. "Timing is slightly different for everyone, but once that happens, the patient usually passes away within two months." Matthew didn't need to register the tension in Samuel's posture to predict his next question. "No one has ever woken up from the coma stage." Matthew spoke slowly and matter-of-factly, trying hard not to emphasize any of his words.

"How long after contracting the virus do patients become comatose?" Samuel finally asked. He turned his head slowly to meet Matthew's soulful gaze.

"Not long," Matthew admitted. "16-18 weeks."

Samuel quickly recalled the last time Matthew was home. They had picked out a lovely bouquet of flowers to be delivered to their standing surrogate like they did every Mother's Day. They never wanted her to forget just how appreciated her gift to them was.

"So, you could soon never wake up ever again?" Samuel asked, even though he knew the answer.

"That is right," Matthew said. "But I would prefer not to think about it until it's too late for me."

Samuel lowered his eyes to the floor. He spoke no words in response. He just gave Matthew a single nod of acknowledgment, letting him know that he assented to Matthew's silent request.

Samuel knew he would not be able to honor Matthew's request not to think about his disease, but he resolved to try his best to make it look like he had. There was no need to ask Matthew about financial details or funeral arrangements. Matthew had been forcing them both to discuss these things in painstaking detail each year since Eternity was born. Samuel knew exactly how much money was set aside to take care of the family.

The service binder he had put together with Matthew was located back home. Matthew was the only person Samuel knew who had prepared a binder with every detail of his final services. Colors, flowers, music, casket—everything was already picked out.

Samuel always found it morbid that Matthew left out no detail in his overly organized plan. But at that moment, sitting there with Matthew, Samuel recognized that this was a final gift of Matthew's to him.

He planned his own funeral so that I wouldn't have to, Samuel admitted to himself.

The realness of the situation started to settle in his body. Samuel knew he was going to lose it. He got up swiftly and declared, "I'm going to warm up your dinner. I know you must be hungry." Samuel hustled around the couch and into the kitchen before Matthew had time to dismiss the idea.

Matthew ate while Samuel stared through the book into the abyss of nothingness that he knew he would soon be facing. The two sat in silence as an invisible clock ticked on in the distance. Matthew took small bites while Samuel retreated to his façade of reading. Lost in his thoughts for minutes, or hours, he was unsure, Samuel's attention shifted as he heard Matthew start snoring. The grumbling air escaping Matthew brought burning tears to Samuel's eyes. Matthew was never so tired that he fell asleep in the midst of eating before. The realization was harder and harder to ignore now.

Samuel sat still for a while with tear-filled eyes, not wanting to wake up the obviously exhausted man. He restrained himself to shallow breaths until he was certain his partner was asleep. He carefully removed the plate of food from Matthew's lap and rested it on an end table. Then, he retrieved a pillow from the bedroom and gently guided it under Matthew's frail head. He would not do anything to risk waking him.

Samuel placed a new log on the fire to keep Matthew warm. He could only imagine the kind of day his husband had been through. Samuel knelt in front of his love and examined Matthew's still body. His hair seemed to have even more gray and white in it than it had just hours ago. The sea of colors it created was incredibly beautiful, but at the same time, it scared Samuel.

Matthew's eyes were outlined by deep charcoal circles which reminded Samuel of a wild raccoon. Patches of skin shaded in purple were turning black all across his face. Matthew's chin looked more chiseled than ever, but not in a positive way. He was gaunt. His skin rested right against his jawbone with no padding in between. His lips were no longer the bright crimson Samuel remembered. They too were faded. Now, they were a light gray color and mottled with little specks of white hiding just underneath the surface.

Samuel could not resist reaching out to Matthew's face and caressing it. He combed Matthew's hair gently with his fingers, starting from the front of his face and running down to the base of his neck, each stroke minutely higher than the last until he was combing through the top of Matthew's head.

Samuel noted the extreme texture change in Matthew's hair with each pass of his hand. Matthew's hair used to be smooth like fresh silk, but now it was tough and wiry. It felt like he was combing sandpaper against his hand. The change sent chills down Samuel's spine, but he could feel Matthew's body relax more with each pass. If this were helping him unwind, then Samuel could stand to be slightly discomforted.

Samuel allowed his hands to feel their way gently down Matthew's jawline, caressing the barely covered bone. It too felt rough, bare, dead. Samuel took in a deep breath and held it with his shoulders high in the air. He closed his eyes to hold in the avalanche of feelings building inside him. It was waiting for just one last sound to release it. He shook his head violently from side to side. *This won't be the moment I falter*, he resolved.

Samuel dropped down and continued tracing Matthew's side. Down his neck, his shoulders, and over the top of his fragile arm, he trailed the back of his fingers. Stopping at Matthew's elbow, Samuel could see fresh needle marks in the crease of his skin. They were either from blood being drawn or from a recent IV port, and either idea caused Samuel's heart to seize and twist inside his chest. It was obvious that

Matthew had gone through so much alone. His body painted the picture that his words wouldn't share.

Samuel was caught in the need to discover just how deep the painted betrayal went. Even with some answers, Samuel knew he was not getting the entire picture of how much Matthew was going through. He peeled back Matthew's shirt just above his stomach, or at least, above what used to be his stomach. Matthew had never worried about having a sculpted body, not even in his teens. He always had a very slight stomach, never a large one. There were so many more important things in life than personal physique. Now he had nothing.

As Samuel traced his fingers down the highways of tar and opal bruises that ran wild over Matthew's ribs, it finally became too much. Samuel removed his hand from Matthew's body and turned back to the fire.

Think of anything else, he instructed himself. *Anything but this, anything but now.*

But of course, he could not do that. After a few minutes passed of not looking and not touching Matthew, the hurricane within Samuel subsided. He was more cautious as his fingers returned to Matthew's body. Samuel found himself tracing a familiar surgical scar on Matthew's abdomen. He ran his fingers up and down the scar slowly, as he had done a million times before over the last two decades. This was a familiar gesture, one that Samuel's mind could find solace in.

As he traced the scar over and over again, he remembered the day this scar was born. The first time he thought he was going to lose Matthew. It was the summer after the first year of college. Matthew had planned a hiking and camping trip to allow them both to unwind from the tough school year.

The Rocky Mountains were beautiful. Samuel had enjoyed every serene moment of the trip. Matthew, on the other hand, had started to cramp up on the way back down. At breakfast, the stomach cramps were so bad that Matthew couldn't bring himself to eat. They both thought the pain was a sign of exhaustion, so Matthew made sure to hydrate himself well. They continued walking down the path.

Over the few hours it took to complete the hike back down the mountain, Matthew's pain shifted from his belly button toward his side. The pain was so bad that every step made him grimace. They were a mere few miles from their car when Matthew realized he could move no further. He held his side tightly and leaned against a tree for support. "I can't move any further." Matthew winced, "You have to go get the car." He slid down until he hit the ground.

Samuel's soul was tormented as he had no idea what was going on. He didn't even answer Matthew's command. He threw his backpack to the ground and took off running down the gravel path to retrieve their car. His mind raced just as fast as his legs. *What could be causing Matthew's pain?* he wondered. *Had he encountered something he was allergic to? Had a spider or snake bitten him?* No matter what the cause, Samuel knew that Matthew's pain was bad if he admitted to needing help. It was extremely out of character for him, and that meant there was cause to be terrified.

Samuel gripped the wheel with white knuckles the entire drive to the hospital. He was petrified. Every few seconds, Matthew would breathe out in pain. When they arrived at the hospital, the medical staff was ready for him. Matthew had told Samuel to call ahead between winces of pain. The hospital took Matthew back immediately but forced Samuel into the waiting room since they were not family. Samuel paced laps around the room until it felt like his legs were jelly. He screamed into the palms of his hands in frustration. It seemed like days passed in wait. No one would tell Samuel anything. The staff wouldn't even tell him if Matthew was alive or dead.

By the time Mama Jene walked through the door, Samuel had convinced himself that Matthew was gone and that the hospital was avoiding telling him anything. Her head was held high as she scanned the room and locked eyes with Samuel. She snapped her fingers and motioned for him to follow her as she approached the desk at full speed. Samuel arrived moments behind her and headed toward the room number the nurse had just said.

As Samuel stood next to her, the nurse started to protest, but Mama Jene stopped her before the words could leave her mouth.

"Honey, you do your job and man this desk. I will take anyone I want to see my son. I expect the doctor to be there to update us when I arrive," Mama Jene said firmly.

The heavy-set nurse puffed in frustration, but Mama Jene's face offered no room for objection. She didn't wait for a response and swung the door closed behind them both. They were both relieved when the doctor—who was, of course, waiting for them—told them both that Matthew was okay.

Samuel loved this memory. Mama Jene was always his hero. She always got what she wanted with very few words. No one stood in her way—or even attempted to do so. It was obvious that Matthew took after her. Samuel had always hoped to be that kind of person for his family.

"The pain was all in his appendix," the doctor explained to them. "Thankfully, it didn't rupture before we got to removing it. Matthew will need to stay with us for a few days for observation, and then he can go home fine."

"Will he be okay without his appendix?" Samuel asked worriedly. The doctor looked at Mama Jene as he responded. "Of course, he will. In all honesty, we have yet to figure out what the appendix does. It is one of the only parts of the body that remain a mystery, even to the brightest of scientists."

* * *

As Samuel continued tracing the scar, he repeated the same words that he heard in his head every time he did this.

"The pain was all in his appendix."

Old emotions swirled around with new ones inside him. Samuel knew this emotional tornado was more than he could hold back. He grabbed Matthew's dishes as quietly as possible and rushed off into the kitchen. He needed to occupy himself out of view as he let his feelings flow through his tear ducts.

Samuel kept himself busy by cleaning the already-clean kitchen. He tried to focus on the old familiar pain that he had already processed and dealt with. It was safer than the new pain that he had not been able to deal with yet.

He replayed in his head the doctor's words over and over as he wiped the kitchen counters. *The pain was all in his appendix. The pain was all in his appendix.*

As he picked up the cookbook he had used for dinner, he recalled what Matthew had said to him that very morning when discussing what to cook.

"Check the appendix," Samuel recalled from their discussion over the cookbook earlier that day.

Samuel thought, *For an organ no one really thinks about, you sure are finding your way into the conversation today.*

Samuel finished cleaning the kitchen. Feeling that his emotions were once again under control, he allowed himself to be with his love.

Samuel stared at Matthew's exposed stomach and listened to the crackling of the fireplace for a long time. Truth be told, he was not staring at Matthew's stomach exactly. His extreme bruising made that difficult to look at. Instead, he focused on the appendectomy scar, which gave him the most amount of comfort.

He stared at it for so long that it made him recall the impromptu pool party Matthew had hosted last year. A few of Matthew's astronaut friends had flown into town for a work gathering and a handful of them had decided to follow Matthew home from work. Matthew prepared food on the grill while Samuel entertained on the deck, watching everyone enjoy their home pool.

One astronaut had told him that an appendectomy was one of the many surgical procedures that were done to astronauts before they were cleared to fly. Indeed, all the men and women at the impromptu party had the same exact scar that Matthew had.

Samuel placed another log on the fire and watched the pile of ash build-up. He would have to clean it out tomorrow before they could make another fire. A small piece of paper clung for its life in the hearth. Samuel assumed it was part of Matthew's letter that had somehow survived his tossing it into the fire.

Samuel thought, *Him and twenty other people who would have the same scar as Matthew. The virus rode to Earth on soil from space. As far as he was aware the virus, through happenstance, was only harming people without their appendices. No one really knows what the appendix is for, maybe it is for this. Maybe it protects us from space viruses.*

Samuel was as still as a statue as he considered this possibility. He secretly hoped that Matthew would wake up soon, so they could discuss his theory.

Samuel was too humble to think that he had discovered some great hidden truth of the world. But he did think that perhaps there was something there to investigate further. He had avoided asking Matthew about treatment plans, so for now he would allow himself the small hope that his connection could be helpful in some way.

Matthew slept soundly for hours, while Samuel hadn't slept at all. He spilled out every thought, memory, and experience he had the moment Matthew opened his eyes. Matthew lay quietly, either pondering Samuel's words or still waking up. It was impossible to tell.

After a millennium of silence, Matthew finally spoke. "Well, that is quite a bit to wake up to. None of us have considered whether the appendix ever factors into medical conditions. It's always just been thought of as useless dead weight constantly threatening to rupture. I will share the idea with our medical teams tomorrow for them to look into."

Samuel couldn't help but smile. The idea that Matthew was going to share his thought with the team gave him hope. Matthew took in a deep, ragged breath as he observed the change in Samuel's expression. He knew he had to preemptively crush Samuel's false hope.

"I want you to be mindful, though," Matthew started. "Even if the team thought this was undoubtedly the cure to my illness, they would have no way of testing it. No large animals have an appendix, and this kind of testing would take the FDA years to approve even if there were any."

Samuel's smile dropped to the ground quickly. "So, even if we did find that this is the solution, they wouldn't be allowed to use it on you while there was time..." Samuel trailed off.

"No," Matthew admitted, "and as I will hopefully survive to be the last known case on Earth, there will not be an opportunity to test it, even if the approvals were expedited. NASA will continue to work with the blood samples they collected from all patients until there is nothing left. If there is something to gain from your insight, it would be assessed by testing smaller animals. But not in my lifetime."

"There has to be something," Samuel started, but Matthew shook his head and cut him off.

"At this point, love, the only thing to do is embrace reality. I am going to die. And very soon."

Samuel tried his best, but he could no longer hold back his emotions. He bawled into his clenched hands. Matthew reached for him but did not have the strength to raise himself up. Samuel noticed this through his teary eyes and moved to the floor next to Matthew and cried into his chest. Matthew rubbed Samuel's hair with the little energy he had. *He was still so very exhausted*, Samuel realized as Matthew's strokes slowed down.

"Let me help you to bed," Samuel offered. He stood up and reached down to help lift Matthew from the floor.

Matthew's translucent eyes flowed with tears as he allowed Samuel to help him stand up. They walked to the bedroom side by side. Matthew fell asleep almost immediately once Samuel had tucked him into bed. There were still wet tears on his cheeks. Samuel retrieved some tissue from the bathroom to dry his husband's tears, then thought better of it. *Best to leave Matthew to rest for now.*

Samuel quietly closed the door, ensuring not to wake Matthew. He knew he had so much to say, and if he could get his emotions off his chest, he could process them. But Matthew was not in the right state to talk about things. He was not about to break Matthew's trust by calling Mama Jene.

Julia was aware, as always. That was Samuel's option; she was whom he had available. Samuel loved Julia and knew she would be a sturdy sounding board for him now, as she always was.

As he headed back to the living room, Samuel pulled his phone from his pocket and sent a short, simple text message to Julia. "Can you swing by today? We need to talk about Matthew's condition."

TWENTY-SEVEN

The **aroma** of fresh maple and bacon wafted into Samuel's nostrils in the morning. The sweetly familiar scent brought him joy. He opened his eyes to see a fresh fire had been started. He lay motionlessly in bed, taking a moment to listen to the crackle and pop of the bacon in a sizzling pan. Matthew must have woken up early and decided to make breakfast. *He must be feeling better today*, Samuel thought. His smile widened. The thought of Matthew feeling better after their conversation last night was cause for celebration. An electric wave of hope shot through his body.

Samuel popped up from the couch with a newfound zeal for life. He was ready to help Matthew in the kitchen, but then he froze dead in his tracks when he realized it wasn't his husband who was cooking. Julia must have snuck past him while he was passed out.

The realization caused his smile to flicker momentarily. Still, he was happy to see her today of all days. *Still, he had lots to talk about with her...* Samuel thought.

"Yum," Samuel exclaimed while rubbing the sleep out of his eyes. "Whatever you're doing there smells absolutely amazing!"

Julia turned to meet his tired eyes. "Well, it's not every day that I get a summons from you. You were passed out when I got here. Based on the time you sent that text, I assumed you had been up all night. I thought I would make us brunch."

"Brunch?" Samuel asked. "What time is it?" he scanned the room in search of a clock that he could not find. "Oh, it's about 11 AM now," Julia answered.

"11 AM," Samuel repeated. "Has Matthew left for work already?"

"No," she replied, looking puzzled. "I assumed he was up all night with you and needed to sleep in as well."

Samuel made his way into the kitchen and poured himself a cup of coffee while he answered. "No, he got home around 9 or 10 in the evening. We spoke briefly, but he fell asleep pretty quickly last night."

Julia put down two plates and pulled out a stool for herself. "Well, the last two days of tests finally caught up to him. I was starting to wonder if he was even human. The man never stops moving."

Samuel nodded in agreement as he took the stool beside her. He shared his late-night theory between breakfast bites. Julia listened quietly and pondered Samuel's words. She sat quietly and contemplated every word of his until he paused in wait for her response.

"Well, as much as it hurts to admit it, Matthew is right. I doubt there's any conceivable way to test and approve a treatment plan before it's too late." Julia took in a calculated breath as she finished speaking. She forced herself to stop talking, giving Samuel time to absorb her answer.

She had prepared for the inevitable for months now. Matthew had been prepping her for this exact conversation since the beginning of their work at the safe house. It was always going to be her that broke the news to Samuel when Matthew was gone.

"I know," Samuel spoke exasperatedly, unwilling to look up from his plate. "But we can't just not do anything. I doubt there's any current legislation around what guidelines to follow when you're illegally infected with a space virus. There has to be something. We have to try something, right?"

Julia took a long sip from her coffee before chiming in. "Of course, we have to try something. I'm just not sure what we can try, what we would be permitted to try."

A concerned expression flitted across Julia's face.

"What is it?" Samuel asked.

Julia paused and debated whether she should share her thoughts or not. Finally, she decided that if it were her partner she would want to know.

"Well," she started, "I was just playing out the scenario of sharing this line of thinking with the medical team looking after Matthew. No matter what they would not be able to do anything for him before..." She stopped that sentence mid-word.

"But," she continued, "doctors are curious. If we share this one thing with them, we can be sure that Matthew will be turned into a human pin cushion for the little time he has left."

The words stung Samuel like an angry hornet. He pulled his hands over his heart instinctively, clasping them together as if to protect himself from the imagined scenario.

She's absolutely right, Samuel thought.

He had watched enough documentaries about scientists obsessed with new discoveries to know that is exactly how the scenario would play out. Samuel's hypothesis would have to be tested thoroughly.

Matthew would be turned into a human guinea pig for the rest of his short life. Samuel realized that Matthew was right as well. Even if they knew for a fact that the new theory was right, they wouldn't be able to act on it in time.

"I cannot allow that," Samuel said.

Tears welled in Samuel's eyes as he considered the gravity of the situation.

"In that case, we cannot share the idea with NASA until Matthew passes. That way, he gets as much peace as possible. God forbid, if this happens again in the future, we'll have armed the medical team with as much knowledge as possible. After he is gone, we hold nothing back. It may take both of us to convince Matthew though. He can be such a martyr at times."

Julia looked into Samuel's eyes, which were now stronger. She offered a single nod in agreement with his words. "But we can't do *nothing*."

Samuel agreed, "I heard you were a first-class networker. Do you think you could find someone outside the medical team that I could talk to? Not about specifics of course. That's confidential. We need to get ourselves someone with medical knowledge that we could chat with hypothetically. I think that would make me feel a little better. A retired doctor maybe, or an experienced nurse, a med student - hell, even a veterinarian. Anyone along those lines would be able to provide a sounding board for my thoughts."

"I will see what I can do," Julia offered. "I do have to get going, though. If both Matthew and I step out of the office, it might raise some questions that we don't need anyone asking. I blocked his calendar out for a personal day today."

Samuel hugged her and thanked her for breakfast. After she drove off, he permitted himself a peek to check on Matthew. He was still sound asleep.

He must have been through a real battery of tests yesterday, Samuel thought as he closed the door behind him.

Samuel tried to busy himself in the meantime. He cleaned up the kitchen, showered, and transferred some more money to Eternity's account. He made a mental note to call and check in on the kids after school. He would need to tell them he had to extend his trip for a few extra days. There was nothing specific Samuel needed to buy, but he talked himself into a grocery run to Alexandria. If he stayed indoors, he would be forever pacing around waiting for Matthew to wake up. *Matthew deserves all the rest he can get*, Samuel sighed to himself.

The small one-screen cinema in town was playing a thriller that Samuel was interested in, so he treated himself to a solo movie experience. Afterward, Samuel stopped at a local bakery and picked up a

German Chocolate cake, Matthew's favorite, thinking it would be a nice treat to lift up Matthew's spirits. He then made one last detour to a touchless carwash station, as the dust had built up on his travels and it was a much-needed stop on his tour.

When Samuel finally arrived back home, he expected Matthew to be waiting for him in the living room or the kitchen. But as he opened the front door, Samuel noticed that the rooms were just as empty as he had left them. It was after 3 PM and Matthew was still asleep. The realization made Samuel's heart pulse over and over like a sonic boom. *Almost 16 hours had passed*, he thought. Matthew couldn't still be sleeping. Matthew never slept that long, ever.

He's progressed to the next stage, Samuel thought.

He ran through all their conversations in his mind. Matthew had said that the comatose stage, the next stage, could happen any day now. "

How could I have been so foolish?" Samuel moaned out loud. "I was out seeing movies and running around even though I *knew* this could happen. Maybe if I had been here, he would have woken up. Maybe if he sensed me near…"

Samuel tried to rouse his partner, but it was useless. Adrenaline began to pump through his system. Samuel did all he knew to do. Tears breaking through, Samuel called Julia and delivered the bitter news. His hand shook as he tightly gripped the phone, the quivering words leaving a bitter taste in his mouth.

After hanging up, Samuel slunk into bed and curled into the fetal position. He covered his eyes with the palm of his hands, the sobbing inevitable. His rational mind was busy reminding him of everything he had learned over the last few days. There was no cure for Matthew's ailment, no patient ever waking up from their coma. This was the first stage of failure for Matthew's body.

It really is happening now, Samuel thought. No longer could he allow himself to be pushed blindly forward by childish hope.

He bellowed as he realized that his children would never see their Papa again. He would soon have to drive back to Nebraska and stare into their eyes and tell the twins that Papa was in Heaven now. This was more than Samuel could bear to acknowledge.

* * *

He didn't know how much time had passed when the front door opened, and chatter filled the hall. Samuel recognized Julia's voice. She was talking to a man he did not recognize. Samuel rushed up and tried to compose himself quickly, drying the sobs that sprang from his soul. They entered the bedroom, and Samuel was immediately taken aback by the man's beauty. His rich blonde hair was parted to his right and his eyes were the color of the ocean, seeming to set in the bronze sand that was his face. His short stature lent him an air of youth. Samuel guessed that he was in his mid-twenties at the latest.

"We came as quickly as possible," Julia said, breaking the awkward silence. "This is my grandson, Adam. He's doing his doctor's residency at Johns Hopkins right now. I asked him to come by and check on our patient."

Adam was already getting down to business as Julia made introductions. He was all business as he set up his stethoscope quickly and began listening to Matthew's heart. After a few quiet minutes, Adam confirmed that Matthew did appear to be in a coma.

"He will need to be taken to a hospital," Adam announced. "His vitals are not great. His body will need nutrients to keep him as comfortable as possible."

Samuel stood stock-still and tried to figure out what to say.

"He wanted to be here for the comatose stage, not at a hospital," Julia interrupted.

"He expected to be in a coma?" Adam asked.

They exchanged a long, steady look. Julia refused to elaborate. Adam realized, as he often did, that some parts of his grandmother's life were closed off to him. He knew that her job would never allow her to divulge the details he wanted to know.

"All of the legal medical directive paperwork has been filed," Julia offered. Adam looked confused.

"He will need many medical supplies if you want him to be comfortable here," Adam insisted.

Julia did not respond. She turned and walked down the hallway, with Adam and Samuel following her, wondering what she was doing. She walked into the study, where Samuel had once rolled around like a carefree child, and winced at the memory.

They assembled in front of the room's empty closet. Julia opened it and pulled the wooden dowel towards her. A series of gears seemed to grind into place, and after a final click, the closet began to turn counterclockwise. Both men were astonished to see what was on the other side: where once stood a sturdy wooden closet, there was now a tall metallic cooler with glass doors. The inside of the cooler was stocked with clear IV bags filled with fluids in different colors, which Samuel didn't recognize, but Adam appeared to be taking inventory as he stepped forward to examine them more closely.

A few different machines were nestled next to the cooler, and there were also some shelves stocked with tubing and other medical knick-knacks. "He was fully expecting this coma, apparently," Adam said, running his fingers along the equipment. "Looks like he has everything that he needs here, and then some."

"That's Matthew for you," Samuel added without being asked.

* * *

Adam banished Samuel and Julia to the living room while he set up the equipment and attached it to Matthew. They sat on the couch and leaned against each other in silence. Samuel finally regained control of his sorrow enough to converse with Julia.

"What do we do now?" he asked with an exhausted breath.

"I'm not sure," Julia answered. "I hadn't thought this was going to happen today. I wanted Adam to fly in and talk to the both of you together. As soon as I deliver the news to the agency, doctors will be showing up here to check on him every day."

The idea was horrifying. Samuel's stomach churned. He could already see lines of gray-haired NASA doctors clustered around Matthew's bed, poking and prodding him while taking notes on their clipboards.

"Can we not tell them?" Samuel asked. "At least not right away? Give me some time to figure out what all this means. From the look of the supplies he stocked, it looks like Matthew should be good for a couple of days at least."

Julia agreed that this was something she could do. She agreed to give Samuel a few days alone to say goodbye in private.

Eventually, Adam joined the two on the couch. "Well, Gran, I can't say that I would have agreed to come if I knew I would be setting a stranger up on life support today. Especially when it's at home, and doubly so when the man isn't my patient. I think that the next time you ask me to fly over I'll be asking a few more follow-up questions."

Julia smiled at her grandson, a smile that could only be learned through generations of love and support. There was no way Adam would be able to stay angry with her now.

"I appreciate you very much," Samuel offered. Adam did not answer. He stared at Samuel and his grandmother, studying their proximity and assessing how much his grandma meant to this man whom he did not know.

Samuel's emotions were drained. There were no tears left in his body for him to cry. It was time to concentrate. He had asked for a medical professional; now he had one sitting in front of him. This was the only chance he would get. He put on his lawyer hat and started asking himself what he would ask.

"I have a few more questions I hope you can answer for me," Samuel asked Adam. "If it's not too much to ask," he added softly.

Adam didn't reply, but he met Samuel's gaze and gave him a silent go-ahead.

"I hope this is not a silly question, but is there any such thing as an artificial appendix?" Samuel asked. "I know there are all kinds of machines that can mimic bodily functions for organs like dialysis machines do for the kidneys, et cetera. I was hoping there was a similar machine for the appendix," Samuel queried.

Adam had a bewildered look on his face. "No, there is not. Honestly, there's no need for one. We still know extraordinarily little about what the appendix does, but the human body can survive just fine without it. It would be a waste to produce a machine that mimics a job we don't even need to be done. Why do you ask?"

Samuel exchanged a glare with Julia as he tried to decide how to proceed while still honoring his freshly signed NDA.

"I was thinking that maybe he would get better if he had an appendix. A common denominator of every patient who has this disease is that they have all had their appendix removed." Samuel admitted.
Adam started forming a few incoherent questions before he realized that there were some elements involved in the case, he would not be able to ascertain. "If there is any validity to your theory, then it's quite a shame. There is no artificial replacement for an appendix. We simply don't have any animal with a similar enough appendix. We do heart valve transplants from pigs because their hearts are so close

to humans. I've even used pigs' livers at times to filter human blood, but unfortunately, they do not have appendices. It's an organ that's almost unique to humans."

Several thoughts spun around in Samuel's head simultaneously. He found himself speaking up again before he fully realized what he was saying. "What about using an appendix from another human, like a transplant?" Samuel asked.

"It's never been done that I'm aware of. There's simply never been a reason to try it," Adam replied.

Samuel was not ready to be defeated. "What about filtering his blood through another person's appendix like you mentioned with the pig liver? Is that possible? I've seen live blood transfusion discussed on TV before, can it work the same way?" Samuel asked.

Julia pulled away from Samuel. She looked at him trying to figure out his logic.

"I have never heard of that," Adam answered, "I supposed it could technically be possible to connect the collateral artery. Typically, these arteries are thought to only supply blood to the appendix. Perhaps there are unknown exchanges that occur. There would be a lot to consider. In this case, the live donor would be receiving blood contaminated with... Whatever... Any disease that the original patient has. If the theory were wrong, another patient would be infected unnecessarily through the process. The donor's appendix could also become quickly overworked, as it would have to filter two bodies' worth of blood at the same time."

Adam continued with some medical jargon about what he would need to do and his best guess for performing such a procedure. Samuel had already stopped listening once Adam said it was possible. Judging by the flare in Samuel's face, Julia knew exactly where he was going with this.

"Absolutely not," she interjected. "There are four kids waiting at home for you. I will not allow you to orphan them for the sake of some wild theory."

She was right, of course. Samuel knew it too, but he wasn't ready to give up just yet.

"Obviously, there isn't any other way to know if I'm right or not," Samuel said. "How could I live with myself if we found out that I could have saved him later? And I did nothing? That alone would kill me inside. The kids would be left orphans just the same."

Julia was left speechless. She shook her head at him fervently. "We have the same blood type. It would be wrong not to try it at least," Samuel begged, looking at Adam.

Adam registered the silent exchange and added his own objection. "Even if you were going to do this, you'd need a seasoned doctor on your side. Someone with way more hours in the O.R. than I have. You'd also need a real hospital environment with support staff in case anything went wrong. Even if everything were going to work out perfectly with surgery, you've got to consider the risk of human and environmental errors when doing such a procedure at home. There's a large chance you'd both die anyway."

Samuel tried to make his voice as firm as possible as he enunciated each word. "If we don't do anything, we'll both die."

"I could lose my license," Adam retorted.

Adam did not know Samuel, but he could feel the depth of his conviction. He could tell that Samuel had spent many years of his life with the mysterious patient. But he would not let his empathy outweigh his logic. He would not participate in this folly.

Samuel could tell that Adam was not going to budge. It was a long shot anyway, and he was out of time. *I have to sway his opinion and I have to do it now*, he thought.

"You were never here," Samuel tried to control the excitement in his voice. "Just set up everything and then leave. Let the cards fall where they may. That's on me, not you. No one has to know you were ever here."

"That would be medically irresponsible of me," Adam answered.

It was time for Samuel to put on his attorney hat. He needed to strike while the iron was still hot. "Adam, it's a win-win for you. If the procedure doesn't work, you were never here. If it does, you get to be the new up-and-coming doctor that discovered the purpose of the appendix. That is a big feather in your cap for someone just starting out in their medical career."

Samuel could see Adam's eyes widen at the mention of that offer. He guessed at Adam's thoughts. A discovery of that magnitude would be monumental for his career. It could establish his position on the medical food chain right from the start.

Adam looked at his grandmother for help. "I don't know, honey," she offered. "Some choices you have to make by yourself."

Julia could guess by the twitch in Adam's eye that he was seriously considering Samuel's offer. "But you have to be able to live with your choices afterward, Adam," she reminded. "Fame cannot quiet ghosts that you're not prepared to live with."

What was that? Samuel asked himself. *It's not time for cross-examination yet. I still have the floor, counselor.* Reading the room, he could sense that there was some family talk that needed to happen here. So, Samuel made a quick exit and went to be by Matthew's side. He couldn't think of anything more to say other than what had been already stated. Either Adam would help or not; there were no guarantees either way.

Samuel tried to find a comfortable spot to lay on the bed without jostling the many tubes and wires that connected to his husband's body. Matthew looked like some kind of half-human cyborg. *He's likely more machine than man at this point*, Samuel thought wearily to himself. He did his best to snuggle against Matthew as he had done a million times before. He wanted to softly whisper sweet memories into his partner's ear. *I can't do anything else to help him, but at least I can do this*, he thought. He desperately wanted to know what Julia and Adam were talking about, but it was impossible to hear their voices over the noises of machinery in the room.

Hours passed by. Samuel listened to the machines hiss and hum and beep. Eventually, Adam appeared in the doorway.

"I will set up the lines to connect the two of you, but you will have to open the flow valve yourself. That way, it is entirely your choice to go through with the procedure. Whatever happens next will be the outcome of your own free will."

Samuel was shaking his head in agreement before Adam was even done talking.

"It will hurt a lot," Adam admitted. "The needles I'll use have to be long to reach your appendix, and I cannot sedate you since you must open the flow valves by yourself. You'll have to lay very still and try to relax as much as possible."

"For how long?" Samuel asked.

"That's hard to say," Adam responded truthfully. "Every heartbeat circulates blood through your body. It takes about a minute for the blood to complete a full cycle through the body. I know nothing about this virus, so I can't guess how much of it could be filtered out in each cycle that passes. This is even assuming that your theory is correct and that the transfusion works. The longer you can stand it, the better chance it has to help—if it is going to help, that is. Hypothetically, we'd see the most amount of improvement after anywhere between twelve to twenty-four hours. Let me leave you with one warning, though. Keep in mind that if you do this, you will be infecting yourself with whatever your husband has. There is no going back from that."

"I have to do this," Samuel declared.

"Julia," Samuel called. She appeared in the doorway quietly. "If this does not work, please call Mama Jene. There's no one in the world who's better prepared to manage our four unique kids. It would kill me to think of them being split up, or worse... Sent away to live with my parents." She pulled his hand into hers.

"Do you want to call them now?" Julia asked.

"No," Samuel responded quickly. "Right now, I'm a wreck. Those kids are hyper-observant. They'd know something was wrong right away."

"You don't worry about a thing. If you decide to do this—against my advice, as I've repeatedly said—I'll make sure those darlings are taken care of. If need be." Samuel already knew that she would stand true to her word. Even if he wouldn't have asked her, Julia would always take care of his family. She always had.

Samuel watched Adam manipulate Matthew's tubing and insert long needles above and below his appendicitis scar. The needles were huge, and the insertion was obviously very painful. Samuel shivered and recoiled away. He did not do well with needles or with pain.

Julia tried to distract Samuel from the thoughts troubling his mind. "Once we're all set up, you'll have to wait a bit before you turn on the valve. I need time to get Adam back to the city and checked into his hotel. He needs to make a public appearance so he can have a credible alibi. Give us about 90 minutes, please."

Samuel nodded. He could do that. He *had* to do that. He could not put Julia or her grandson in danger, not after everything they had both done for his family.

The cool gel from the ultrasound machine brought goosebumps to Samuel's skin.

"Lay very still," Adam directed. "This is going to hurt."

Samuel tightened instinctively as the needle pierced his skin. "Holy crap," Samuel winced. "That feels like a turkey injector being jammed inside me."

"You have to try to relax!" Adam ordered, "I know it hurts a lot. I warned you it would."

Samuel tried to take deeper breaths and not look at what was happening to his body. He could feel Adam adjust the angle of the needle inside him. The pain made him want to vomit. Samuel closed his eyes and tried to focus on his breath. He had not noticed before now, but he could hear the windchime from the front yard. The soothing sound washed through his body. When the second needle went in, he did not open his eyes. He gritted his teeth and held his breath, praying for the ordeal to be over as soon as possible.

When Samuel re-opened his eyes, Adam was securing the needles with tape.

"This will help keep the needles from moving as much as possible," Adam shared. "If you move around too much, you'll run the risk of pulling them out of place. Then Matthew's blood will just pool around inside you."

"Ok," Samuel agreed. "Got it. Still as granite."

Julia set a timer for 90 minutes and reminded Samuel not to start the flow tube before then. She agreed to come by the following night to check in on Matthew. She had already keyed the information into her work calendar, so it would look like a normal visit.

Samuel could hear the sound of Julia's car driving over the dirt in the old driveway.

"Ninety minutes. Just ninety minutes. Lay still and don't move, you can do this." He spoke to himself to stay focused.

He tried to concentrate on the beautiful sound. It was always so peaceful. Samuel's mind drifted back to a pleasant memory of playing outside with the kids while Mother Nature whistled through the chimes. He could see the kids' tiny hands struggling against the mighty wind, trying to control the kites that they were flying that day. Matthew was lifting the twins up in the air and pretending that the kite was going to carry them away with the wind.

The distraction worked. Before he knew it, his phone vibrated with a notification letting him know that ninety minutes had passed. Samuel took in a big breath, stared at his husband, and said, "I have been lost without you. I took too long to realize you needed me. It's time to mend my broken compass." Then he turned on the flow valve.

Nothing happened,

"No!" Samuel groaned in panic.

Adam was too far away to help him, and he wouldn't do it even if he was right there. Samuel frantically toggled the valve switch open and closed again. *Maybe it wasn't set up, right?*

"Please, please, please," Samuel begged aloud.

After an excruciatingly long moment, blood began to ooze through the tubes and inch its way slowly toward his body.

Samuel watched the blood from his own abdomen tiptoe its way toward Matthew, as quiet and stealthy as a thief in the night. He found himself mesmerized by the realization that this is the closest they have ever been. Nothing they had ever done together, not even in their most intimate of moments, would bring them this close ever again. They were one person in this moment. The same life force that flowed through one of them now also flowed through the other. It was overwhelming. Tears found their way out of Samuel's eyes.

After the intense realization wore off, Samuel found himself staring at the transfer. The exchange was making him dizzy. He closed his eyes and tried not to think about what was going on. He knew he had a long night ahead of him. He couldn't allow himself to move, let alone pass out or vomit.

Samuel had forgotten that even giving blood made him lightheaded.

"You are not losing blood. You are just swapping it," he tried to convince himself. He attempted to hang on to that idea as if it would make his current condition any better.

The nausea slowly dissipated once Samuel closed his eyes and focused on the sounds around him.

He was relieved. Laying in a pool of his own vomit all night would have been unbearable. He tried to guess how much time had passed but refused to look at his watch. He knew from experience that that would only make things worse.

By now, it must have been hours since I opened the flow valve, he thought.

Samuel assumed that would be the worst of it. He thought too soon. Something brushed against his toes, just beneath his skin. He desperately wanted to reach down and scratch the itch, but he knew he could not move. He wiggled his toes in the hopes of some minor relief. No luck. The tickle eventually morphed into a stinging ache. After a while, it changed again from a sting to a burn. Samuel squeezed his eyes shut. He knew that if he looked down, he would see the flames rising from his feet. His skin had surely turned to ash. Yet still, he could not move; he had to endure this new ordeal motionlessly.

Samuel swallowed hard. He imagined the physical sensation was strong enough to force his saliva down toward the end of the bed. The water from his spit would surely quench the fire there. His hands balled into fists as the fire spread up his feet and wrapped around his ankles. He twitched his toes quickly, imagining them fanning out the fire, but it was no help.

"Arghhh," he screamed.

He had to get up, but he knew he could not. He looked back at Matthew, imagining how much he had endured all by himself, all this time. He was overcome with a wave of shame. How could he give up already? He resolved not to move and bear the pain. But he knew he needed help. Before the pain got too unbearable, Samuel began reciting the Lord's Prayer to the room. He said it over and over, each time a little louder than before. He hoped that God would hear his pain and help him.

But God did not intervene. Samuel continued his recitation until the burning sensation dulled and morphed into something else. His muscles started to contract and cramp. The cramping rose past his ankles and up his legs. He could not decide if this was better or worse than the burning. Though the cramping wasn't as painful as the burning, the urge to move and turn around was now much higher. He would never make it through the night fighting against this.

Suddenly, another voice broke into Samuel's consciousness.

"What have you done?" Matthew mumbled softly. His voice was so quiet it was barely intelligible.

Samuel snapped his head towards him at once, forgetting all about the pain and the cramping. Matthew spoke! *That meant he's awake*, Samuel thought.

"Don't move, my love." Samuel ordered, "It looks like the transfusion is helping. I have only continued to do what you have always done for me. I made sure that our fates would always be intertwined."

"No," Matthew tried to resist in a fierce whisper. "The kids." But before he could finish the sentence, he fell back asleep.

Samuel called Matthew's name a few times. Matthew did not answer.

Stay calm, he instructed himself. *The fact that he woke up, even for a moment, is a good sign. Maybe he just needs more time.*

The cramping now spread to his groin, but Samuel didn't care. He could endure this; he would endure this. The transfusion was working. The wrenching pain was beginning to take a toll on him. With each cramp, he fought against his body not to move. He had to remain still. Each cramp weakened him. He could feel his eyelids getting heavy with fatigue.

"Don't sleep, you can't sleep," Samuel tried to yell out. "You cannot move."

He tried reciting the Lord's Prayer again. He could barely hear the sound coming out of his lips. His eyes were getting too heavy to hold open. Finally, he lost the battle, drifting quickly to sleep beside his husband.

TWENTY-EIGHT

The room was full of mechanized beeps and hums when Samuel regained awareness. The bright lights around him blurred his slowly opening eyes. He was in a mental fog. He couldn't remember where he was or what was going on.

"Well, there he is," a joyful chuckle announced.

Samuel tried to turn towards the speaker. It was a man in a long white jacket. The man was mumbling a few things too rapidly for Samuel to understand. He couldn't concentrate enough to figure out whether the man was scolding him or asking him a question.

"Can you hear me?" the voice repeated with less chuckle and more concern behind the words.

Samuel tried to remember how to speak. Something was keeping the words from coming out of his mouth. He coughed and cleared his throat.

"I can hear you, but I have no idea what is going on," he answered finally in a raspy whisper.

The blurry lights finally came into focus, and so did the figure in front of him. Samuel realized that the man in the white coat was Adam. He tried to sit up, but as soon as it was apparent what he was trying to do, Adam's hand was on his chest.

"I am going to need you to lay still and take it easy. Do you know where you are? What do you remember?"

Samuel was confused but obedient. Looking around, he saw that he was in a room with striped grey and blue wallpaper. It was unfamiliar to him. He was lying in a stainless-steel framed bed with paper-thin sheets. The air smelled strongly of bleach and ammonia, and the room was very cold. Looking at his arms, Samuel saw that there were tubes protruding out of them. He was connected to several annoying machines. Their noise was what had woken him up. One of the machines began to beep faster as Samuel's heart realized his situation.

"I am in a hospital," Samuel answered Adam, "but I don't know how or when I got here."

Adam made a few marks on his clipboard and nodded in confirmation. Samuel's suspicion was indeed correct.

"That's right. You are in a NASA hospital," Adam reassured Samuel. "You've been here for a few days now. Your appendix nearly burst. It almost doubled in size and was extremely inflamed when they finally took it out. It'll be a few more days before we can take your stitches out, so you'll need to take it easy for a bit. No sudden movements. I have you on a morphine drip for the pain. I also have you on a few medications that may make you feel groggy or disoriented for a bit. That's normal. The procedure was a little bit more intense than a typical appendectomy."

Samuel lifted the sheet, and his eyes examined the gauze taped to his abdomen. The memory of what had happened before slowly began to rise in his consciousness.

"Matthew?" Samuel questioned. "He spoke to me before I passed out. He was awake for a moment."

Adam smiled at his patient. It was a huge, ecstatic smile.

"He did," Adam confirmed. "He has been awake quite a bit since then. He is such an inspiring man. Sometime after you passed out, he regained consciousness. He realized what had happened and called an ambulance to bring you here. He had all the evidence disconnected and hidden away by the time the paramedics came around. There were doctors waiting for you with a prepped OR when you got here."

Samuel was overjoyed. Matthew was awake. He could barely control himself and let Adam finish his words.

Grandma filled him in on all the details. Matthew had arranged for Adam to oversee Samuel's post-op care, and as his primary care provider, he had been granted access to all his medical information. It seemed that the appendix had been designed to capture and store the virus. Matthew's infected blood had filtered into Samuel and cleared out of Matthew's system, thus saving him. Early lab tests suggested that the appendix had trapped the virus from doing any harm to Samuel's body and may have allowed his body to produce antibodies to fight it. Unfortunately, it had been overworked and couldn't do its intended purpose. It had been too much.

Samuel absorbed the information. His theory had been right; it had worked: he was alive and so was Matthew. Trying to keep up with the conversation, he added, "I'm not sure if the virus was trapped from doing anything else to my body. I felt extreme burning radiating up from my legs and hitting my stomach right before I passed out. I also had some major cramping by the end. Have I been assessed? Are you sure I'm free of the virus?"

Adam's face was very serene as he answered. "One hundred percent sure. Our bodies always respond to fighting infections by raising our core temperature. In this case, I assume it was rising quickly due to the sudden viral overload in your system. Your body overreacted. The cramping you felt is a normal sign of appendicitis." It's essentially your body's way of saying, 'Get this out of me.'

"Where is Matthew?" Samuel asked. "Is he okay? Why is he not here?" Adam nodded quickly in response to Samuel's questions.

As soon as the inquisition was over, Adam answered. "Matthew is fine. As I said, as soon as he woke up, it was like he picked up right back to normal. He checks in on you every few hours. He has been sharing what happened with some other medical professionals and infected patients in an effort to save them. Your bravery may very well have saved more lives than just Matthew's."

That sentence sent a familiar tingle through Samuel. It was a mixed sensation of pride, excitement, and joy. He tried not to let it overtake his thoughts.

"That is great news," he tried to sound as humble as possible. "But really it was your bravery in taking a chance on my crazy idea, and your medical knowledge that allowed all of us to be alive and well today. I'm glad the world is gaining a doctor with such compassion toward his patients. It will be a better place as a result. I am sure that's why Matthew made sure you would be in charge of me."

Samuel's cheeks raised slightly at the edges. He did not mind passing the credit off. Of course, he had taken a risk, but it was for the man he loved. Nothing in the world would have prevented him from taking the leap to try and save him. Adam, on the other hand, had risked his career and his arduous schoolwork for someone who was essentially a stranger. Adam was the hero today. Samuel was not going to let anyone take that title away from him.

"I get the distinct impression that I will be answering to Matthew for quite some time," Adam sheepishly grinned at his patient.

"That would not surprise me," Samuel answered.

A phone call pulled Adam out of the room, but he promised to be back soon to check on his patient. Samuel lay motionless and took in everything that had transpired. *What a roller coaster!* Never in a million years would he have imagined that he could endure all this and come out victorious.

He had found Matthew. Matthew was okay and back to normal. He was already working, of course. He had a beautiful family, his family… Panic started to set in at the thought.

The kids have been alone for days! And no one has checked in on them! He fumbled frantically for his phone and dialed the home number.

The phone rang and rang and rang. Samuel let it ring for what seemed like hours, but no one picked up.

He glanced around the room in an attempt to tell the time. He found a clock just beneath the TV set that read 4:30.

The kids should be home from school by now, he thought. *What day is it anyway?* Adam said he had been out for a few days. That meant that it was likely a weekday by now. Samuel clawed at his wrist for his call box before realizing that he had left it in Nebraska. His babies were left all alone with no way for anyone to reach them. He could feel his temperature rising and the annoying machine behind him beeping faster and faster.

* * *

A painful lunch of baked chicken, boxed potatoes, and pudding was still settling in Samuel's stomach when the door opened, and Matthew walked in. Samuel thought he was going to jump out of his own skin at the sight of Matthew. He had more color in his skin and more bounce in his step. He was clearly healthier than Samuel remembered seeing him before.

"Have you come to spring me?" Samuel asked pleadingly.

Matthew grinned like a fox in a hen house. "Not quite, my love. But soon." Matthew found a safe place to sit at the foot of Samuel's bed and began to rub his legs gently.

"Sounds like we are going to have matching scars now," Samuel said, gesturing towards his abdomen through the blankets.

Matthew followed his look and stared through the blanket. "Maybe not an exact match," he confessed, "I think yours will be slightly worse. That was absolutely a reckless choice you made. What if—"

Samuel shook his head from side to side, not allowing Matthew to continue. "There was no choice," he fumed. "A choice implies that there are two paths to pick from. Two outcomes you can live with, even if one is less than ideal. The two options I had were either to do nothing—and lose you for sure—or do something and have a chance at keeping you. That was not a choice. Family sticks together, no matter what. Our fate is intertwined, Tater, whether you like it or not."

Matthew considered Samuel's words for a moment but ultimately decided that it was better not to continue the argument.

"Because of your genius, at least three other patients stand a good chance of recovering as well," Matthew shared as a peace offering.

Samuel allowed himself another moment of pride as he answered. "I'm glad I could help, but I can't take credit for that. It was just a happy byproduct of my trying to save you. You were all that I cared about."

Samuel felt a pang of guilt as he said these words. The admission felt selfish and bad, but it was true.

But Matthew could hear the dismissal in his partner's voice, and he wasn't having it. "Byproduct or not, it doesn't change the fact that all of this happened because of you. No one cares whether or not you set out to save these people. Their families only care that their loved one will be able to come back home because of you."

While Samuel did not totally agree with Matthew's logic, the painkillers were making it too difficult to sustain an effective argument at the moment.

"I can't reach the kids," Samuel suddenly remembered. He was getting worried again.

"They are fine," Matthew calmed, "They should be here very shortly. I sent Julia to pick them up after school and bring them here. I figured that after all this time apart, we should all be in the same room together. Adam isn't willing to release you yet, but I didn't want that to stand in our way."

The idea of his family all together and well in the same room touched Samuel's soul. It brightened a dark, forgotten corner of his heart that he thought would never be repaired. It was like his deepest fantasy was about to come true. He felt like he was waking up for the first time in months.

Samuel recalled the feeling of completion his family brought him. He could feel phantom sparks of electricity on his limbs as they returned to function. He stared into the sea-blue eyes watching him from the end of the bed and allowed decades of emotions to rush over him.

Because of this man, everything in Samuel's life was perfect. He could enjoy parts of his life that he never would have imagined enjoying before. The pain, the joy, the sadness, the excitement, the struggles—all of them were necessary to transform him from the naive country boy that he was to the successful patriarch he is today. The priceless journey of self-transformation all began by looking into those same skyful eyes, many years ago.

The End